Miss
Burton
unmasks a
Prince
A Regency Romance

D0095524

OTHER BOOKS AND AUDIO BOOKS
BY JENNIFER MOORE

Becoming Lady Lockwood

Lady Emma's Campaign

Miss Burton unmasks a Prince

A Regency Romance

a novel

Jennifer Moore

Covenant Communications, Inc.

Cover image: *Young Woman Hiding behind A Venetian Mask* © mammuth. Image courtesy of istockphoto.com

Published by Covenant Communications, Inc.
American Fork, Utah

Printed in the United States of America
First Printing: April 2015

21 20 19 18 17 16 15   10 9 8 7 6 5 4 3 2 1

ISBN: 978-1-62108-913-1

For James, Ben, Andrew, and Joey—
Yes, this is a kissing book.
No, you don't have to read it.

Acknowledgments

Anytime a mom undertakes a big project, it requires sacrifice from everyone around her.

Of course, first of all, I want to say thanks to my super-supportive, wonderful husband, who picked up pizza numerous times and understood when date night meant working on my computer next to him on the couch.

Thanks to my kids, who had to fend for themselves at dinnertime more than once and have learned that when I'm writing, they have to remind me of things—a lot.

I'm so grateful for the great ward I'm in, my kids' friends' parents, other sports moms, grandparents, aunts and uncles, neighbors, and others I probably don't even know about. Thank you for having my back and for supporting me and my busy family so I could do this.

Thanks to my groupies: Josi, Nancy, Becki, Ronda, and Jody. You rein me in and keep me from making a serious fool of myself and at the same time challenge me to be better. I want to be you guys when I grow up.

To my writing friends, I love this community and the support and love I get from all of you. Thank you for cheering with me when things went well; and when they didn't, thanks for picking me up, dusting me off, and setting me back on my feet again.

To my readers: Amanda Kimball, Melissa Fugazza, Josi Kilpack, Nancy Allen, Becki Clayson, Cindy Hogan, and Angela Woiwode. Thank you for your honest feedback, even though sometimes it's not fun to hear it. I know you want me to succeed, and I'm so grateful for you.

I cannot thank Covenant Communications enough, especially Stacey Owen and Kathy Gordon. You make me look good and are the most delightful people I can imagine working with.

And last of all, I want to thank my Heavenly Father for putting me where He did, with people who I love surrounding me, and for teaching me to believe I can do hard things because I am His daughter.

Chapter I

Unfortunately, Thornshire Castle was not haunted. No weeping prisoner languished in the dungeon; no ravenous wolves prowled the surrounding woods. There was not even a menacing highwayman lying in wait on the road from Portsmouth. These unfortunate discoveries made Meg Burton's first trip to England an abysmal disappointment.

Meg wrapped a warm cloak around her shoulders as she stepped into the early morning air, clutching her book in the crook of her elbow. She glanced behind her once as she rounded the corner of the garden wall, glad to see she'd not been followed. Her lady's maid, Bessie, would surely wish her to remain inside on such a cold day, and the ensuing argument would no doubt end with Meg's compliance.

Looking up, she sighed. Did the sun ever shine in England? Everyone had assured her that spring was on the way, but Meg had yet to see any blue sky since her arrival two days earlier.

She looked about to get her bearings and turned toward the forest, judging the structure with the domed roof she'd seen from the window of her bedchamber to be in that direction. Walking down a garden pathway with the gravel crunching beneath her slippers, she saw that the gardens, even in the dead of winter, were immaculately tended. Not a bit of overgrown brambles or thorny stems to lend an air of foreboding to the grounds. Everything was tidy. And beautiful. And uninteresting.

Her mother had approached her six weeks ago with the news that Meg was to take a sea voyage with her elder brother, Daniel, and that their distant cousin, the Duke of Southampton, had agreed to sponsor Meg for a London Season. She had imagined a grand adventure filled with romance, excitement, and danger—a far cry from the limited society of Charleston, South Carolina.

How could it be otherwise? Her cousin's new wife, Serena, was a *princesa* from Spain, who had escaped a French prison and had been secretly smuggled from the country by a band of Spanish guerillas and British officers. Meg sighed as she thought of how thrilling the adventure must have been.

It was while they were at sea that Daniel had told Meg the real reason for their journey. Their father's business had fallen upon hard times. With the rumors of war in the North and the British seizing American vessels in the Atlantic, it was no wonder the merchant trade suffered.

"Meg," Daniel had told her while they had leaned upon the rail of the gunwale, watching Charleston become a small speck upon the horizon, "It's up to you to save the family. You and your pretty face." He'd winked as if it was all a joke, and she was privy to it. "You must find a husband in London. And not merely any husband but a rich one to raise our fortunes. Mother and Father are depending upon you."

The truth of it had settled like a stone in her belly as the boat carried her toward a marriage that would benefit everyone, it seemed, besides her. She felt betrayed. She was to be used, like a voucher in a business transaction. Her parents hadn't even had the courage to tell her themselves. And she felt trapped. No doubt Daniel had accompanied her in order to make sure she did not fail. However as the voyage continued, the sting of the situation abated, and Meg reassured herself that romance and adventure still awaited. How could they not when she would be attending royal balls and living in an ancient castle?

A voyage to London in 1812 was no small feat, with tensions rising between America and England. The British naval blockades had concerned the captain, but a fair amount of luck and the good name of the Duke of Southampton had made the journey uneventful—aside from Bessie's constant seasickness. Without her maid to attend to her, Meg was forced to remain in her cabin or the passenger dining room unless her brother agreed to accompany her above decks. Daniel, however, was quite taken with some of the young ladies on the ship, and he himself remained in the dining room for the majority of the voyage.

Meg kicked at a pebble, watching it skitter across the path and into the mud. She pulled the cloak closer as she stepped into the shadow of the trees and then into the forest. The duke had explained that the forest was newly planted during the time of his grandfather and there was no dense underbrush or vicious beasts to fear. It was well appointed with lovely, nicely spaced trees and clear paths for riding or walking. Meg wondered what her cousin would think if he should see the untamed forests of Appalachia and the hazards that lurked within: bears, thieves, even Indian tribes still lived deep in the hills.

As soon as they arrived at the castle and she first laid eyes upon the stone turrets and weathered battlements, she had hoped her luck would turn. With a name such as Thornshire, how could it not be filled with secrets, hidden rooms, or discontented phantoms?

But it was not the case. The castle was welcoming and well lit and warmly decorated. Upon their arrival, they learned that, while the castle was not occupied by malevolent spirits, it did contain one Spanish prince. An unwed Spanish prince: *Príncipe* Rodrigo Fernando de Talavera—Serena's brother. The news had seized Daniel's interest immediately and set him planning ways for Meg to win the prince's favor.

Meg had learned from casually questioning the housekeeper that the prince rode a white stallion. But even the fantasy of a handsome prince galloping on his noble steed was squelched when Meg perused the periodicals in the duke's library. The House of Bourbon, Spain's ruling family, was famous for their overindulgences and indiscretions, and a picture of King Ferdinand VII was all it took for Meg to realize that the prince was undoubtedly selfish and lazy like his uncle. The idea of the flaccid man riding a horse at all was comical.

In the days since their arrival, they'd not seen one glint from the prince's golden crown, which was perfectly fine with Meg.

She emerged from the trees into a clearing. In the center, beneath early morning wisps of fog, was a large pond, the ice thin and melting. Directly in front of her, a Greek-columned gazebo stood on the banks. Interspersed between the columns were classical statuary and wrought iron benches. In the summer, it must be an ideal place for a garden luncheon, she suspected, but now it was muddy and colorless, just like the rest of England. Hidden among the shadows of the leafless trees—with the occasional squawk of a crow and a cold, howling wind—the gazebo was the perfect location to lose oneself in a Gothic novel. Meg shivered in anticipation.

She'd not bothered to pin up her hair or to wear a bonnet as she was sure she'd meet nobody this early in the morning, and in truth, what was the point of sneaking away to a wild setting to read a contraband book if one did not allow her hair to flow freely over her shoulders? The feel of the wind lifting her loose curls gave her a little thrill, as she imagined how very scandalous she must look.

While Prince Rodrigo had been conspicuously absent, the duke's sister, Lady Vernon, had been more than obviously present and had wasted no time getting Meg outfitted for the Season. Lady Vernon had no daughters of her own, and her enthusiasm for Meg's debut was exhausting. She had arrived at the castle with piles of gowns, fabric scraps, lace, ribbons, bonnets, slippers, and various other fripperies Meg didn't even recognize. Lady Vernon had insisted that Meg's auburn hair and large brown eyes, combined with her own fashion sense and French seamstress, would make Meg one of the most sought after debutantes in town. Meg was overwhelmed to say the least. She'd had no idea that a Season would require such excessive planning.

When the modiste had asked Meg's opinion about the colors or styles of the gowns, she had attempted to answer, but Lady Vernon had hushed her, treating her like a child, and Meg finally just nodded and allowed the two women to make the decisions for her wardrobe. She ground her teeth, remembering that on top of everything else, she had not even been allowed to choose the script upon her own calling cards.

Meg set her book carefully upon a rock near the shoreline of the pond; then she bent over and picked up a smooth pebble about the size of an egg. She measured the weight in her hand for a moment before stretching her arm back and throwing it as hard as she could at the frozen pond. The stone made a satisfying crunch as it broke through the melting ice. Meg stepped off the gravel path, placing her feet as carefully as possible upon the muddy ground as she made her way to a group of rocks at the water's edge. She picked up another stone, slightly larger than the first.

"I do not wish to wear an apricot-colored gown," she said, her voice echoing strangely in the quiet of the clearing. She threw the rock as forcefully as she could, not waiting for it to hit the ice before she picked up another.

"I wish I had never come to England." *Crack.*

"I will not spend my days embroidering screens or practicing on the pianoforte." Her voice was growing louder, but with each stone, she felt as if she were casting away her frustrations.

"Thornshire Castle is the dullest place upon the earth. It could use an ancient curse or a decent ghost." *Crack.*

She spotted a large stone, partly buried. As she dug the mud away from it, she slipped, falling to her knees, but continued to wrench the stone free. Once she'd lifted it, she stood and turned back to the pond, heaving it over her head with both hands.

"I do not care for the favor of an earl, a baron, a Spanish prince, or any other rich man!" she cried, hurling the stone with all her might toward an unbroken section of the ice she expected to shatter quite dramatically.

But the feeling of relief did not come, as the instant the rock left her hands, she saw that it was soaring toward a man holding the reins of a horse, who must have just emerged from the forest. The large stone hit the ice in front of him with a crash, breaking through and launching muddy water over the man's breeches.

Meg gasped.

The horse startled.

The man quieted the animal and then turned. His expression was one of disbelief as he looked down at his wet clothing and then lifted his gaze to Meg.

For an uncomfortably long moment, they stared at one another until Meg collected her wits.

"I beg your pardon, sir. I did not see you." She turned toward him, slipping again in the mud and tripping over her skirts. She scrambled to her feet and, looking up, saw the man's gloved hand extended toward her.

Meg held up her hands to show her muddy palms, but the man did not withdraw his offer. He simply curled his fingers toward his palm twice, reopened his hand, and waited.

She brushed off the mud as well as she could, wishing she had remembered to wear gloves herself this morning. Didn't Lady Vernon tell her a young lady should never leave the house with her hands uncovered? Why had she chosen today of all days to rebel against propriety?

Meg placed her hand into the man's, and his fingers tightened around hers as he slid his other palm beneath her elbow and pulled her onto the path.

"Are you injured?" he asked, releasing his grip, and pulling a handkerchief from his jacket pocket.

She took the offered handkerchief and wiped her hands on it, wincing as the dark mud stained the white fabric. "I am not injured."

"What is your name, miss?" The man stood unnaturally straight as he looked down at her.

Meg was startled. It was the very essence of impropriety for a gentleman to presume that she should wish to begin an acquaintance. They should be properly introduced. But, a quick estimation of his lack of social proficiency, unshaven face, wrinkled clothing, and care of the horse told her that he was no gentleman: a servant perhaps. And as such, it would do no harm to treat him kindly. Besides, he spoke with a foreign accent, which would explain his unfamiliarity with the British rules of decorum.

"Margaret Burton," she said. "But everybody calls me Meg."

"*Margarita*. It is a lovely name."

Meg's cheeks heated, and she lowered her face to hide the redness she knew was spreading in splotches over her fair skin. She had never considered her name lovely, but to be honest, it had never been spoken in a deep, accented voice by a handsome stranger in a mysterious forest. In fact, had a man who was not her relative ever used her Christian name? She shook her head at her preposterous thoughts and, in an effort to transfer the attention from herself, changed the subject.

"What are you doing here? I had expected to be the only one wandering the grounds at this time of morning," she said more bluntly than she'd intended. She looked past him at the horse that had stepped closer to the pond. A white stallion. A pure-bread Andalusian, if she wasn't mistaken. "Is this the prince's horse?" she asked, admiring the beautiful animal.

The man regarded her flatly. His eyes squinted the slightest bit before he answered. "Yes, this is the prince's horse—Patito—and he is thirsty. If you will move aside, Margarita." He led the horse to the edge of the water and allowed Patito to drink. "How timely that we arrived just as you created a nicely sized hole in the ice."

Meg stepped closer, running her hand along the stallion's long neck. "Hello, Patito," she said softly then turned to the man. "You surprised me as I was . . . uh . . ." She should have thought before she began to speak.

He raised an eyebrow. "You were . . . ?"

Meg looked back toward the pond. "I suppose I was relieving my frustration."

"Is that what you call it in America? In Spain, it is known as throwing rocks." When Meg did not answer, he continued, all traces of humor gone from his voice. "It appears we are both far from home. And longing to return, if I interpreted your 'frustrations' correctly." He let out a breath and lifted his gaze to the sky, squinting and wrinkling his nose. "I have not seen the sun in months."

The look on his face was so miserable that Meg's heart went out to him, but she also felt a sense of relief and camaraderie. Here was someone she could relate to. In a matter of minutes, this Spanish servant understood her better than anyone she had encountered in England so far. "I imagine Spain is much warmer—and sunnier."

He nodded his head once, and she noticed just how deep brown his eyes were. His dark hair was pulled back in a queue at the base of his neck but was not tidy.

She again directed her attention to the animal beside her, running her fingers over the raised bosses behind the stallion's ears, characteristic of his breed. Patito regarded her with intelligent eyes as she continued to make conversation with his handler. "Do you tend His Majesty's horses?"

The man's eyes narrowed and an expression of annoyance crossed his face, but it passed so quickly Meg wondered if it had even been there in the first place. He studied her for a moment before answering. "*Sí*. Yes. I tend His Majesty's horses."

"And you did not tell me your name, sir." Meg hoped to put him at ease; evidently, speaking about his employer was uncomfortable for him. The prince must be a cruel master, a tyrant. Further proof that he was someone whose acquaintance she did not seek. Americans had no tolerance for tyrants.

"Carlo." He inclined his head. "Now, what could possibly upset a young woman to the point that she must relieve her frustration in such a violent manner?" His lips quirked as if he were repressing a smile.

Meg crossed her arms and looked back across the pond. "You're mocking me."

"I assure you, I am not. I only seek to understand and perhaps alleviate the source of your distress."

She looked at him, trying to discern whether he was teasing.

When she did not answer, he said, "I believe you spoke of a particular gown and a ghost and, if I remember correctly, the prince himself. How have these things upset you?"

Meg's cheeks heated again, and she looked down. "Of course I had not intended to be overheard. I do not wish to sound ungrateful when the duke has extended such a warm welcome and proven so amiable."

When she raised her eyes, she saw Carlo was watching her. He nodded, encouraging her to continue.

"The duke's sister has chosen some gowns for me to wear in London, but I'm afraid our tastes are a bit dissimilar. You see, Lady Vernon assures me an apricot frock will be the height of fashion this year, but with red hair, I . . ."

As she spoke, Carlo glanced up at her hair, which Meg knew was a wild, untamed mass. Why had she not at least tied it back in a braid?

She clamped her mouth shut, feeling foolish. These matters were certainly none of his affair, and a man would not be interested in such things.

"I would not describe your hair as red. It appears to me a beautiful shade of ginger—*bermejo*." He tipped his head as if truly considering the problem. "Yes, such an exceptional color deserves special consideration. I fully understand your frustration."

He must be teasing. Surely he did not take such a thing as seriously as he pretended. Meg decided she'd had enough of this conversation. The more she spoke with Carlo, the greater fool she was making of herself. If only she could start over. He could happen upon her as she stood in the gazebo, her cloak billowing around her, her hair blowing in gentle curls away from her face. She would appear pensive and beautiful and tragic . . .

"And the ghost," he said, interrupting her thoughts.

"I do not think you are taking me seriously, sir. I should return to the castle. I have undoubtedly been missed by now."

Carlo stepped across the path, picking up Meg's book and looking at it before extending it toward her. "I wonder if your fondness for the supernatural extends from the books you read?"

"I do not have a fondness for the supernatural," Meg said. "I was simply disappointed that my first visit to a castle turned out to be so ordinary."

"A ghost or an ancient curse would make it less so?"

"Obviously. But there's not even a skeleton in the dungeon. I checked myself. There is nothing but old dishes and damaged barrels. And the doors to both towers are locked."

Carlo pressed two fingers over his twitching mouth, but it was not enough to prevent a burst of air from escaping his nose. He attempted to disguise it by coughing into the tunnel of his fist, but Meg knew he was laughing at her.

She snatched the book from him and turned toward the trees.

"I am sorry," he said behind her. "I did not mean to laugh."

Meg continued to walk away without looking back. She would have to visit the gazebo another day.

Carlo cleared his throat. "I believe you also mentioned the prince." His voice was quiet, yet it carried through the clearing.

Meg stopped walking. Her heart sank. And her anger dispersed. She could not see Carlo's face, but she imagined that all traces of humor had gone. If he said anything to the prince, His Majesty would surely be offended. He would likely tell his sister and the duke, and Meg would no longer be welcome at Thornshire Castle. When would she ever learn to watch what she said?

"I did not mean any disrespect to the prince."

"Have you met His Highness?" Carlo asked.

Meg turned. "No. I have not had that pleasure."

"Yet you said that you do not care for his favor. Or did I misunderstand?"

Meg wished the ground would open up and swallow her. She had made a blunder, and Carlo would report it to his master. She squared her shoulders, determining to explain herself. "I did say that. Of course, as I said before, I did not intend for anyone to hear."

Carlo took a step closer, his gaze never leaving her face. She wished she could read his expression. Was he angry? Was he so loyal to his prince that he would expose her offensive words? "I should wonder why you so dislike a person you have not met."

How could she possibly tell Carlo that she was annoyed with the prince because she was expected to ensnare him with her womanly charms? She could not bring herself to explain her family's need for her to marry a man of wealth and her abhorrence of the very idea. It was humiliating. She settled upon her secondary reason for disliking His Majesty. "The prince has avoided our society since my brother and I arrived. I figured he must be either disagreeable or proud to slight us so." She looked at Carlo and saw no censure, no anger, nothing but surprise in his expression.

She gave a small smile. "I am sorry if I offended you. My mouth often speaks before my mind has a chance to censor my words. The truth is I have never met a prince, and surely my attitude has been colored by my inexperience. Please do not tell him what I said."

"I will not tell the prince of our conversation," Carlo said, his eyes still upon her.

Relief flowed like a wave over Meg. She hadn't realized how tightly she had been holding her shoulders. "Thank you."

"Do you think you are being entirely fair toward His Majesty?" Carlo patted the horse's neck, but he continued to watch Meg with an unreadable expression.

"No, I realize I am not. However, I do not think my opinion should matter if I am never to be acquainted with the man. And even if I do, it is highly unlikely that I will meet with his favor."

"And what makes you believe that is the case?"

Meg paused a moment before giving her answer. She spoke slowly, still forming the thoughts as the words left her mouth. "The prince is surely used to always having his way. I am certain that in his entire life, he has never been told that he must do something he did not wish to do. Women undoubtedly fawn over him, agreeing with everything he says in an attempt to win his heart. But I do not believe a title makes a man more worthy of a woman's affection, and I do not wish to pretend to be someone I am not in order to secure a rich man." Meg was certain she would regret her words. She knew the time would come when she would have to do precisely the thing she dreaded—attempt to win over a man simply because he was wealthy. But she wanted Carlo to know how repulsive the idea was to her. In fact, it seemed imperative that he understood—that *someone* did.

She did not know why she worried about Carlo's opinion, however. It could be because he was removed from the society she found herself thrust into. He had listened to her, even seemed to take her concerns seriously, aside from the ghost, of course. For whatever reason, the thought of Carlo's disapproval saddened her. How silly, since he was only a servant and she would leave for London in a few weeks. But at Thornshire Castle, it would be nice to have a friend.

"I must go," she said, gathering her cloak around her muddy dress and tucking her book back beneath her arm. She patted Patito and then looked at Carlo, who said nothing, only continued to watch her with his chin turned slightly to the side. The man had impossibly straight posture. What she wouldn't give to know his thoughts. "I have spoken too freely today; please forgive me."

Carlo nodded his head once, acknowledging her request. "*Margarita*, it was a pleasure to make your acquaintance. Perhaps you will return to cast your frustrations into the pond another time?"

Meg blushed at the reminder of her ridiculous actions. "I love this spot. I hope to come back here another day to read." She glanced past him at the perfectly situated gazebo. "If I have the good fortune of being able to escape my lady's maid, elder brother, and Lady Vernon once again, I shall do it."

The edges of Carlo's lips lifted in a half smile, deepening a crease on his cheek into a dimple that created a tumbling feeling in Meg's stomach. "I am certain that such an undertaking will not be a problem for you, Margarita Burton. I expect you are precisely the type of woman to succeed."

Chapter 2

Rodrigo stood on the gravel path after Meg had gone, staring at the place where she'd disappeared into the trees. He thought for a moment, trying to put a name to the strange emotions the woman had roused inside him. *Bewildered* came to mind. As did *charmed* and *perplexed*; but above all, she had left him feeling amused to the point where a smile tugged at the corners of his mouth. The unexpected meeting had nearly caused him to forget his purpose for hurrying to this spot so early. He'd gotten word one of his trusted emissaries would arrive this morning; Rodrigo could only hope the man had not been compromised and apprehended leaving France.

Stepping from the path, he tied Patito's reins to a low-hanging limb and sat upon the gazebo steps to wait. If there was one thing he'd become adept at since he'd escaped from Spain, it was waiting. Napoleon's armies had invaded his homeland five years earlier and replaced Rodrigo's uncle, King Fernando, with the preposterous clown, Joseph Bonaparte. Nearly a year ago, Rodrigo had narrowly escaped when his parents had been taken by the French army. He may have escaped Spain, but he found himself a virtual prisoner, living under guard in England. The only access to information about his country came from British newspapers and intelligence gathered by messengers operating in secret. And many of these had not stayed alive long enough to return with their reports.

Rodrigo stood and began to pace. He gritted his teeth, frustrated with his inability to take action. He'd hidden in London for months and then, after his sister's wedding, in Southampton, where he communicated with the parliament at Cádiz as they attempted to create a new constitution for Spain. But too much depended upon the outcome of the war for his influence to have any significance. And it was weeks, often months, between missives, which left Rodrigo feeling immeasurably helpless to do anything for Spain.

He'd been persuaded, both by Spanish and British powers, that in England, he and his sister would be protected and of more value to their country, as they were the only members of the royal family who had not been taken by the French.

Rodrigo had not only been unable to stop the invasion of Spain and subsequent capture of his family, but he was now confined to the duke's estate, living in the dower house, constantly guarded and completely useless when it came to saving his people or his family. The British government had made quite clear the terms of his asylum. Between the limitations explained to him as measures to keep him safe and his own distaste for the situation, he had very little freedom. He felt like a child, asking permission to ride his horse or take a walk, never leaving the immediate area alone. Even now, he was certain soldiers stood just out of sight in the trees. If it weren't for his desire to ensure his sister's safety, he would have abandoned this plan months earlier. As it was, he fully intended to leave the instant he had word of his parents' whereabouts.

He stopped and lifted a stone, throwing it at the frozen pond. The crack it made as it broke through the ice echoed through the clearing, and Rodrigo smiled. Perhaps Meg was onto something.

His smile grew as he remembered the look of frustration and determination on her face. Such an expression did little to mar her features; it may have even enhanced her attractiveness as her eyes flashed with emotion. He would not want to be the cause of that woman's bad humor.

He threw another stone. He was no longer simply worried about the messenger's news; the unacceptability of an apricot-colored gown upon a lovely ginger-haired American had moved to the forefront of his mind.

Rodrigo had surprised even himself when he'd given her a false name, but it was even more shocking that he'd taken the deception further and led Meg to believe that he was his own stable hand. There was just something about Meg Burton that had intrigued him, and when he'd heard her disparaging estimation in regards to the noble class, he'd not wanted it to color her impression of him.

He'd have never imagined he would pretend to be a servant so that a woman wouldn't discover that he was truly a *prince*, but it was apparent that it would take more than his title to impress Margaret Burton. Such a challenge he could not turn down.

Rodrigo had been saddened when their visit had ended and Meg had left. Excepting of course his sister's and the duke's, it had been a long time since he'd enjoyed anyone's company. He'd staunchly avoided mingling in society after it had become obvious that he was being paraded like a show horse by mothers of single young ladies. No doubt the idea of their daughters becoming *una princesa* outshone the fact that he was a homeless refugee whose lands were currently overrun with French, British, Portuguese, and Spanish armies, with no guarantee he would ever return to his holdings. And regardless, he would not betray his homeland by choosing a wife from among the British aristocracy. His parents had already planned his marriage to a woman from the noble houses of Spain—Evangelina Gualtierrez, daughter of the Duque de Acerenza—and he fully intended to honor their wishes. He moved back to the gazebo steps and sat again.

Though his title was prince, Rodrigo was not the heir to the throne, although with every other member of the royal family either held under siege or captured, he had assumed the brunt of the leadership responsibilities, performing them from afar to the best of his ability. The Spanish definition of prince was not the same as it was in Britain. Every person in the royal family was referred to as *principe* or *princesa.* But the title of "prince" was simply too much for the *ton* to pass up. Title was everything to the British. And to most of Europe.

Not so with Meg. She felt exactly the opposite. And while he had no doubt that she had been sent to the castle to win his favor, he found the idea of spending time in her company pleasant.

It was ironic. He had finally met someone with whom he was willing to sit through dinner parties and attend dull concerts, and she wanted nothing to do with him—or at least she wanted nothing to do with the prince. But *Carlo* . . . She didn't seem to have any aversions to a stable hand. Perhaps she felt she could be easy in his presence, not forced to put on airs to impress him.

The very idea fascinated him. He'd never met a person who did not know the truth about him, and he realized Meg might actually come to know the man behind his title. He had the rare opportunity to discover what it would be like to truly have a friend without wondering how much of her affection was influenced by his station. His heart beat faster at the implication, and he contemplated for a moment whether it was the excitement of his plan or the young woman at the center of it that caused its acceleration.

His thoughts were interrupted, and he came to his feet when a cloaked man stepped from the forest followed by two Spanish soldiers.

"Your Highness." The man dropped to his knee and bowed his head. "I came as soon as I was able." He rose, and Rodrigo could see from the man's unshaven face and clothing still bearing the stains of seawater that he spoke the truth.

"What news do you bring, Esteban?" Rodrigo asked.

"I am sorry to report that our sources have still found no signs leading to the location of your parents. It is as if they have disappeared."

Disappointment struck Rodrigo forcefully. He let out a heavy breath.

"Joseph Bonaparte maintains his assurance that the king and his family are welcome guests in France and that no harm has come to them," Esteban continued.

Heat flushed through Rodrigo's body as his discouragement was replaced by anger. "Guests that cannot communicate with their family and are kept hidden? Guests who were removed by force from their homes while their countrymen were slaughtered and their lands were burned? The French have a skewed definition of hospitality." He walked to the gazebo and sunk down on one of the benches, indicating with a gesture for Esteban to do the same. Rodrigo rubbed his eyes and his jaw. "Do you think there's a chance they are still alive?" he asked in a quiet voice. Simply saying the words aloud caused a lump to grow in his throat.

"I am nearly certain that they still live, Your Highness. The Republic is not secretive about their, ah . . . executions." He stopped speaking, but Rodrigo nodded for him to continue. "Our intelligence network in France is extensive, yet there has not even been a rumor of such a thing."

"Even with this network, there is no trace of them," Rodrigo said, mostly to himself.

"I am sorry, Your Highness. We had assumed your parents would be with King Fernando at the Chateau de Valençay, but our contacts there assure us they have not arrived."

Rodrigo's thoughts spun. There must be someone who knew his family's whereabouts. They had not simply vanished into thin air. He and Serena had been so confident in Esteban's mission. He gritted his teeth, feeling helpless. If only he could go himself. If he only had a clue as to their location, he was certain he could find them. Gold simply had to cross the right palm, and he'd have the information he needed. Then it would be a matter of a rescue mission, and he had the best soldiers in all of Spain at his disposal, surely—

His mind snapped back to the present when Esteban cleared his throat. "Thank you, Esteban. You must wish to wash and rest. My advisors and I will meet with you tomorrow to receive your full report if that is satisfactory."

"Again, I am sorry I did not have more to tell you." Estaban stood and bowed, pointing his toe in the courtly manner befitting the prince's station. "I have heard a rumor that a British colonel is to be received here at Thornshire Castle."

"Yes, a friend of my sister's, Colonel Jim Stackhouse."

"A man of his rank will surely be able to provide information we do not have access to. Perhaps he will have an idea of your parents' location or at least know where to look."

Rodrigo nodded.

Esteban gave Rodrigo a pouch of missives from the Cortes Parliament in Cadiz and then departed; the soldiers bowed to the prince and followed.

Rodrigo returned Patito to the stables and then walked slowly toward the castle. He needed to read through the missives, but first he must give the news—or lack thereof—to Serena. He dreaded telling her that the thing they had hoped for had failed.

He figured that the family and their guests were likely in the dining hall eating breakfast, so he made his way to the kitchen entrance and directly up a back staircase to the duke's private apartments, as he typically did in order to avoid formalities and houseguests. He sent a startled maid for Serena and paced around the edges of the drawing room.

He only waited a few moments before his sister joined him.

"Rodrigo, what news?" she asked, closing the door behind her.

"*Lo siento*, Serena." He took her hands in his. "Esteban found nothing. Not even a rumor of our parents."

Serena's face fell, and she looked as though she would weep.

"I am sorry. I had hoped he would be the one."

"I know, Rodrigo. You take too much on yourself. It's not your fault."

"You are wrong. Their fate is my responsibility, and with Fernando still imprisoned as well, the future of Spain falls to me—to us."

Serena's eyes still held sorrow, but she folded her arms and lifted her chin in her stubborn way. "And what would you propose? Returning to *España* to fight? Journeying to France to search for *papá y mamá* yourself?"

"That is precisely what I should do." He could match her stubbornness.

"But you could be hurt—killed even." Serena's voice rose to a high pitch, and panic flashed in her eyes.

"Such a thing would be preferable to hiding in England like a craven," Rodrigo muttered. He would welcome the pain of a fight to the impotent helplessness that wrenched in his gut.

"It would do no good," said a voice.

Rodrigo and Serena both turned as the duke joined them. He closed the door behind him and crossed the room to Serena, putting his arm around her shoulder.

Rodrigo felt a small twinge of jealousy. It used to be that he was the one to comfort his sister. A loneliness he'd only known the last few months swelled inside him.

"Spain needs you, Rodrigo. The parliament of Cádiz depends upon you and Serena. You are a link between the Cortes Parliament's plans to reform the government and the monarchy. You represent hope for the future. Hope that one day your country will return to its former glory. That is not something to be taken lightly."

Rodrigo knew the duke was right. "But I must do something. I am useless here, hiding like a coward, tended like a child." He balled his fists. How could they not see his frustration? If only he had a rock and an icy pond to throw it in.

Serena spoke to him softly. "*Hermano,* I worry about you. You are so unhappy. Your clothing is disheveled and filthy. You remain day and night in the dower house and do not join us for meals or gatherings."

"You know why I do not associate with the British *ton*, Serena."

"You would like our guests. The Burtons, from America. They are quite amiable, and a bit of society would do you good. It would distract you from . . ." No doubt Rodrigo's scowl was the reason she allowed her words to trail off.

Rodrigo looked between his sister and her husband, an idea solidifying in his mind. He spoke in English for the duke's benefit. "It happens that I did make the acquaintance of Miss Burton earlier today." He could not help that the sides of his mouth pulled slightly at the memory.

Serena's eyes widened. "It must have been a meeting of some note. I haven't seen you smile in months."

Rodrigo ignored his sister's insinuation. "The meeting was . . . interesting to say the least, and because of it, I have a rather unusual favor to ask of you."

The duke and Serena looked at each other and then at Rodrigo. He knew they must be envisioning all sorts of potential scenarios.

"Miss Burton saw me today, looking . . ." He swept his hand downward, indicating his rumpled and soiled clothing. "And because of this, she assumed I was a stable hand."

"I can see how one would make that mistake." Serena raised her eyebrows and wrinkled her nose at his ensemble.

"I did not correct her," Rodrigo said.

The duke stepped forward. "Your Highness, I apologize that you were put in such an awkward position. I will fix this misunderstanding at once. I assure you, Miss Burton meant no disrespect. She is American and, as such, is not completely familiar with—"

"I do not want the mistake corrected," Rodrigo said. He watched as both Serena's expression and the duke's clouded with confusion. They both squinted and tipped their heads slightly as if someone had synchronized their movements. The sight was diverting, and Rodrigo almost laughed. He was finding humor in the oddest places today.

"For the first time in my life, I had a conversation with someone who did not have to watch their words in an attempt to say only that which is appropriate for royal ears. I found I quite enjoyed it." He paused to allow his words to sink in. "I do not want Miss Burton to know that I am Principe Rodrigo de Talavera."

"Do you intend to avoid her for the entire time that she is at Thornshire?" Serena asked.

Rodrigo clasped his hands behind his back. "Exactly the opposite. I intend to continue to spend time in her company, but I desire my true identity to remain concealed. For this, I will need your compliance. I cannot carry on the charade without help."

The duke shook his head. "This is highly irregular. Miss Burton is my guest, and I will not be part of a hoax. I do not like this deception or the idea of making sport at the expense of the young lady's sensibilities."

Rodrigo lifted his hands in a gesture meant to calm. "I assure you I have no intention of damaging her feelings. I simply want to continue the friendship in the way it began."

He took a breath, turning toward the fireplace. He felt foolish explaining himself in this manner. He was not used to having to justify his whims to anyone. Placing his hands upon the mantel, he gazed at the fire as he spoke. "I have not enjoyed myself so much since coming to England as I did having a simple conversation this morning. If I told Miss Burton that I had misled her earlier, I'm afraid any chance of our acquaintance following the same path would be ruined. We would be relegated back to our social roles." He felt vulnerable, exposing himself thus, but it was essential to have his sister's and the duke's compliance.

He could only imagine the wordless conversation—raised eyebrows and hand gestures—his sister and her husband were carrying on behind his back.

"It is quite probably the only opportunity I will ever have to know someone in this fashion, and I understand it is highly unusual to wish for such a thing." He continued to plead his case as he watched the flames licking over the logs. Inside he squirmed at the idea of having to explain himself. He was used to being obeyed without question. "But as the entire household and Miss Burton will leave for the London Season in two weeks, the deception will necessarily come to an end." The room was silent for a moment before Rodrigo turned around to face the others.

Serena was looking at her husband with a small smile. She lifted her shoulders in a shrug.

The duke's arms were folded across his chest, his brows pulled together. He turned to face Rodrigo. "I will insist that Miss Burton does not feel as though she has been made a fool of, and you must reveal yourself before she leaves for London. Or I will do it for you."

Rodrigo frowned. He did not like the idea of telling Meg she had been deceived. However, his concern was slightly remedied with the expectation that if he were to allow her to get to know him, to trust him, she would inevitably understand why he had misled her. Although he didn't want to reveal himself, he understood why the duke was insisting upon it. There was every possibility that she could find out the truth at the masque, and of course Rodrigo would never want to hurt her. But in the meantime, Rodrigo would have two weeks of friendship, and exposing the truth was a small price to pay to spend time with the young lady until then.

"I agree completely to your terms," Rodrigo said finally. He was surprised by how important this was to him. "I have already promised Serena that I will attend the masque the day before you and your guests leave for London. A fitting place to reveal myself, do you not agree?"

"But what do you intend to do about the other guests?" Serena said. "The Poulters know you already, and you cannot mean to avoid Colonel Stackhouse. Not when he's traveling all this way from the military hospital in Chelsea to spend time recovering in our company."

"We shall have to be creative, I think," Rodrigo raised his brows.

"It will be a delicate operation to be sure." The duke tapped his finger against his lip. He held his hand out to Rodrigo. "But I think Miss Meg Burton—given her love of adventure—is the perfect person to inspire an escapade of this nature."

Rodrigo took the duke's hand and shook it, a smile forming on his face. "I could not agree more."

Chapter 3

Meg leaned back against the pillows she had arranged on the library window seat and rested her book on the blanket that covered her legs. She sat with her feet pulled onto the cushion, her small space enclosed on three sides by the bay windows, and the other by heavy drapes. It had rained constantly for two days, spoiling her planned excursion to the gazebo. But she'd discovered the library window seat and found that with the drapes closed, it was just the spot to remain hidden. Her own secluded realm. The space was dimly lit, gloomy, and rather cold, but even the chill was a tolerable exchange for her privacy.

The diamond-paned windows had a splendid view of the front gardens, and if she leaned her cheek against the cool glass, she could just see the doorway to the duke's stables. She'd found her gaze pulled toward that particular section of the property more often than she'd like to admit, but since she had met Carlo in the woods two days before, there had been no sign of him.

Movement at the main gates caught her eye, and she turned her head to watch as a carriage approached accompanied by a group of men on horseback. When the company arrived at the entrance, Meg managed to catch a glimpse of colorful skirts and wraps as three women exited the conveyance, but she could not make out any particulars through the blurry water-trails on the window. Servants with umbrellas hurried to escort the visitors out of the rain and carry luggage into the house. Grooms hurried from the stables to lead the horses and carriage away. Meg tried but could not discern whether Carlo was among them.

She waited until she figured the company had enough time to be welcomed and shown to their rooms before peeking out of her sanctuary.

When she saw that she was alone, she made her way to her bedchamber to change her gown for supper.

Serena had told her very little about the Poulters. Only that they were old friends of Lady Vernon's. She wondered nervously about the new guests but did not have to wonder for long. Bessie bubbled over with information when she came in to help Meg dress.

"Lady Vernon and Lady Featherstone are the best of friends," Bessie said as she arranged Meg's hair. "Ever since they were young girls. Lady Featherstone's father's estate is near to here, and of course, Lady Vernon grew up at Thornshire Castle as the elder sister of the duke. Every year, they prepare for the Season together, and the night before they depart for London, they throw a masquerade ball at Thornshire. It's been a grand tradition since the two of them made their bows in the Queen's drawing room over twenty years ago."

Meg raised her brows. After only a few days among the duke's servants, Bessie was sounding as British as King George himself.

Bessie began to fasten Meg's curls, chattering around the hair pins that she held clamped in her teeth. "Lady Vernon's sons are all grown and married, except for her youngest, who is in His Majesty's Navy. Lady Featherstone arrived today with her son, the new earl, and her two younger daughters. Her eldest daughter is married. The late earl died tragically two years ago. Rumor has it, she's got her mind set to marry off her two younger daughters—and of course the earl—as quickly as possible."

Meg should have been thrilled with this news, but instead, a heavy brick of dread settled in her stomach. Here was her first opportunity to attempt to catch the eye of a member of the aristocracy. What type of man was Lord Featherstone? Would he be interested in her? Would she know how to keep his interest if he were?

Lost in her thoughts, she hadn't noticed that Bessie had finished and was waiting for Meg's approval.

"Thank you, Bessie. You did a lovely job," Meg said, studying her reflection. Bessie had managed to tame what Meg's mother referred to as a "crimson thicket" into sleek twists, arranged so that a few curls surrounded her face and fell down to her shoulders. The dress Meg had chosen was robin's egg blue, and one of her favorites, as the color complemented her auburn hair and light-brown eyes.

She left the room, closing the door to her bedchamber, and found her brother, Daniel, waiting for her in the hallway.

"And where have you been all day?" he asked. "No doubt you discovered a hideaway where you could read to your heart's content." Daniel smiled at her and offered his arm.

"You look very handsome tonight," Meg said, noting his crisp white shirt and smartly tied cravat. Her brother had no doubt been making good use of the valet the duke had procured for him. The man obviously knew how to choose clothing, as the dark blue of Daniel's coat muted the unfortunate hair color he shared with Meg.

He tipped his head in a thank you, grinned, and flipped a curl off of his sister's shoulder. "And I see Bessie has miraculously tamed your wild hair into submission." Daniel stopped at the landing above the great hall and turned toward her. He glanced once over his shoulder before speaking, all teasing gone from his expression. "Lord Featherstone owns a grand estate in Somerset. From what the steward tells me, his mother is eager for him to marry." He took Meg's hand from where it rested on his arm and pressed it between both of his. "Meg, I hope you remember what I said. Father is counting on you—I am counting on you."

The weight in Meg's stomach grew, and she thought she was going to be ill. "I remember, Daniel." She turned away and started toward the stairs.

He held onto her hand, pulling her back toward him. "Just take your lead from the other ladies. Speak about easy things, like the weather. For heaven's sake, do not mention the ridiculous Gothic romances you read or indulge in any of your strange fantasies. And don't forget to smile. Your smile will win over any man." He tipped his head, trying to catch her eye. Apparently he thought he'd bestowed a great compliment.

"Anything else? Would you like me to learn German or master the harpsichord before supper?" Her tone was more curt than she'd intended.

"Meg, I know it's not what you want. I would never wish you to be unhappy. Perhaps the earl is wonderful." He ran his fingers through his hair. "If only you hadn't been so picky in Charleston. You understand why you must do this, don't you?"

A rush of anger overcame Meg, but she managed to keep her temper in check. How often must she be reminded of the ship maker's son with his greasy hair and simpering smile? Was it too much to want a man who could carry on an intelligent conversation? She pulled her hand from Daniel's and started down the steps. "I understand, and I will do my best not to humiliate you." She had accepted her duty and would see it through, but she was insulted nonetheless.

"Meg—" Daniel began, but he didn't have a chance to finish what he would have said. At that moment, a group of people entered the Great Hall. Meg recognized Lady Vernon, and she assumed the tall thin man whose arm she leaned on was her husband. The remainder of the party was unfamiliar to her, and she stopped upon the stairs and allowed Daniel to catch up to her, unsure about facing them alone.

Before there was a chance to feel the least bit awkward, the duke and Serena, ever the perfect hosts, entered the main hall and graciously introduced Meg and Daniel to their new guests.

Besides Lord Vernon, who she had correctly assumed was the lanky man accompanying Lady Vernon, Meg was presented to Lady Featherstone and her three children: Anthony Poulter Lord Featherstone, and his two sisters, Lady Lucinda Poulter and Lady Helen Poulter.

The four members of the Poulter family had the brightest shade of blue eyes Meg had ever seen, and it was all she could do not to stare. She carefully curtseyed the way Lady Vernon had taught her.

Lord Featherstone in particular looked unimpressed with her attempt. In fact, he looked unimpressed with everything. The way he held himself and the look upon his face as he gazed around at the hall gave Meg the impression that he was making a conscious effort to keep his lip from curling in a sneer of contempt. He fixed his brilliant eyes upon her, taking in everything from her hair style down to her slippers, and she felt as though her worth as a person was being placed upon a scale in his mind. The feeling made her stomach turn.

Lady Featherstone took her hand, and Meg's gaze was pulled from the earl's bright eyes and captured by his mother's. "And how lovely that you have traveled from America for the Season. Rachel has spoken of little else for months."

Meg did not know to whom she referred to until Lady Featherstone waved her hand toward Lady Vernon. Meg had not known that Rachel was her Christian name.

"Thank you. Her ladyship has been most gracious to help me with my wardrobe and preparations," Meg said.

"Of course she has," Lady Featherstone said. "She has wanted a daughter of her own, and how could she not dress you up and dote upon you when you are such a handsome young woman?" She reached out a hand to one of her daughters, motioning her closer and then holding onto her elbow. "My Helen is coming out this year as well. She'll be delighted to have a friend." Lady Featherstone spoke in a matter-of-fact manner that Meg was uncertain how to interpret. "Now, did His Grace say your name is Miss Meg Burton?"

"It's Margaret, actually. But I go by Meg."

Lord Featherstone made a sniffing noise.

Meg's face colored, and she glanced at the earl. Did the noise signify his disapproval with her name? Or was her nervousness causing her to be extra sensitive? But before she could wonder more about his reaction, Serena excused them and led Meg toward where Lord Vernon, the duke, and Daniel were speaking to a man she had not noticed earlier.

"Miss Meg Burton, if you would allow me, I would like you to become acquainted with my dear friend, Colonel Jim Stackhouse."

Meg nodded her consent to the introduction.

The man turned, and it was all Meg could do to maintain her countenance. The side of Jim Stackhouse's face was marred with an uneven red scar that began at his forehead and passed through his eye, over his cheek, ending below his ear. He wore a patch over his eye, and his graying hair hung loosely to his shoulders, no doubt in an attempt to cover his disfigurement.

"How do you do, Colonel?" Meg said, hoping he could not hear from her voice that her throat had gone dry. Even without the scar and patch, he appeared menacing. A thrill skittered up her spine, and she tried not to look too interested at his injury.

His face was weathered and wrinkled, and his good eye scowled at her beneath a heavy brow. He looked to be no older than fifty, but she found it difficult to judge. She wondered if his many battles had aged him. The only thing that prevented him from looking like an evil villain or murdering pirate was the gold-trimmed regimental jacket he wore.

"A pleasure," he growled.

Meg did not think any words could have been more the reverse of his expression. She did her best not to cringe as his eye moved over her, but she was secretly delighted that a person so interesting and potentially dangerous had joined their party. The evening could hardly be tedious with such a dinner companion.

Serena slipped her hand into the crook of his elbow. "Colonel Stackhouse rescued me when the French attacked Sevilla, and he saw me safely from Spain." She looked at him with utter admiration, as if he were a kindly grandfather instead of a maimed war veteran. "He saved my life."

The colonel's face softened for a brief moment when he looked at Serena. He patted her hand before turning back to the men and continuing his discussion.

While she feigned interest in the men's conversation, Meg took the opportunity to study the gathering. Lord Vernon stood to the side nodding and smiling between the two groups while Lady Featherstone and Lady Vernon spoke together animatedly—Lady Vernon in her excited voice, and her friend in clipped tones that Meg decided was an indication of a more straightforward temperament.

Once Meg was able to look past the shock of their dazzling blue eyes, she saw that the Poulter siblings were not at all alike.

Lucinda was definitely the more confident of the sisters, while Helen appeared to be shy and timid. Perhaps it was because Lucinda was older, Meg thought. Both sisters were exceptionally beautiful, but where Lucinda's high cheekbones and pointed chin were all sharp angles, Helen appeared much softer. Her cheeks were rounded and her expression more pleasant and approachable.

The earl continued to look around the hall as if there were a foul odor that hovered just beneath his nose, which he was too polite to mention. His hair was fair like his other family members', and Meg noticed that he continually stroked his thumb and finger across his upper lip. When she looked closer, she was able to see a thin layer of whiskers that must be the beginnings of a mustache.

As she watched, Helen attempted to say something to her brother but was interrupted by Lucinda. Though she could not hear their words, she saw that the elder siblings conversed without allowing Helen to get a word in; even their body language seemed to shut her out.

Meg felt a swell of pity for the young lady. She understood all too well how it was to be the youngest sister. She didn't feel an overwhelming desire to get to know the rest of the family but thought she would like to become better acquainted with Helen.

Supper was announced, and the group made their way into the dining hall.

As they moved to the table, Meg overheard Lucinda speaking to Serena. "Will your brother be joining us this evening, Your Grace?"

"No, I am sorry. His duties keep him quite busy at the moment."

Meg did not much appreciate the reminder of the prince and the arrogant way he had avoided them since their arrival. No doubt his "duties" consisted of eating and sleeping and believing himself superior to his sister's guests.

It was thanks to their hosts' hospitality and attention to detail that the room was arranged so that a dinner party of eleven felt intimate and comfortable. Meg found herself seated between Lucinda Poulter and the earl. The Ladies Featherstone and Vernon sat on the other side of the table, chatting like young girls.

Conversation flowed around Meg, and she listened, feeling completely out of her element as the company discussed the events that would take place during the Season. Although he did not speak to her, Meg felt Lord Featherstone's eyes upon her more than once, and she concentrated on using the best possible manners as she ate.

Lucinda leaned toward her. "Miss Margaret, Helen is so looking forward to her debut, and you must be as well."

Meg swallowed and dabbed her napkin against her lips before answering. "Please call me Meg."

Lord Featherstone harrumphed again, and this time she was certain her name was the reason for his displeasure. She chose not to acknowledge his reaction, instead thinking of the way Carlo had called her Margarita, making her feel as if her name were the most beautiful word he knew. The thought brought a smile to her lips.

Meg looked up, meeting Lucinda's overly polite gaze. Her raised brows and stretched smile weren't fooling anyone. "Yes, I am quite looking forward to London and the Season. I am just now realizing how ill prepared I am."

Lucinda's eyebrows drew together, and her bottom lip pouted out in a show of concern. "I'd imagine it is quite a shock traveling to someplace so civilized from the wilds of America."

Wilds of America indeed—Charleston is one of the largest cities in the United States with a population of nearly 25,000, not a frontier town with log cabins and Indian raids. Inside Meg's mind, she regarded Lucinda with a tipped head, partially lidded eyes, and a flat stare. But outwardly she managed to maintain what she hoped was a refined expression. "Yes, undoubtedly London will prove to be very different from Charleston," Meg said.

"And you are so fortunate in your sponsors. Lady Vernon is truly an expert when it comes to town fashions. She has the best eye for style and color, and her modiste is second to none."

Meg glanced across the table at the woman in question just as Lady Vernon stole a glance down the table at Colonel Stackhouse and shuddered.

Lucinda continued. "She advised me on my wardrobe last Season, choosing the most exquisite gown of lilac for my debut ball. Thereafter, lilac became all the rage."

"I am sure it was lovely," Meg murmured, cutting a piece of pork and wondering how this topic could possibly become any less interesting.

"But, you know, it's not enough to merely wear a beautiful dress. There is much more to being an accomplished young lady than simply looking the part."

Meg swallowed and nodded. "You are right, of course."

"For example, my sister and I both play instruments, embroider, sketch, speak Italian and German, and arrange flowers."

"Very impressive," Meg attempted to nod approvingly as if these sorts of skills were a regular accomplishment of young ladies of her acquaintance, but inside, her stomach clenched. She had a passing knowledge of French and a pathetic ability at the pianoforte. Improving her talents had not been a matter of extreme importance as she'd attended school and helped her father manage his business.

"And what occupies your time, Meg? What sorts of activities do you do?" Lucinda's brilliant eyes were trained upon her, and though she did not turn her head, Meg could feel Lord Featherstone had stilled. He was awaiting her answer as well.

"I . . . well, I help my father with his bookkeeping. He is a merchant, you see. And I spend much of my time studying poetry and reading books."

Lucinda's expression did not change, though her eyes widened the slightest bit. "Your father works in trade? That is charming, dear," she said, nodding slowly, and doing little to mask the condescension in her voice. "I'm certain you perform your tasks wonderfully."

Meg's heart sank. She was in no way able to compete with the British ladies when it came to talents. And this was only her first exposure to the *ton*. What would the remainder of the Season be like?

"The development of one's mind is of utmost import," Lord Featherstone said.

Meg turned her head toward him. She felt her face relax into a grateful smile. He had saved her from embarrassing herself further with her lack of accomplishments. Perhaps she had misjudged the earl after all.

"Although it is important to consider what types of edification to choose," he continued, stroking his insubstantial mustache with the tip of his forefinger. "A lady should shun literature that puts radical ideas into her mind, especially such things as novels or modern poetry, focusing instead on things that improve her ability to manage a household and make appropriate social connections."

Meg's smile froze on her face. Her insides heated.

"It certainly would not do for a lady to form opinions that disagree with her husband's, for example." Lord Featherstone looked down at Meg as if she were a young child in need of a gentle reprimand. Meg would not have been surprised if he had patted her on the head and told her to go play with her poppets.

She opened her mouth but could not think of anything to say that wouldn't be extremely rude, so she closed it. She looked around the room, but aside from the two women across the table, the only person paying any attention to the conversation was Colonel Stackhouse, who regarded her with interest as if waiting to see how she would answer.

Lord Featherstone apparently thought that his words were being well received and continued. "It is appropriate that a young lady not concern herself with matters better left to gentlemen, focusing instead on maintaining a pleasant disposition. But certainly a bit of reading in order to add to her competence as a conversationalist is to be seen as a benefit. It is as King Henry said, 'The empty vessel makes the quietest sound.'"

Meg blinked. *Did the earl just misquote the bard?* This was an atrocity that she could not allow to pass without setting the record straight. "Sir, I am afraid you misunderstand Shakespeare's meaning. The boy in *Henry V* is musing on the babbling of the French soldier and the fact that in all his speaking the soldier said little. The boy paraphrases the proverb, 'The empty vessel makes the *greatest* sound,' meaning those with the most to say are often the least intelligent, while a wise person does not need to use so many words."

The moment the utterance left her mouth, Meg knew she had made a mistake. Lord Featherstone's face reddened, and his eyes narrowed. Meg glanced down the table, relieved to see that Daniel was too occupied with Helen to have overheard her blunder. The discomfort at their end of the table became palpable until Lady Featherstone took the attention away from Meg by speaking rather loudly.

"Colonel Stackhouse, Her Grace tells me you have been in Chelsea recovering from an injury."

Meg was astonished. Surely her correction of the earl's misunderstanding of Shakespeare was not as gauche as bringing up a man's deformity.

The colonel glanced up at Lady Featherstone, gazing flatly at her for a moment. "I should think the answer to your question is rather obvious, madam." He directed his attention back to his plate.

Apparently Lady Featherstone was not to be deterred by the colonel's clear wish to terminate the discussion. "And does your wound still give you discomfort, sir?"

"Discomfort?" The colonel set his silverware down and leaned back in his chair. "Madam, I was stabbed through the face with a French bayonet that flayed open my skin and popped my eyeball like a grape. I think discomfort is a rather mild term for such a sensation, don't you?"

The ladies at the table gasped, and Lord Featherstone whispered, "Oh my," as he put his hand over his mouth.

Meg, however, leaned forward in anticipation of a ghastly tale. This was quickly becoming the most entertaining evening of her stay thus far, and she didn't want to miss a moment of it.

Colonel Stackhouse glared at Lady Featherstone, but to her credit, the countess did no more than raise her brow. "I am quite skilled with herbs and ointments, sir," Lady Featherstone said, her voice remaining even and calm. "If you would allow me to inspect your injury, I believe I could create a salve that will relieve any itching and ease the soreness."

"That will not be necessary," the colonel said, returning to his meal.

"Mother, really . . . ," the earl said.

Lady Featherstone did not acknowledge her son or the shock in his voice. "Oh come, Colonel. If you think to spare my genteel sensibilities, you are speaking to the wrong woman. A salve will even help the scar to heal much more smoothly."

The colonel looked as if he would argue but perhaps did not want to draw more attention to himself by continuing to refuse. A war seemed to take place in his expression before he finally said, "Very well, madam. I thank you for your concern."

The servers began to clear the plates, and following Serena's lead, the ladies excused themselves to the drawing room. As they were leaving, Lord Vernon spoke up for the first time since the company had sat down to supper. "At which battle did you receive your wound, Colonel?"

Meg slowed down, hoping to hear some of the gruesome details.

"It wasn't a battle at all. Only a minor skirmish near Badajoz. Pointless, really."

Lord Featherstone nodded his head knowingly and stroked his fuzzy lip. "One may think that, sir. However, even the smallest engagements are important. As the poet said, 'But what good came of it at last? Why that I cannot tell, said he. But 'twas a famous victory.'"

Meg's head whipped around. Her eyes met the colonel's, and she saw that he was every bit as appalled as she. The man did not only misunderstand Shakespeare, but Southey too. She clenched her fists, digging her fingernails into her palms, and hurried from the room before her mouth got the better of her and she corrected the man again.

Lucinda waited for her in the hall and linked arms as the two walked to the drawing room to wait for the men to finish their port. "I should like to provide a bit of advice, Meg. I hope you will not take offense."

"Of course not," Meg said, knowing she would likely do just that. Although she had only known Lady Lucinda Poulter for a matter of one meal, she had already surmised her to be the calculating type of female that other young ladies ought to be wary of.

"Perhaps it is not the case in America, but in Britain, a lady does not correct a gentleman. You would not want to give the impression that you are a bluestocking."

Meg's skin tightened. It was one thing for Lady Vernon to give her never-ending tips on lady-like decorum, but Lucinda too? "Perhaps I simply wanted to give the impression that I have an intelligent thought in my head."

She felt Lucinda cringe. "*That* is even worse."

***

When the men joined them, they played at cards and listened to Helen perform on the pianoforte. Meg did her best to avoid Lord Featherstone. She did not wish to speak to a person so completely unfamiliar with classical works, although she could not help but notice that he watched her throughout the evening. Though he did not say or do anything inappropriate, the way he watched her made the hair rise on the back of her neck.

Two hours later, the members of the party began to separate and bid one another good night. Meg and her brother walked through the great hall toward the staircase.

Daniel glanced behind him to ensure that they were not within earshot of the others then leaned in to begin a conversation. "What did you think of the earl? He is handsome, is he not?"

"I suppose," Meg said, the image of wispy facial hair lingering in her mind. "He certainly does not know his poetry."

"One cannot have everything," Daniel said, winking as they began to walk up the stairs. "And Helen is such an agreeable young lady. And very pretty, don't you—"

They were interrupted by Lord Featherstone calling to Meg as he hurried to catch up with them.

Meg and Daniel descended the few steps to the base of the staircase.

The earl stopped and gave a small bow. "Miss Margaret Burton, I wondered if you might accompany me tomorrow for a ride in my chaise. That is, with your brother's consent, of course." The earl looked to Daniel for permission.

Daniel nodded. "Certainly."

Meg did not know what to say. Why would the earl ask to take her for a ride after she had apparently insulted him? Either he was unaffected by her words or was not one to carry a grudge. She was still formulating an answer when the earl spoke.

"Very well, shall we say eleven o'clock?" Lord Featherstone bowed quickly and took his leave.

Daniel bumped Meg's shoulder with his and waggled his eyebrows as they turned back to the stairs and climbed to the upper floor. "I told you no man could resist your smile. This is going to be easier than we had supposed."

Meg's head began to ache, and she wondered whether it was the trout they had eaten or the thought of spending time with Lord Featherstone and his horrific grasp of literature that made her stomach queasy.

Chapter 4

The next morning when Meg awoke, she was delighted to see the sun shining through the windows of her bedchamber. The brightness ignited optimism, and she found herself looking forward to something new, even if it was an outing with Lord Featherstone.

After breakfast, the earl accompanied Meg through the great hall and out the main entrance to his chaise. A beautiful dark horse was harnessed to the carriage. A Yorkshire Coach Horse, Meg thought, recognizing the long legs and elegant body; until now, she had only ever seen the breed in a reference book.

Lord Featherstone assisted her into the chaise and handled the reins himself, driving down the road, farther into the duke's estate. Meg tipped her head back, enjoying the feel of the warmth on her face as she admired the grounds. She took a detailed accounting of the scenery around them. With the sun shining, England was a completely different place. The meadows were beginning to sprout green grass, birds chirped, and buds clung to tree branches.

The earl did not seem to want to enjoy the serenity of a late winter's morning and instead filled the silence by describing his holdings in Somerset. Though Meg had yet to learn anything about the man himself—aside from his inability to grow a full mustache—she did learn that he had an income of 15,000 pounds per annum, an estate of more than 10,000 acres, which required a bailiff, land agent, and auditor to manage in his absence. Not to mention various other properties that accompanied lesser titles he had inherited. Lord Featherstone informed her that Hawthorne House itself had 34 bedchambers, a ballroom, extensive gardens, stained glass windows, a large conservatory, and a dining room to rival that of any estate in England.

Meg nodded and smiled in all the right places, but the earl apparently did not expect her to answer, so she allowed her mind to wander as he talked, specifically to the elegant horse pulling the carriage. Did Lord Featherstone realize that the horse would perform better if given her head? He held the reigns so tightly that it looked painful for the animal, and in Meg's opinion, the man was a bit too free with the whip.

She had almost resolved to mention it when movement between the trees caught her eye. She turned her head to look closer. There were people in the forest. It was most certainly a band of outlaws, she thought. "I think there is someone in the woods, my lord," Meg whispered.

Lord Featherstone peered in the direction Meg indicated, and they both saw the flash of color and glint of metal between the trees.

"Most likely poachers," he said, turning his gaze back to the road. He sniffed, and his lip curled as they moved past the spot. "The duke will undoubtedly need to be informed. Britain prosecutes such criminals severely."

"For hunting in the forest?" Meg asked, looking back over her shoulder.

"They are stealing the duke's animals," the earl said, his eyes narrowing. "If they are apprehended, they will be transported for a minimum of seven years."

"What does that mean, *transported*?" Meg began to feel the sinking feeling of unease.

He shrugged and ran his finger over his upper lip. "Deported, consigned to seven years of hard labor, and never allowed to return upon penalty of death."

"Perhaps they are simply trying to feed their families," she said. She was horrified with the injustice of it all. "How can the duke own the animals when they could at any moment walk in and out of his forest?" She tried not to allow her voice to rise, though she was not entirely successful.

He looked down at her, shaking his head and patting her hand where it rested in her lap. "Miss Margaret, do not concern yourself. Such things are not a lady's affair. You must put them out of your mind and leave these matters to men." He wrapped his hand around hers.

Meg bit down on her lip to prevent herself from arguing further. She lifted her hand away. The earl's touch had been the opposite of comforting. Her throat ached, and her eyes began to prickle. It was yet another reminder of the self-importance of the aristocracy and her reasons for wanting to avoid the entire upper class.

Lord Featherstone must have considered her silence to indicate agreement, and so continued to regale her with descriptions of his wealth and importance, which in his eyes were apparently all that mattered, and Meg thought the carriage ride could not end quickly enough for both her sake and the horse's.

When they neared the castle, she had readied herself to make a dash for her sanctuary in the library when she saw that the duke awaited them near the front entrance.

He waved and smiled, and once the carriage came to a halt, he held out his hand to help Meg step down. "A lovely day, is it not?"

"Yes, and we have had a nice tour of your estate. It is so very beautiful with the sun finally shining," Meg said.

He laughed. "I imagine the English weather takes some getting used to after the warm climate of South Carolina."

The earl joined them, and the duke turned to him. "I thought with the clear sky, it would be an excellent time to flaunt my new racehorses, if you are still interested." The duke's smile grew larger, and his enthusiasm was nearly tangible.

"I'd be delighted, your grace," Lord Featherstone said, tipping his head.

The duke turned to Meg. "Would you join us, Miss Meg?" He offered his arm, and Meg did not even hesitate.

Thoughts of escaping Lord Featherstone's company dispersed as she anticipated a tour of the duke's stables. She slipped her hand beneath her cousin's elbow. "Thank you, Your Grace. I would dearly love to see your horses."

"If you are not too tired from this morning's excursion," the earl said. "Perhaps you would prefer to rest during the heat of the day. I wonder if the stables will keep a lady's interest."

Meg made sure to turn away before she rolled her eyes. "I will endure it the best I can, my lord."

The duke squeezed her hand, where it rested on his arm, and when Meg looked at him, he gave her a quick wink.

Meg smiled, hoping that the duke's wink indicated that she was not the only one to find Lord Featherstone's assumptions about her absurd.

When they stepped through the doors, the smell of animals and straw assaulted her senses, but she felt comforted by the familiarity of it. She'd spent countless hours at her grandfather's horse farm. It took a moment for her eyes to adjust, and she looked around in awe. The duke's stables were grander than the Royal Exchange building in Charleston. The ceilings were high and the stalls spacious, separated by wooden partitions. Uniformed grooms moved purposefully as they tended to the animals, some leading the horses outside to the track for exercise, some feeding, and some cleaning the floors.

A stable hand led the earl's Yorkshire coach horse into a stall and filled a trough with water as another brushed the animal after its outing with the carriage.

Meg scanned the rows for one horse in particular, and finally, near the other end of the stable, she spotted the white head of Patito.

The duke led them past the stalls telling about each horse as they passed. Meg was in love. Some of these breeds she had only read about in equine reference books. The duke certainly had an eye for high quality horseflesh as well as beauty.

When they reached Patito's stall, Meg released the duke's arm and stepped closer. "Hello, Patito," she said in a soft voice, patting his neck. The men continued to talk, and she allowed the stallion to nuzzle her cheek. Meg's heart jumped when Carlo stepped around from the other side of the horse. She'd thought him pleasant-looking before, but with his face clean shaven and his dark eyes wide with surprise, she was caught off guard by how handsome he was.

When she opened her mouth to greet him, he shook his head, placing a finger in front of his mouth and looking pointedly over her shoulder.

Meg realized how inappropriate it would be for the duke and Lord Featherstone to see her greet a servant familiarly and so held her tongue, but she could not help the contentment she felt at seeing him. She gave Carlo a small smile, patted Patito one last time, and made her way to where the men were waiting.

She noticed the duke nod politely to Carlo, but Lord Featherstone did not appear to notice any of the servants or acknowledge their presence.

Carlo kept his head bowed, which looked unnatural for a man who stood so straight. He stepped back into the shadows, and Meg's insides squirmed uncomfortably. A groom must remain subservient in the gentlemen's presence, she reminded herself.

The duke and earl had stopped in front of a stall and were admiring a black horse when she rejoined them. Meg was taken aback by the animal's beauty.

"A Thoroughbred," she said. "He is so majestic." The horse was obviously bred for racing, with a lean body and long legs.

She stepped closer, but the earl stretched out his arm, blocking her from moving closer. "Be careful, miss. An animal like this is spirited. I'd not want you to be frightened."

"Oh, I shan't be frightened, sir. My grandfather owns a few of this breed, though they are older. And I quite enjoy riding them, *especially* if they have a bit of spirit."

Lord Featherstone made the sniffing noise that Meg was beginning to loathe. "It is a pity your education in appropriate behaviors was so neglected." He looked down at her with a sad smile. "Though your enthusiasm is delightful, such an activity as riding a racehorse is hardly suitable for a lady."

Meg did not answer. Her throat was tight, but this time it was not from the despair of injustice. The earl infuriated her with his condescension. It did not appear that she and Lord Featherstone had any topics on which they could agree, especially as they concerned her. The idea of remaining with the earl and withstanding his barbs suddenly seemed more than Meg was willing to bear. She was emotionally exhausted from merely a few hours with the man.

"I am sorry, gentlemen, please excuse me. I believe I'll take your advice, my lord, and rest for a few hours," Meg said, dipping in a curtsey. She kept her eyes on the stable floor, not wanting to see Lord Featherstone's arrogant expression and not wanting the duke to see the discouragement she knew she would not be able to hide.

"Come, I will accompany you back to the castle," said the earl.

"No, thank you, I will be quite all right alone. Continue your tour."

Lord Featherstone nodded. "With such a delicate constitution, it would be best . . ."

Meg did not stay long enough to hear the remainder of his words but hurried from the stable toward the castle glancing back only once to see Carlo's gaze on her from the shadows. She rushed down the path, into the great hall, and up the staircase.

When she arrived in the library, she stopped when she heard a snore; peeking around the back of the wingback chair near the fireplace, she saw Colonel Stackhouse. But when she realized her footsteps hadn't awakened him, she tiptoed to her spot on the window seat and closed the curtains, grateful to be alone as she fumed.

Meg opened a book and tried to read, but even Ann Radcliffe was unable to distract her from her irritation. "Not a suitable activity for a lady indeed," she muttered. "Well, my lord, perhaps you would prefer it if I were to misquote Shakespeare and recount the number of drawing rooms at Hawthorne House."

She rubbed the back of her neck, which she realized was painfully tight. Angry tears sprung to her eyes, and she swiped them away. Was this the life she was destined for? A life with someone like the earl? A man of wealth who cared little for the people beneath him and less about a woman's opinion? The idea of marrying a man like Lord Featherstone was simply too repulsive to consider. How could her family expect this of her?

As she considered all the things that had unsettled her, she thought of how the earl had treated the poor horse. Was this how the aristocracy treated their wives? She had never seen the duke behave in any way but kindly toward Serena, but perhaps he was an anomaly. How could she guarantee she would not find a husband who was cruel and controlling? How could she form an attachment in a society she wanted no part of?

Meg sighed and leaned her head against the cool of the window. A movement drew her attention, and she turned to focus her gaze on the lane that ran from the stables to the side entrance of the castle. Carlo stood there, waving one arm at her, holding the reins to Patito and a beautiful dark Thoroughbred. When she waved back, he beckoned to her and then motioned toward the saddles on the animals. She saw the dark horse was equipped with a lady's saddle, and she sat up straighter. She pointed at herself and raised her brows, tipping her head toward him.

Carlo nodded, raising his own brows and smiling.

Meg flung aside the curtains and hurried out of the library as quietly as possible so as not to wake Colonel Stackhouse. She skipped down the stairs before whirling around and running back to her bedchamber for her riding coat.

Chapter 5

Rodrigo tapped his foot as he waited for Meg. As soon as the men had left the stable, he'd saddled Patito and one of the duke's Thoroughbreds and hoped he would find Meg at her spot in the window seat. If not, he supposed he would have had to send a servant for her, but gratefully she was precisely where he'd seen her so often the last few days as he'd gone back and forth to the stables to tend to Patito. He'd been trying to devise a way to see Meg again, only to have the opportunity fall directly into his lap.

The dark horse was not a young racing horse such as the one she had admired with the duke but one a few years older, and much gentler. But he would not tell Meg that. Not after seeing the way the earl's words had affected her. He'd realized that Meg was not a lady he would ever tell that she was not capable of something; first of all because she would likely do it anyway, but mostly because he would never want to be the one to cause such a disheartened expression on her face. It had stung him to see, and he'd immediately felt the need to give her a chance to prove that she could indeed manage a spirited Thoroughbred. Even if it was just to prove it to herself. But despite this, the idea of Meg riding a dangerous racehorse was more than he was willing to entertain until he saw how she handled herself on horseback.

This young woman and her well-being had moved to the center of his thoughts in the past few days. He'd seen her reading in the window and had contemplated for hours what sort of books she found interesting. He already knew she favored unconventional romances, and she longed for adventure. She was intelligent. He could tell that immediately by how she spoke and studied the world around her. In fact, he was surprised how much he knew about Meg Burton after only interacting with her one time.

She hurried out of the castle and joined him much sooner than he had anticipated, wearing a brown riding coat and hat. Her eyes shone with an excitement that soon enveloped him and made a ride in the country sound like the most wonderful activity imaginable.

"Carlo! Patito! Are we to go riding?" She clasped her hands together, her face shining.

The stallion whinnied, and she patted his nose.

"I believe you mentioned having some experience with this breed." Rodrigo nodded toward the dark mare, and Meg moved toward the horse, reaching up to run her hand along the animal's neck.

Meg nodded. "My grandfather raises horses on his farm outside of Charleston." She took the reins and pulled the mare's head lower to stroke her nose. "What is her name?"

"Bonnie." He could not help but be impressed with the way Meg handled the animal. She showed no fear, speaking softly and moving smoothly so as not to startle the horse.

"Hello, Bonnie," Meg said in a gentle voice, keeping eye contact with the mare. She continued stroking the horse as she moved to study the animal's trappings. Meg expertly checked the saddle's cinch, making sure the strap was tight and adjusting the stirrup before she turned to Rodrigo. "I do not typically ride sidesaddle. On my grandfather's farm, he allows me to wear breeches and sit astride. But I am up to a challenge." Her eyes twinkled. "That is, if you and Patito think you are prepared for a race."

Rodrigo's brow lifted on its own volition. *A race?* He had not done anything for the sheer diversion of it for longer than he could remember. "Patito and I accept your challenge." He inclined his head. "I'm afraid I did not think to bring a mounting stool," he said.

"Oh." Meg's cheeks colored slightly as he stepped closer to assist her onto the horse, and even though Rodrigo did not want to cause her any embarrassment, he found it to be incredibly charming to see her blush.

Meg placed one gloved hand on the saddle pommel and the other upon his shoulder. She stepped into his linked hands and bounced a few times before they both lifted together, and she situated herself upon the saddle, slipping her foot into the stirrup and arranging her skirts.

Once he was certain Meg was securely seated, Rodrigo mounted Patito and turned to her. "Are you ready?"

Meg looked thoughtful. "I think Bonnie and I should become used to one another before we show you and Patito how ladies lead the pack."

Rodrigo felt a lightness inside at her words, an impulse to grin like a fool. He'd not grinned in years. Meg seemed to contain an endless supply of joy that seeped into him when she was near.

He watched Meg as they rode down the path away from the castle. She had not misrepresented her skill with a horse. She sat straight in the saddle, looking at ease as she balanced in what he could only imagine was a horribly uncomfortable position. She led the mare masterfully, understanding when to allow Bonnie freedom and when to retain control. She spoke softly but firmly to the animal, and occasionally he noticed Patito reacting to Meg's voice as well. *It seems he wasn't the only male having a difficult time resisting this young lady's charms.*

After a few moments, she turned toward him and grinned. Then suddenly she spurred Bonnie with her foot and riding crop. The horse leapt forward under Meg's encouragement and broke into a full-out gallop.

Patito needed no urging. He sprang after them, and they followed Meg and Bonnie away from the path and through a meadow.

Meg glanced back once then leaned forward, pushing her horse faster.

Rodrigo followed, both exhilarated at the competition and at the same time terrified that Meg might be thrown and injured. He knew she would be furious to know he had such thoughts, so he kept them from showing on his face. He ground his teeth and gave Patito his head. The stallion surged toward Bonnie, and when they neared, Meg reigned the mare in, laughing.

The sound penetrated into his heart, warming him from the inside, and Rodrigo made it his personal mission in the next week and a half to hear Meg's laughter again—often.

Her cheeks were flushed, and her hair was coming loose from its bindings. She pushed the curls out of her face with a flip of her fingers. "Carlo, I cannot thank you enough. I had resigned myself to a day of boredom."

"As had I."

"And you are certain the prince doesn't mind you riding his horse?"

Rodrigo studied her face for an instant and then shook his head. "Patito needs to be exercised." He turned the horse toward a hill that rose from the meadow floor.

"He seems to favor you," Meg said, urging Bonnie to follow.

"*Sí.* We have been friends for a long time." Rodrigo patted the stallion's neck, careful to be as honest as he could, even as he maintained the ruse necessary for them to remain so comfortable with one another. "He is one of the only companions that accompanied me from Spain."

"Do you miss Spain?"

Rodrigo's throat tightened. He missed his homeland so much that at times it was painful. "Nearly every moment," he said.

"I am sorry."

He turned toward her and tried to muster a smile. "But today for the first time in months, I have had something else to occupy my mind, and for that I must thank you."

Meg regarded him thoughtfully, and he wondered how much of his frustration was evident in his expression. "Is it painful to speak of your home? I would love to know more about Spain."

"What would you like to know?"

Meg tipped her head, as if she were thinking. "Have you ever seen a bullfight?"

"Yes. Of course." Unsurprisingly her mind had jumped to that exhibition. Her fascination with the sensational was utterly enchanting. And she wasn't the kind of lady to behave squeamishly as so many British women did when he discussed the violent performance—or its gruesome end.

She looked at him expectantly, obviously waiting for him to tell her more.

"Margarita, *la corrida de toros*, it is—"

Meg shook her head and let out a groan. "Please don't say it is not appropriate for a young lady or I might scream."

The look on her face saddened him as he wondered how often Meg had been discouraged from learning or trying new things. "I was going to say, *la corrida de toros*, it is something you would love."

"Truly?" Her face brightened.

"*Sí*. It is very sensational. The toreadors, they are masters who have trained for years. The bullfighter learns the quirks of the bulls as he confronts the animal with his capote and maneuvers out of reach of the animal's horns, at times coming within inches of being gored." He demonstrated with his hands the swish of the cape and the near miss of the bulls' horns.

Meg watched, enraptured by his description. "The entire performance is filled with pageantry, costumes, a parade, and music; but mostly it is the tradition that makes it special. The tradition of *festival*, of celebration."

"Tell me more. What else happens at *festival*?" Meg's eyes were alight with excitement, and he loved that his words had been the cause.

"Of course, no gathering would be complete without a feast, and Spaniards love to eat. Supper is much more informal than it is in England, often lasting late into the night. And the food is delicious. Pastries, fish, chicken stew, fresh fruit. And delicious desserts I have yet to see in England. I particularly love *turrón.*"

"It all sounds wonderful. I would love to travel to Spain." The light in her eyes dimmed, and Meg's expression changed to wistful.

Rodrigo thought there was nothing he would like better than to watch the delight on Meg's face as she experienced *festival* for the first time.

Then the truth spread like a shadow over his mood. There was no *festival.* Spain was in turmoil. His countrymen were dying and their livelihoods torn away. Even when this war ended, would the country he loved ever recover?

They reached a stream, and Rodrigo dismounted then moved to Bonnie's side to assist Meg. She put her hands on his shoulders and leaned into him as he lifted her down from the saddle. When he moved to back away, Meg reached out a hand to touch his arm.

"I didn't mean to make you more homesick."

He looked down at her caramel-colored eyes, aware of how close they stood to one another. He had not thought it possible for a person's expression to touch him so deeply. "You did not. I simply allowed my mind to wander. I apologize."

She nodded. "I understand."

"I imagine you do."

They led the horses to the stream and allowed them to drink. Rodrigo worried that he had cast a pall over their outing and tried to think of a way to bring Meg's smile back. "Tell me about Charleston. You said your grandfather raises horses?"

Meg nodded, running her hand over Bonnie's neck. She glanced at him for a moment and then turned back to the mare. "Yes, racehorses. I learned to ride at his farm." She sighed. "Charleston, my family, all of it seems so far away." She continued to stare at the horse as she spoke, her hand moving automatically in the same repetitive motion. "I'd always dreamed of embarking on a grand adventure. Sailing across the sea to visit a castle seemed so magical, but now that I am here, I realize nothing is how I had imagined. I will likely never return home."

Rodrigo was taken aback. Why would Meg believe that she was not to return to Charleston?

Meg turned toward him with a start, and he wondered if she purposely changed the topic. "I forgot to tell you, Lord Featherstone and I saw poachers in the forest. I hope you will be careful if you and Patito ride in there."

At the sound of his name, the horse lifted his head toward her, and she rubbed his nose. It seemed Patito was smitten.

"I would guess they are not poachers," Rodrigo said. "More likely soldiers. The prince and his sister are under heavy guard."

Meg tipped her head to the side and ran her teeth over her lip as she considered this information. "I imagine it is frustrating for them," she said, "living in constant fear. It would make one's house seem like a prison." She patted Patito's neck.

Rodrigo turned the horses back toward the road.

"I should return to the castle," Meg said. "Lady Vernon expects me this afternoon for a gown fitting."

"Has the issue with the apricot dress been resolved to your satisfaction?" Rodrigo hoped the change of subject would lighten the mood as he helped Meg back onto the horse.

"I am afraid not." She took the reins from him, and once he was astride Patito, the horses began to walk side by side back toward Thornshire Castle. "Lady Vernon is quite adamant that I wear it to Lady Harrison's musicale. She has even ordered a head dress with feathers for me. I shall either look like an Indian chief or a chicken." Meg shrugged her shoulders, her eyes rolling.

Rodrigo fought the impulse to laugh at her sentiment. Even when she did not intend to, Meg managed to lift his spirits, but right now, she looked so unhappy.

"I wish we didn't have to return so quickly," Meg said. "I have enjoyed this more than any day since I arrived in England." She rode with her gaze down.

They rode to the stables, and he helped Meg dismount. One of the duke's grooms took Bonnie away but knew that Rodrigo preferred to care for his own horse.

Meg's melancholy hung over them, and the air felt heavy. Rodrigo cast his eyes around, looking for something to say that would return her good humor.

"Did I tell you what *Patito* means?" Rodrigo asked as Meg patted the stallion's nose.

Her eyes squinted in confusion. "I assumed it was simply a name."

"In Spanish, it means small duck—duckling."

A smile stretched her lips. It grew, lifting her cheeks and finally reaching her eyes, igniting the sparkle he had not realized had been so obviously missing until it was returned. "The prince's white stallion is named *Ducky*?"

Rodrigo nodded. He smiled himself at the laughter in her eyes.

"How did such a powerful animal come to have a name that is so . . ."

"Sweet?" Rodrigo offered.

Meg giggled. "Yes. Sweet."

"When Patito was a foal, he and his mother were housed in a large paddock that contained a pond. A duck built her nest near the pond, and when the ducklings hatched, they followed their mother in a line. Patito followed too." Rodrigo smiled, remembering how comical it had looked to see the horse following along as if he were one of the ducklings.

"I adore that story." Meg laid her hand on her chest, sighing. "Patito, you are a warrior with a gentle heart." She leaned close and kissed the stallion's nose.

Rodrigo would not have ever imagined a time would come when he was jealous of his own horse.

Chapter 6

A BEAD OF SWEAT ROLLED down Meg's back as she took the dance master's hand and allowed him to lead her from the floor. They had been practicing for hours, beginning directly after luncheon. Her feet hurt, and she was utterly exhausted.

"Much better, miss," Mr. Crenshaw said. "But there is more to a dance than simply memorizing the steps. A lady should appear to glide across the floor." He swept his hand in front of him with his palm down. "Effortless grace is one of her best assets."

"I understand," Meg said, hoping this little speech was an indication that their lesson was over. The steps in England were much more formal and complicated than what she was used to, and the idea of blundering the sequence in front of a ballroom full of elegant ladies and gentlemen made her insides shudder.

"You are such a beautiful young lady," Lady Vernon spoke up from where she sat on a chair near the wall. "It is too bad that you clomp around like a . . ." She waved her hand in front of her, as if searching for the right word but apparently gave up. "Well, anyway, you shall simply need to practice. The ball is in less than two weeks, and I know you will want to demonstrate your proficiency for all the handsome gentlemen who will attend." She smiled, obviously anticipating the event more than Meg.

Meg nodded. It had been an incredibly long and disheartening day, and she didn't have it in her to pretend to be enthusiastic about anything at the moment. Least of all noblemen who were much more likely to be impressed by the accomplished young ladies with titles and large dowries than an American merchant's daughter.

Lady Vernon had spent the morning listening to Meg pound out the repertoire of songs she knew on the pianoforte. The countess's smile had been kind, but she had determined in only a few minutes that Meg would need to work with a music instructor if she was to prepare a song for Lady Harrison's musicale.

"I do not think it is necessary for me to perform," Meg had said. "Surely there are others who are much more accomplished to fill the time."

Lady Vernon had shaken her head. "It is the custom for all the young ladies who will come out this Season to present. It gives the gentlemen an opportunity to view them in their best light."

Meg did not think her pathetic attempts to play the instrument while wearing a gown that made her skin look pale and sallow was her "best light," but she had learned to simply nod, discouraging further analysis of her shortcomings. She wished it were some other venue where she would not stand out as the least accomplished young lady.

The gown fitting that followed had been no better, and the feathers in her hair were the least of her worries as Lady Vernon and the modiste discussed the ways to conceal the freckles on Meg's upper arms, where her gloves wouldn't reach. It was decided that she would be better off wearing longer sleeves.

Serena had joined them and asked to see Meg's Season wardrobe. "Oh, Meg. *Qué hermoso sera*. You will be so beautiful," she said, holding up a cream-colored gown. "And this; you must try this on for me, *por favor*."

"Thank you," Meg said, smiling as she stepped behind the privacy screen and changed her clothes for what felt like the thousandth time.

Serena clapped and asked Meg to spin around and even spent some time admiring and discussing the bonnets, fans, gloves, and ribbons Lady Vernon had chosen. Serena's presence had made the entire experience much less grueling, and Meg even began to feel excited about the gowns. It was refreshing to receive compliments instead of criticism, and Meg found herself laughing more than once.

Meg realized that Serena reminded her a bit of Carlo. Perhaps it was the way she listened to Meg's opinion, instead of simply telling her what was best. *Or it might be her accent*, Meg thought.

Before Serena had left, she'd held up the dreaded apricot gown. "I do hope you're not intending to wear this particular dress to the musicale," she said. "My dress will be precisely the same color, and what a disaster that would be for us to arrive together."

Lady Vernon and the modiste had immediately begun reassessing the gown choices for Lady Harrison's musicale, and just before Serena left the room, she caught Meg's gaze and winked.

Meg pondered on the meaning behind the duchess's action. Did Serena know how she felt about the gown? But how could she? Meg didn't have time to think about it for long before the dance master gave a small tug on her hand, and she was quickly transported back to the present.

"And now, miss, if you will demonstrate the five positions of dancing . . ."

When the dance instruction finally ended, Meg fled to the sanctuary of her window seat in the library, but her reprieve only lasted an hour until it was time to change for supper.

When she reached the top of the stairs with her hair arranged and wearing a fresh gown, she saw Lord Featherstone, Colonel Stackhouse, and Daniel standing together in the main hall.

Even though she could not hear what they were discussing, she could see by Daniel's posture that he was uncomfortable. He stood rigidly with his arms folded and brows furrowed. Colonel Stackhouse was listening to Lord Featherstone, whose back was turned to Meg. The colonel's face was unreadable.

Meg stepped quietly down the stairs, so as not to disturb the men, and as she approached, the earl's words became clear.

"It is bad enough that cotton prices have risen in the extreme, but my steward tells me that we shall have to begin to find another source for sugar. I know I am not alone in my opinion that the former colonists owe us the courtesy of discontinuing trade with our enemies. Why, it is no secret that the Royal Navy has been forced to employ privateers to seize American cargo ships bound for France."

Meg stopped with one foot in the air. The arrogant earl must know that the navy's action was costing her father his very livelihood.

Daniel looked up, his gaze meeting hers. His face was pale with anger, and she saw lines of tension around his lips. He shook his head ever so slightly, indicating that Meg should remain silent.

Colonel Stackhouse's eye darted to her quickly, but he continued to regard the earl without acknowledging Meg's presence. "If I understand you correctly, sir, you are saying that the Americans should stop acting like an independent nation and work harder to serve Britain's global interests."

"Precisely," Lord Featherstone said, nodding once. And even though Meg was behind him and could not see his face, she could tell by the motion of his arm that he was stroking his upper lip whiskers.

"And, Miss Burton, what is your opinion on the matter?" the colonel said without taking his gaze from the earl.

"I . . ." Meg didn't look at Daniel but could see from the corner of her vision that he was attempting to catch her eye.

Lord Featherstone turned and stood aside as Meg stepped down the remaining stairs.

She looked between the two men. Colonel Stackhouse stood quietly, awaiting her reply, and Meg had fully decided to play the entire matter off as if she did not understand such issues and change the subject—until the earl blinked and lowered his chin. That slight movement portrayed such a wealth of condescension that Meg's hands clenched, and a flood of words poured from her mouth.

"I believe that exact attitude, the British blatant disregard of rights, not to mention contempt for international laws upon the high seas is the reason that there will most assuredly be another war between Columbia and Britannia." Meg turned her head from the colonel to the earl. His bright eyes were half-lidded, and he held a small smile as he appeared to humor her, and she could not help but continue.

"And if you would condemn American merchants for trading with the French, perhaps, England would care to explain how the Indians attacking frontier settlements have come to be supplied with British weapons." Meg's legs were trembling.

"Meg," Daniel stepped toward her and placed his hand beneath her elbow. "This is hardly the—"

"Dear Miss Burton," Lord Featherstone interrupted her brother, "I admire your loyalty to your homeland. It is quite adorable." He shook his head from side to side slightly, his face still exhibiting that expression that looked as if he were speaking to a person of slow wits. "But you understand America has no hope of defeating His Majesty's Navy."

Meg pulled her arm from Daniel's grip and turned her entire body to face the earl directly. "It is true, sir. Although the continual illegal impressment of Americans to serve in the British navy has provided many men with an excellent training in naval warfare, however unwanted it might be." The issue of impressment had been a topic of heated discussion in Charleston ever since the Chesapeake-Leopard affair, and the thought of men taken forcefully from their families to serve for years aboard a foreign warship heated Meg's blood further.

"I think you would be surprised, sir. The shipyards in Massachusetts produce top quality vessels. But even if America didn't have the resources to attack the British fleet, the fact is, England's soldiers are spread about the globe. Even now, more and more are sent to the peninsula, not to mention India and other holdings of the crown. I would not be surprised if the United States decided to put pressure on Britain by invading the Canadian colonies. Strategically, it is the perfect—"

"Margaret," Daniel spoke more forcefully.

When she allowed her anger to abate to a simmer, Meg saw the horror on her brother's face. This sort of topic certainly was not among those deemed suitable for a young lady, and she had undoubtedly offended the men. Colonel Stackhouse continued to study her, and Lord Featherstone's lips had pressed into a look of such disapproval that they had almost completely disappeared.

She closed her eyes and released her breath, willing a pleasant smile to her lips. "But perhaps we should change the topic to one a bit more suitable for a dinner party." Meg forced her arms to relax and tipped her head to the side. "Lord Featherstone, I have not yet thanked you for the lovely flowers that were delivered to my room this morning. And I believe your mother said you spent the day shooting in the duke's forest. And did I hear that you are planning a fox hunt?"

***

Meg excused herself directly after supper, claiming that her long day had quite worn her out. She trudged up the stairs and down the hallway to her bedchamber. After she stepped inside and closed the door behind her, she sagged against it. Today had been one of the worst days she could remember. She had failed at every attempt to be an accomplished young lady, and even worse she had disappointed Daniel—again.

The dance instruction and music had been grueling. She had hoped for the time to go for a ride on Bonnie with Carlo or at least to read for a few hours. She didn't care if she was being overly dramatic as she indulged herself for a moment, envisioning pulling on a cloak and wandering grief-stricken through the woods. But as tempting as the idea was, she knew it wouldn't make her feel better. All she really wanted to do was sit on the floor and weep.

A knock sounded behind her, and she opened the door for Bessie to help her undress. Her lady's maid chattered on as she unpinned Meg's hair, pulling it back into a braid so it wouldn't be so difficult to manage in the morning.

And finally when Meg was left alone, she found she was too tired to even cry herself to sleep.

***

Meg woke disoriented and looked around in the darkness, trying to discover what had awakened her. She listened for a moment and, finally deciding it had been nothing, turned over to go back to sleep when she heard it. A scratching on the door.

She pulled the bed coverings to her chin, straining her ears, and after a moment, it came again. But this time the scratching was accompanied by what she thought sounded like a chain being dragged over the floor.

Meg's heart began to race. Surely she was imagining it. But when she heard the scratching for the third time, she mustered her courage and climbed out of bed quietly. She pulled a wrap around her shoulders and stepped to the door.

Her mouth was dry, and her pulse sounded in her ears as she opened the door of her bedchamber just a crack and peeked out. A large window at the end of the hallway provided a bit of moonlight, and Meg was relieved when she saw nothing. She opened the door wider and looked around the doorframe in the other direction. A jolt of terror shot through her when she saw a flash of white and heard the jangle of chains.

She pulled away from the door quickly, breathing heavily. She hadn't imagined it. Something white was floating in the hall, glowing in the moonlight. An apparition? Her pulse sounded in her ears, and she breathed heavily. Her legs trembled, and she wanted to cry out or hide under her sheets, but the compulsion to investigate overrode her fear. She stepped into the hallway, creeping toward the place where she'd seen the ethereal form.

When she reached the end of the corridor, she stood in the shadows, trying to calm her breathing. She held onto the wrap with shaking fingers, attempting to gather her nerve to round the corner when she heard the chains jangle again.

A delightful surge of terror crept down her spine. She did not believe a true phantom could hurt her, and if she did not follow it, she would possibly never have another chance to see where it disappeared to. Meg closed her eyes, took a deep breath, then stepped around the corner.

In the hallway, she found not a specter, but *Carlo*. He crouched on the carpet, and it appeared that he was attempting to wrap a length of chain in a large white sheet.

Meg gasped.

Carlo raised his head. Even in the dimly lit hallway, she could see from his expression that he had not expected to be discovered.

He took a step toward her, and she stumbled back.

Carlo placed one finger to his lips, apparently hoping she would not scream. "Margarita . . ."

"Carlo, what are you doing?" she asked in a loud whisper.

He dropped his arms to his sides, took a step back, and glanced toward the sheet on the hallway floor before looking back at Meg. "I was trying to imitate a ghost." He placed his hands on his hips. "But I never dreamed you would be bold enough to chase me."

"A ghost?" Meg furrowed her brow. "Why would you do such a thing?"

Carlo looked decidedly uncomfortable. "You mentioned that you wished the castle was haunted, and . . ." He shrugged.

Meg looked from Carlo to the bundle upon the floor and then back as the entire scenario suddenly made sense. "You pretended to be a ghost in order to frighten me?"

Carlo's eyes widened, and he shook his head. "No, of course not. I only—"

But Meg didn't allow him to finish. She rushed toward him, and he lifted his hands as if to ward off her displeasure. "Carlo! I cannot believe you would do such a thing." She held out her arm and pulled up her sleeve. "Do you see this? Gooseflesh! I truly thought there was a ghost in the hall."

"I am sorry. I—"

"This is the most exciting thing that has ever happened to me!" She was still whispering, but somehow a twitter of a giggle entered her voice. "I was terrified when I heard the scratching . . . and then the chains. Terrified! Do you see? I am still trembling." She kept her hand held out in front of her to demonstrate.

Carlo's face had relaxed into a relieved smile, and Meg realized she had not seen the expression on him before. She also noticed that it was extremely handsome and that the moonlit shadows served to emphasize his high cheekbones and shroud his face partly in darkness. The dimple in his cheek deepened. For some reason this caused another chill to travel over her spine.

"Thank you for giving me a deliciously terrifying adventure," she said, wrapping her arms around herself. She closed her eyes and blew out a sigh. "It was completely wonderful."

Carlo tipped his head to the side. "I am glad you apprehended me. For such a reward, I would willingly humiliate myself again."

Meg was touched by his words; Carlo had not only done something thoughtful for her, but he had also placed himself in a dangerous situation. If a stable hand were discovered creeping through the castle hallways late at night, she did not know what his punishment might be. Their lightness of her mood was quickly replaced by a more serious tone as they stood together.

For a long moment he held her gaze, and in the shadows she tried to discern his expression. Though he was still a step away, Meg could feel the heat from his body. She became extremely aware of Carlo and his nearness, and she quickly recognized that they were together in the middle of the night, and she was wearing only her nightclothes.

He seemed to realize the same thing and took a step back. "Come. You have had enough adventure for one night. I must return you to your bedchamber." Carlo took her hand and looked at her thoughtfully before tucking it beneath his elbow and leading her down the hallway.

The door was still open, and Carlo stopped. Though he still held Meg's hand, he allowed her to walk the few remaining steps alone.

Meg turned in the doorway, stifling a yawn. "Thank you again, Carlo. I feel lucky to have such a friend."

"*Dulces sueños,* Margarita. Sweet dreams."

Chapter 7

RODRIGO WALKED DOWN THE PATH to the dower house feeling more contented than he had in years. To be honest, he felt positively giddy. Assuming a man could feel such an emotion.

He'd left the castle directly after seeing Meg to her room, not returning to the side hallway to fetch the "haunting equipment"; instead he'd sent a servant. The duke's well-trained man no more batted an eye at that strange request than he had when Rodrigo had sent him to procure the items in the first place.

Rodrigo could not remember doing anything so spontaneous or absurd—and for the sheer diversion of it. It had been foolish to creep around the halls in the dark of night wrapped in a sheet, but at the same time, he'd felt a rush of nervous excitement and could not attribute it only to the successful execution of a clandestine mission. He'd been anxious to see Meg's reaction.

He had imagined her peeking out of her doorway and closing the door quickly, delighting in the fact that the castle was indeed haunted. But he would never have guessed in a million years that Meg would chase a ghost down the hall. The memory of her finding him brought a rumbling sensation very much like a laugh deep in his chest.

The entire situation had been silly and childish, and he should at this very moment feel completely ridiculous. But as he'd watched Meg's expression as she realized what he'd done and seen her confused face soften into pure delight, he'd not regretted his actions one bit. He only wished he had thought of the entire scheme sooner.

When he reached the dower house that the duke had been gracious enough to allow him to occupy with a small staff, he made his way directly to the study, where he sank into the soft chair behind the desk. He leaned his head back and allowed himself to bask in the glow of the night's events—the image of Meg in her nightclothes with her face flushed and her eyes wide as she smiled at him, the feel of her warm hand as he'd seen her to her bedchamber, and her smile when he bid her good night. His heart stuttered for a moment, and then he put the memories carefully away to examine later. When it came to shelving thoughts that might elicit too much emotion, he was certainly an expert. He sighed and lifted a pile of papers closer. It would be a long night, and he could not put off his task any longer.

He'd been working closely with the Cortes Parliament at Cádiz. They consulted him as they formed a new constitution for Spain. The entire issue of the country's government had been in upheaval for years, even before the French invasion and Napoleon's installation of his brother as the ruler. The factions within the country that had been at odds split farther apart, some embracing the French ideals, some clamoring for the return of King Fernando. The Cortes Parliament sought to rule Spain, doing away with the monarchy entirely. Rodrigo was torn between loyalty to his family and the ideals of equality the interim government was attempting to implement.

He had spent endless hours poring over documents and composing missives to recommend reforms as well as compromises. For a moment, his thoughts turned to his carefree days as a young prince. He'd been relatively sheltered from the unrest in Spain as he'd traveled. He'd basically occupied every moment engaged in pursuit of diversion or leisure. But necessity had forced him into the position of representative for the monarchy, and he did not permit himself to dwell in regret.

Rodrigo worked through the late hours of the night and into the morning without the luxury of sleep. He wanted to ensure that the missive he was drafting was ready as soon as a messenger was found to deliver it.

When he finally finished, the early-morning sun peeked through the curtains, shining bright lines across the wood floor and climbing up the walls. He stretched and made his way to his bedchamber to dress and then, after a hurried meal and word to his guards, left for the castle.

He was fatigued, but before he allowed himself to rest, he hoped to meet with Colonel Stackhouse, and he determined to do so while the remainder of the household was likely still asleep, supposing that a military man would not be lounging in bed late into the day. When he arrived at the servant's entrance, he stopped a footman. Upon inquiry, he learned that the colonel had indeed eaten breakfast hours earlier, and the rest of the household was either in the dining room or had not yet made an appearance.

"Please inform the colonel that I will meet with him at his convenience in the library," Rodrigo said. The man sent a servant to fetch Jim and then accompanied Rodrigo to the library, ushering him through a small side office. Rodrigo peeked through the door before he entered, relieved that the library was empty save for a maid who knelt before the hearth, lighting a fire. The footman excused himself.

While he waited, Rodrigo stepped over to the window seat and pulled aside the curtains. A thin blanket lay on the seat and at one end, a cluster of throw pillows. He smiled thinking of Meg arranging everything just how she wanted it. The view of the duke's garden from this vantage point caught his eye, and he tried to imagine Meg's thoughts as she'd looked at the same scene. Glancing around the small space, he saw books and periodicals piled at the end of the bench. He hesitated briefly, feeling as though he were intruding on something private, but his curiosity got the better of him, and he picked up one of the piles of books.

Some of the books, he realized, did not belong to the library but had Meg's name written inside the cover. As he'd expected, she had quite a collection of Gothic romance novels. It seemed that *Romance of the Forest* was her favorite, since it was the most worn. He also found a book of poetry. Many of the pages had bits of paper marking them, and some of the passages were underlined. Again he was not surprised.

One book, hidden almost out of sight between the cushion and the window pane, appeared to be brand new. He pulled it out and looked at the title. "Rudiments of Genteel Behavior."

Opening the cover, he read the inscription.

Miss Margaret Burton,

As it is apparent that your training in the matters of etiquette and politeness has sadly been neglected, I thought you might benefit from reading this book. Please accept my best wishes for your continued improvement.

Your well-meaning friend,
Anthony Devon Poulter, Lord Featherstone

Rodrigo's stomach burned as he thought of Meg's embarrassment upon receiving such an offensive gift. Etiquette and politeness indeed. Meg had more politeness in her small toe than the pompous earl. Imagining Meg with such a man sickened him. Lord Featherstone would only stifle the vibrant, intelligent young lady. She would never entertain the idea, would she?

He glanced at the book again and tucked it back where he'd found it, thinking that he'd not mind seeing the arrogant man at the business end of a French bayonet.

Rodrigo set the pile of books back down, carefully arranging them in the same way he had found them, and lifted a slim volume bound in moleskin. Thumbing through it, he saw it was a sketchbook, and while Meg was not a master artist, her sketches were interesting enough that he was engrossed in the small volume.

Some of the drawings were fanciful: a woman in a cloak standing upon a bridge with her hair blowing across her face, a pirate brandishing a cutlass, a skeleton clapped in irons hanging from a stone wall. A puff of air escaped his nose, and even though he was alone, he fought to hold in an amused snicker.

Other drawings seemed more true to life: a stone fort upon an island, the riggings of a ship, a close view of what appeared to be the sparse beginnings of a mustache. One drawing in particular tugged at his heart—a foal following a family of ducks. He could not help the smile that grew on his face as he studied Meg's representation of Patito's story.

"Likely one of the better ways to discover a person's character."

Rodrigo started when he heard the voice and, turning, saw a man he assumed was Colonel Stackhouse. He wore a patch over his eye, and Rodrigo cringed inside when he saw the jagged scar that extended over the colonel's forehead and down his cheek.

The man waved his hand toward the sketchbook Rodrigo held, and the books that remained on the window seat. "Observing the books they read. However, in the case of Miss Meg Burton, the periodicals and the *Times* that she scours on a daily basis seem to be more telling. I've rarely encountered a young person with such an understanding of international politics. If my advisors paid half the attention to the enemy's tactics as that young woman, I might be looking at you with two eyes, Your Highness." The man bowed. "Colonel Jim Stackhouse at your service."

Rodrigo nodded his head in acknowledgement. He would have liked to ask the colonel more about Meg, but the way the man studied him already made him feel as if the colonel knew more than Rodrigo was willing to say. "Principe Rodrigo de la Talavera. I thank you for meeting with me, sir. My sister speaks quite highly of you, and I cannot begin to express my thanks for rescuing her and bringing her safely from Spain. For this, I am forever in your debt, Colonel." Rodrigo blinked at the prickling in his eyes.

The colonel's damaged face softened into a semblance of a smile. "Serena is one of the finest women of my acquaintance, sir."

Rodrigo raised his brows at the man's familiar use of his sister's Christian name but did not comment on it. He would forgive this man any breach of etiquette after the way he'd risked his own life to protect Serena.

"She tells me that you have some questions and you think I might be able to provide some answers," the colonel said.

Rodrigo nodded, motioning toward the chairs near the fireplace. "Please have a seat." He replaced Meg's sketchbook and drew the curtains back, returning them to their former position before he took a seat by the fire.

Colonel Stackhouse watched thoughtfully, and Rodrigo attempted to appear as if he were simply a naturally tidy person, instead of concealing evidence of his intrusion into Meg's personal things.

"Colonel, my sister and I hoped you might have some information about our parents. They were taken from Madrid months ago, and though we've employed emissaries to learn anything of their whereabouts . . . or fate"—Rodrigo's throat tightened on this last word, and he swallowed hard—"we have been unable to discover anything. At the very least, we thought you might have an idea where to search or whom to ask."

The colonel nodded. "It's surprising that with all your resources, you've been unable to find anything. But I do not see it as a sign they have not survived."

Rodrigo's chest clenched, but he was grateful the colonel did not mince words. He would rather have the truth, no matter how difficult to hear.

The colonel pushed out a heavy breath and settled back into the chair. "Your Highness, I firmly believe the key to winning a war lies in understanding one's enemy. I have fought the blasted French for decades." He spoke slowly, and Rodrigo had the impression that the colonel did not speak at length often so he had better listen.

"The emperor is a bit less predictable than his predecessors, but when it comes down to it, we must realize the reason your parents—and the rest of the royal family—were taken. They were not killed as a demonstration of power. Napoleon knows that the Spanish people are too devoted to the monarchy, and such an action would only ensure further rejection of his brother. I believe the emperor has been surprised to encounter resistance from the militia bands in the hills as it is.

"The obvious reason for abducting the royal family is to dishearten the people and increase their loyalty to Joseph. And if you do not mind my saying so, Your Highness, I'm quite surprised they have not attempted something of this sort with you and your sister. It's not exactly a secret that she married the Duke of Southampton, and while you have an admirable detachment of guards, it would not be impossible for the French to find and seize the two of you as well."

Rodrigo frowned. "Do you truly believe Serena to be in danger?"

"I believe both of you to be in danger. To Spain, you represent hope. You are a beloved prince and princess, a symbol of what the country once was. Certainly you can see how this makes you a thorn in the emperor's side?"

"And what would you recommend, Colonel?" Rodrigo's stomach was sick at the idea that the colonel would want to relocate Serena, but he would do whatever was necessary to keep her safe.

"What I'd recommend is keeping the two of you locked up in the Tower of London, surrounded by an army of dragoon guards until this war ends. But I will not brave Serena's temper by mentioning it." A strange expression crossed the colonel's face, and Rodrigo realized the man was attempting to make a joke, and by its clumsy execution, how rare an event such a thing was.

"With your permission, I'll post some more British troops on the duke's estate and around Southampton. Simply as a precaution, you understand."

"I do not think such a thing is necessary."

"You must know that the safety of a foreign diplomat does not rank among the army's highest priorities, and the guards assigned are not exactly—" Colonel Stackhouse narrowed his eye as he studied Rodrigo. "You intend to leave."

"Yes."

"And why would you do such a foolhardy thing?"

"I intend to rescue my parents. The first whisper of their whereabouts, and I mean to find them." Rodrigo lifted his chin, daring the colonel to oppose his decision.

The colonel was silent for a moment regarding Rodrigo with his one eye. "I do hope when the time comes you will consult with me for a bit of strategy before you go barreling across the channel. Rescue missions are something I have a bit of experience with. I will, of course, see to further safety measures for your sister."

"Thank you." Rodrigo could not keep the relief from his voice.

"It's a weighty responsibility that's been thrust upon you. Even if we successfully drive the French out of Spain, your country has an enormous amount of mending to do. And I do not simply mean repairing damaged property."

Rodrigo's shoulders sagged. "It's true. The problems began long before Napoleon's invasion. And my family is a large part of it."

"But you have been working with the Cortes, am I correct? It is a valuable thing you do, attempting to negotiate a compromise."

"Yes, but we must hope that King Fernando acknowledges the new constitu—" Rodrigo's words broke off when he heard voices outside the library. Women's voices. He immediately recognized Meg's as one of them. He looked at the colonel, who must have seen panic in his eyes. "Excuse me, sir."

Colonel Stackhouse's face remained impassive. He pointed to the door leading to the side office, and Rodrigo had just slipped through when he heard the library door open behind him.

Chapter 8

MEG PAUSED WITH HER HAND on the library doorknob when she heard Helen calling to her from down the hallway. She turned her head to look back the way she'd come.

"Miss Meg," Helen said, as she approached. "I am sorry to bother you. I wondered if I might have a word with you?"

Meg had come to be quite fond of Helen in the past few days, though they'd never had a chance to speak privately. "Of course, Lady Helen. And please just call me Meg."

"And will you call me Helen? It is so nice to have a friend." Helen smiled shyly.

Meg linked her arm through Helen's. "Perhaps we could talk in the library?" She pushed the door open, and the familiar smell of leather and books wrapped around her. Her eyes were drawn to the far wall as the door to the small office closed. Undoubtedly a servant, Meg thought, noticing the fire crackling in the hearth.

The ladies walked into the room and sat together upon a sofa. The room wasn't bright. The cloudy sky muted most of the sunlight through the uncovered windows, and aside from the fireplace, the only light came from candles that flickered around the room. But Meg didn't want to risk revealing her secret place on the window seat by opening more drapes.

She studied the other woman's face for a moment. Helen's gaze was turned downward, and she picked at her fingernails as if she were nervous. Meg decided that if there was going to be conversation, it would be up to her to begin it. "What is it you wanted to ask me, Helen?"

Helen raised her eyes quickly, and Meg was again startled by the bright color. She just as quickly lowered them, and her cheeks reddened. "It is about your brother. I wondered if you might tell me what sort of things appeal to him. I hoped to find some topics of conversation that would keep his interest."

Then you should talk about pretty young ladies, Meg thought. Daniel declared himself hopelessly smitten nearly every month. It seemed he continually found a new "true love," but he just as quickly lost interest as soon as another attractive woman caught his eye.

Meg did not want to see Helen become the latest injured party. "Maybe you should speak about subjects that are interesting to *you*," Meg said. "I am sure there are a great many things that you enjoy. Music, for example. Your performance on the pianoforte the other night was exquisite."

Helen shook her head, and her dark golden curls bounced slightly. "I hardly think a gentleman wants to hear about my favorite sheet music or composers."

Meg reached to squeeze her hand, and Helen looked back up at her. "Nonsense. Your activities and concerns are every bit as important as those of anyone else. Do not pretend to be someone other than Lady Helen Poulter in hopes of impressing a man."

"I suppose I am worried that no gentleman will find Lady Helen Poulter remarkable enough," Helen said softly.

"Then you simply have not met the correct gentlemen. There are a great many things about you that are remarkable, and any man would be a fool not to perceive them." Meg smiled, hoping to reassure her new friend.

"You really are a bluestocking, Meg," Helen said.

"Don't tell Lady Vernon," Meg whispered conspiratorially.

Helen smiled in return, and the ladies sat in a companionable silence for a short moment before Helen spoke. "What a time we shall have tomorrow when we go to choose our costumes for the masque."

Meg felt a shiver of excitement at the thought. She could not wait to choose an exotic costume for the ball.

Helen's shy expression returned, as did the color flooding her cheeks. "Is there a specific costume you believe Daniel might be pleased to see me wear?" she asked.

Meg resisted the urge to shake Helen's shoulders but was spared the necessity of answering when a servant stepped into the room.

"Pardon me, Lady Helen, but the music instructor awaits you in the conservatory."

She thanked him and turned to Meg. "Please excuse me," Helen said. "I am rather uneasy about the sonata I have chosen for the musicale. I am afraid I will never play Beethoven as well as I should."

The reminder that she would be performing as well made Meg's stomach dip uneasily, but she kept a smile upon her face. "I would not worry. That poor musician is rumored to still be at the Bohemian spa in Teplitz. I do not think he can hear Lady Harrison's pianoforte from such a distance. And even if he could, I think he would be quite pleased with your effort in regards to his work. I do hope you have a lovely practice session."

"Thank you, Meg." Helen squeezed her hand and left the library.

Meg crossed to the window seat to push aside the curtains, but she spun quickly when a voice startled her.

"A pity you do not follow your own advice, Miss Burton."

Meg saw the colonel stand from the chair facing the fire. She pushed her palm against her chest. "Colonel Stackhouse, you startled me." Meg took a moment to regain her composure, and as her breathing slowed, her eyes narrowed. "Sir, why did you not reveal yourself sooner? It is quite discourteous to eavesdrop on a private conversation."

The colonel stood, and Meg squared her shoulders. She would not allow this man with his gruesome scar and frightening manner to intimidate her. Luckily Helen had not completely shut the library door. Meg didn't like to admit it, but the colonel quite unnerved her, and being alone with the man . . .

"Please have a seat, miss." The colonel indicated a chair near the fireplace with a gracious bow. The corner of his lips twitched slightly, and she had the distinct impression that he could read her thoughts.

"Thank you." Meg sat on the edge of the chair and smoothed her skirts over her legs, avoiding his gaze.

The colonel sat back into his chair. His hair was tied into a queue, and his face was clean-shaven. Even the patch over his eye seemed to be positioned with more care than she'd previously seen. Perhaps his injury was not bothering him as badly as it had been.

He offered no apology for concealing his presence, and from his expression, she did not think he was likely to. He watched her for a moment, as if waiting for her to speak.

Meg thought back to what the colonel had overheard, and finally spoke to fill the uncomfortable silence. "I do not understand your meaning, sir. If you mean that I should follow my own advice and practice the pianoforte, I do not believe it is a pity at all that I neglect it to such an extent."

"I was referring to the counsel you gave Lady Helen in regards to impressing a gentleman. It's a shame you do not follow the course you recommended."

Heat spread up Meg's neck, and she fought to keep it down. She gazed at the painting above the fireplace, attempting to look as though his words did not affect her. "I'm afraid I do not know what you mean." She knew precisely what the colonel meant, and it was humiliating. But it was also none of the man's business.

The colonel shifted in his chair, resting his ankle upon his knee. "Perhaps I am mistaken, then, miss. But what did you think of Lord Featherstone's reference to Southey's *After Blenheim*?"

Meg remembered perfectly the moment the colonel referred to and knew that he had seen her reaction when the earl had quoted the poem. "I believe . . . it was unsuitable for the earl to use antiwar poetry in reference to the battle where you were injured." Her stomach clenched as she thought of just how inappropriate the earl's words had been. "The reiteration of ''twas a famous victory,' indicates that the narrator does not understand why war happens; he's merely repeating the words he's been told. I have to believe that perhaps the earl did not fully understand Southey's meaning."

Somehow the colonel managed to look at her intently and still keep an expression that neared exasperation. "Based on your reaction that night, the earl's misrepresentation disturbed you deeply. Poetry is quite important to you, is it not? You're well versed, and not merely for recreation, but as a serious student of morality and theme."

Meg nodded slowly. She was unsure of the direction in which this conversation was moving.

"You might say, I would assume, that poetry is one of the most central parts of your life. And from the few days that I have been at Thornshire, I have gathered that books, specifically novels, are quite important to you as well, and yet the earl does not approve of young ladies indulging in either of these things. And what would the man think if he knew of the periodicals you read?"

Meg did not say anything. She stared at a spot upon the library floor, hating that he could see through her so completely.

The colonel leaned back in his seat, steepling his fingers. He was quiet for a moment before he spoke again. "I believe you mentioned that your father is a merchant in Charleston."

Meg nodded again, feeling as though her head might break off her neck if she continued to do nothing but bob it up and down all morning.

"I imagine the trade embargo must be difficult for the import/export business. A man left with few resources might resort to sending his daughter to London to find a rich husband—"

"Please excuse me, sir." Meg had had enough. She didn't know what the colonel's intentions were, but he seemed determined to either humiliate her or expose her as a swindler. She stood. Her face burned, and her fists shook as she pressed them against her legs. She turned to go, but the colonel's words stopped her.

"Miss Burton, I recognize that we do not always have the luxury to live our lives the way we wish." His voice remained low, but Meg could still feel every word pierce into her heart. "I can see from your reaction how unhappy this arrangement makes you. If there is one thing I understand, it is the importance of doing one's duty, no matter how painful."

Meg turned back toward him, swallowing against the constriction in her throat. "Then you can see why I have no choice, sir."

The colonel's gaze did not waver as he regarded her. "In the spirit of giving advice, Miss Burton, might I offer you some?"

Meg did not trust herself to speak. She lifted her eyebrows and pressed her lips together, waiting for the colonel to tell her something she was certain she did not want to hear. She would have put her hands on her hips if such a thing was not so unladylike.

"As I have spent my life as an observer of people, I have discovered that no matter the association—master, servant, allies in a battle, family members, friends—the same holds true. The correct relationship will make a person bloom. He becomes more himself, his talents deepen, his personality grows, and he thrives. But the wrong relationship will produce the opposite. The things that were once so vital no longer matter. His talents disappear, his individuality fades, and he wilts." Jim placed his foot back on the floor and leaned forward. "I do not know you well, miss, but I would not want to see a person so passionate about life and learning cease to exist because she was seeking to impress the wrong person."

Meg's eyes filled, and she refused to blink and allow the tears to spill over. "Would you recommend that I condemn my family to a life of poverty, sir? Simply so that I could continue reading romance novels?"

The colonel exhaled through his nose in a huff. "Poverty? In America? I do not believe there is such thing. Not when a man is willing to work hard. There are endless opportunities. Perhaps your family will go west or purchase some land and grow cotton." The colonel shrugged, and his face contorted in an expression Meg thought might be a smile. He settled back into his chair. "I'm certain you have other interests besides books. You have an astute understanding of war tactics. And unless I am mistaken, I believe I saw you riding the other day. You are a skilled horsewoman."

Relief washed over Meg. The colonel had not set out to ruin or embarrass her. Quite the opposite, he acted as if he cared about her situation. She felt a connection with this man, who, through only a few interactions with her, seemed to understand. And though he did not speak compassionately, she felt the honesty in his words. There had not been many at Thornshire who cared about Meg's opinions.

She perched again on the edge of the chair, a relieved smile on her face. "Thank you, sir. I do love to ride."

"And you seemed very happy in your companion."

Meg's smile grew as she thought about Carlo. The memory of the ride and the way he had surprised her the night before grew inside her chest like a warm bubble. "Yes, my friend, Carlo. He is wonderful. He tends Prince Rodrigo's horses."

Jim's eye squinted, and his head tipped slightly to the side.

Meg stopped as she saw the colonel's expression. Her throat went dry as she realized that she may have given away a confidence. Carlo had taken her riding in secret. Would he be punished for accompanying a lady alone? And on the prince's horse.

The colonel remained silent, but Meg could not, not when her friend might face some sort of discipline. In a country that transported a man for killing a bird, what would be the penalty for Carlo's actions? "Please Colonel Stackhouse. Do not say anything to the duke or Her Grace. Carlo simply thought to do something nice for me, a favor. Please do not report him to the prince. I . . . it was my fault. He should not be punished."

The longer the colonel remained silent, the bigger the lump in Meg's throat grew. Her eyes burned with tears. Her heart was beating loudly. She considered what she must do to protect Carlo. She would plead with the duke if she had to. Could she convince Serena not to say anything to her brother if Colonel Stackhouse told her?

Jim's expression did not change, but he murmured, "Carlo?"

She brushed her fingers across the tears leaking down her cheeks. "Colonel, I am begging you. Please do not tell anyone. He has been most kind to me, and I could never forgive myself if he were punished for it."

Colonel Stackhouse blinked and looked up. He seemed to notice that Meg was near the point of sobbing and jolted in his seat. "Miss Burton, dash it all, do not weep. I understand the value of a good friend, and I will keep your confidence. Please, I beg you, do not start blubbering."

Meg thought she might sink to the floor or throw her arms around the colonel, so great was her relief. She let out a sigh that was choked by a sob.

"Thank you, Colonel," she said, although he may not have understood her through her hitching breath.

"I'd not thought to cause so much distress, miss. I seem to have a knack for upsetting women." He rubbed the back of his neck. "Let us talk about less troubling things. Perhaps you'd give me your opinion of the rumors that Napoleon thinks to invade Russia."

Meg was nearly numb after the range of emotions the colonel had managed to elicit in such a short time. The swing in her mood gave her the distinct compulsion to giggle in relief. She scooted back in her chair, careful to maintain appropriate posture as she considered the colonel's question. And made certain that she was calm enough to answer rationally. "In my opinion, sir, France is making much the same mistake of spreading her resources too thin, just as England has done."

The colonel said nothing but motioned for her to continue. "Speak freely, miss. I seek to know your true thoughts on the subject."

"Russia is the largest potential ally for both parties. Napoleon would be a fool not to attempt to get the czar on his side or at least prevent him from siding with enemies of the *Grande Armée*, but to invade Russia is a mistake. The campaigns on the peninsula are wearing down the emperor's armies. Many cities have been under siege for more than a year, and the militias in the mountains undermine the morale. Should Napoleon muster a large enough force to march into Russia, he will leave his troops in Spain without reinforcements, Paris abandoned and ripe for a coup, and the Cossacks to contend with."

The colonel's mouth turned down, and he rubbed his fingers over his chin. "I wonder if you would ever consider working as an advisor. Your understanding of the conflict and its ramifications is remarkable."

"Thank you, Colonel. But I'm afraid we are not on the same side." She smiled. "I could be accused of fraternizing with the enemy."

"Are we enemies then?"

"You and I are not, I hope, but I fear our countries will soon be hostile once again."

"We shall see whether—"

Meg and the colonel turned toward the library door when they heard Lady Featherstone's voice. They both stood.

"Colonel Stackhouse, I waited in the dining room for you all morning, only to find that you had eaten hours ago." The countess entered the room carrying a jar and a face cloth. While still practical, Lady Featherstone's expression seemed a bit softer today.

Meg curtseyed, and from the corner of her eye, she saw the colonel perform a rather stiff bow.

"Good morning, madam. Am I to presume you are here to torture me with more of that foul smelling concoction?" he said.

"It helps with the itching, and you know it is true. You are just too stubborn to admit it," the countess said, waggling her finger as she walked closer to the fireplace. She turned her bright eyes toward Meg and nodded. "Good morning, Meg. I hope I have not interrupted anything."

The colonel folded his arms across his chest. "Miss Burton and I were just speculating about the emperor's next move. It is a very important discussion, and—"

Lady Featherstone pushed down on the colonel's shoulder until he sat in the chair. "Nonsense. I am certain Miss Burton does not want to spend the entire morning talking about military strategy. Now sit still and let me look at this." She began to pull on the colonel's patch, as he attempted to hold it in place while arguing with her intentions.

"Please excuse me," Meg said, fighting back a laugh. "I must . . ." But neither of them seemed to be listening, so she did not bother coming up with an excuse to escape the library.

She picked up a few books from the window seat on her way out. As she walked down the hall toward her bedchamber, she thought of her strange conversation with the colonel. Her emotions had been completely unpredictable, swinging from one extreme to the other, and she tried to analyze what had set them off. It had been upsetting and humiliating to realize that the man had deduced her family's financial situation and Meg's part in its restoration, but that had been nothing compared to the utter despair she felt when she'd thought Carlo might be in trouble.

Meg had been ready to throw herself upon her knees and beg for mercy for a man she hardly knew. Her reaction had wholly astonished her, and she did not know what to make of it.

She remembered the colonel's words, "I understand the value of a good friend." The sentiment described Carlo perfectly. Her heart felt light as she thought about the events the night before and the gentleness of his expression when he had bid her good night.

An idea began to form in her mind, and she grinned as she decided how to implement it. She left the books in her bedchamber—nothing could convince her to return to the library with Colonel Stackhouse and Lady Featherstone arguing inside—and headed toward the dining room.

Her grin grew until a giggle burst forth, and she pressed her fingers against her mouth. The idea was forming into a plan that pushed her fears about the musicale and the need for a rich husband far enough away to forget about them altogether. First, she would need to speak with Serena and then with the cook.

Chapter 9

RODRIGO ALLOWED THE REIGNS TO go slack, and Patito immediately turned toward the duke's stables. "*Que desea para un dulce?* Are you hoping for a treat?" he muttered, but his mind was not upon the horse. His thoughts had been a confused jumble since overhearing Meg's conversation with Colonel Stackhouse the day before.

He'd gone over every word they'd both said, countless times, and had always arrived at the same conclusion: Meg was no different than all the other young ladies he had met in England. She was after a wealthy husband and would go to whatever ends necessary to secure one. She had said as much herself. Hearing this from Meg's own mouth had stunned him. Rodrigo knew logically he should employ the same course of action he had come to rely on and avoid the lady completely. But the very idea of missing Meg's company produced such an uncomfortable feeling that he shied away from it. He returned to the conversation he'd overheard, reviewing it again.

Rodrigo looked up and noticed that Patito had brought them to the stables. Out of habit, he raised his gaze to the library window, but Meg was not there. She had not been there at all the day before either. And he did not understand why this was so concerning to him. Was she still distressed? Had she taken ill? Or was she simply busy with the other ladies, preparing for a season and concocting schemes to ensnare a rich husband? An image came into his mind of Meg smiling and flirting with the gentlemen of the *ton*, and Rodrigo's stomach turned inside out.

He hated that Meg was willing to sacrifice her own desires and marry a man for his fortune. It seemed such a waste. But even more, he hated the idea of her losing herself. Just as the colonel had said, it would be a pity to see a person so passionate about life and learning cease to exist. He felt a rush of anger when he thought of her parents putting aside Meg's happiness for their own purposes, but something akin to pity replaced the emotion as he thought of how difficult it must be for them to put such pressure on their daughter. This feeling took him by surprise. It was not at all something he had ever considered as he'd regarded all of the young ladies of the *ton* with distaste. So why were things different with Meg? What made *her* so different? He remembered how she had laughed as the horse galloped across the meadow and then how she'd understood so compassionately when he'd spoken of Spain. Why was he allowing emotions to dictate his actions when it came to Meg Burton?

Rodrigo dismounted and led the horse into the stable. As he'd mulled these things over, one thing became certain. He would not reveal himself to Meg. Not before the ball. If he was to ascertain her true feelings for him, he needed to keep his secret as long as he could. And a selfish and vulnerable part of him wanted Meg's approval, not as a man with a title, but as himself. Or, he supposed, as Carlo. He wondered how she would act if she knew the truth about him. Would she flirt and pretend to be the lady she thought he wanted? He would never have believed her capable of such deception until she had confessed the same to the colonel.

But just as soon as he made up his mind to sever contact with Meg, the resolve fled as he remembered the sound of her weeping when she spoke to Colonel Stackhouse. She'd been nearly beside herself with worry for him—for Carlo—and the thought of the prince's stable hand being punished had brought her to tears. The sound of her voice hitching as she'd pleaded with the colonel not to reveal their friendship had sent a jolt through his heart as he'd imagined her distress, yet at the same time, he had felt as if he'd been wrapped in a warm blanket. Did she really feel so strongly about a servant? Could she really feel so strongly about *him*?

The hope that the idea produced was nearly painful. Rodrigo wanted nothing more than Meg's good favor, and he wondered why. She was, after all, an American, and if he did return to his holdings and his country, his loyalty to Spain and to the wishes of his parents would lead him to marry the woman they'd chosen for him. The thought was not as comforting as it once had been. He had only met Evangelina Gualtierrez twice, and though she was truly a Spanish beauty, she had not aroused feelings inside him the same way as the ginger-haired American woman.

In the few hours he had spent in Meg's presence, she had filled him with joy and touched a place within him he thought had been destroyed upon the plains of his homeland when his parents were captured and his beloved country had erupted into a war zone. The feelings she elicited in him were addicting.

Perhaps he would see if Meg wanted to take a ride with Patito and Bonnie later today. The thought brought a smile to his face.

Rodrigo closed the stall gate behind Patito and fetched some grain to fill the animal's trough. He moved to the box where he kept the horse's brush but stopped short when he saw a roll of parchment tied with a length of twine, sitting on top of the lid. His mouth went dry as he lifted the scroll. Was it a missive from Spain? A threatening letter from the French? A ransom note? Colonel Stackhouse's warning moved into his mind, and he took a sharp breath.

He slipped off the twine and unrolled the parchment. It was much larger than a typical piece of writing paper. It appeared to be a map. The parchment was worn and wrinkled, and he noticed that the edges were burned. Crimson stains of what looked like blood were splattered and streaked across it. Rodrigo sucked in a breath. Had a messenger died to bring this map to him? He squinted, tipping the parchment toward the window, but the light filtering into the stable wasn't bright enough for him to make out the words.

Rodrigo carried the map out of the stable, ignoring the protesting whinny from Patito at his neglect. He stepped into the sun to study the map.

For a moment, he could not understand what he was looking at, but as he examined it further, the tension in his shoulders relaxed as apprehension turned into confusion and then melted into amusement when he began to recognize the depiction.

Bold script scrawled across the top of the page:

Warning: Ye who hold this map, take heed. Chart your course, but beware. A brutal fate awaits he who steals a buccaneer's treasure.

A large rectangle at one side of the map was labeled *Haunted Castle*, and in parentheses beneath, it said, *Beware of* el fantasma *in chains.* A chuckle rose into his throat at Meg's use of the Spanish word for ghost. For there was no doubt in his mind that Meg Burton was behind this.

Landmarks of the area around the castle were drawn and labeled. A dashed line snaked through the estate, marking a path and terminating at a large *X.* The line began exactly where Rodrigo was standing, outside the stables—or as the map-maker had labeled them *Blackbeard's Stockyard*—and though he could see precisely where it ended, he still followed the longer route.

Rodrigo could not help the tingling excitement that skittered over his skin. He felt like a young boy, and even imagined himself an adventurer in search of riches. This entire situation was utterly ridiculous, yet his heart was light, and he was as eager as a child anticipating Three King's Day. How did this woman have such an effect on him?

He walked past the cook's herb garden, which according to the map was "soaked in marauders' blood," climbed a small hill (*Gallows-meat Bluff*), and crossed over a wooden bridge (*Traitor's Plank*) that spanned *Doubloon Creek*. The path led him behind the carriage house (*Blade o' Fortune Brig*) and into the forest, which the map-maker claimed was the hideout of "murderers, marauders, and sea-wolves." Finally he stepped into the clearing with the pond (*Jolly Roger Lagoon*), and obeying the instructions to beware of "mermaids that might lure him into the sea," or the "ghosts of mercenaries that had been hung at low tide," he followed the dotted line toward the *X*.

Rodrigo walked up the steps into the gazebo, his stomach fluttering. His fingers tingled in anticipation. It was not difficult to spot the treasure. A small trunk sat on one of the benches.

Kneeling on one knee, he lifted the lid of the treasure chest and found it filled with small wrapped packages. He lifted one and, looking closer, recognized that each bundle contained a cake of turrón. How he had missed his favorite Spanish sweet. A treasure indeed!

He threw his head back and laughed heartily. It had been so long that the sensation took him by surprise, but he had apparently not forgotten how to do it. It felt so unbelievably invigorating to release the tight hold he kept on his emotions.

He stood and walked to the edge of the gazebo, laughter still bubbling inside him. "Margarita," he shouted, "where are you hiding?"

A movement at the edge of the clearing caught his eye. He strode toward it and found Meg hiding behind a tree. He grabbed her hand and pulled her along the path to the gazebo. Before she could protest, he broke off a bit of turrón and popped a piece into her mouth and one into his own, then he pulled her down to sit on the bench next to him.

"How did you possibly find turrón in England, Margarita Burton?"

Even while she chewed on the sticky treat, her eyes twinkled with mischief. She swallowed and smiled, tipping her head playfully. "A lady should not reveal all of her secrets."

"You will not tell me how you were able to perform such a miracle?" He broke off another piece, put it into his mouth, then offered the rest to Meg.

She shook her head, indicating for him to finish it. “It was not actually so remarkable. I asked the Duchess Serena about it. She told me it is one of her brother’s favorites, and she described it to the cook.” She glanced at the piece he held in his hand. “I hope the flavor is right.”

Rodrigo searched her face for a moment but determined that she was still ignorant as to the identity of Serena’s brother. “It is perfect. The taste is exactly as I remember.” He broke off another piece, chewing and swallowing before he spoke. “And how long did you hide in the trees, waiting for me to arrive?”

Meg placed a hand over her mouth. “Were you so intent upon the map that you did not see me following you?” She schooled her face into a serious expression, waggling her finger at him. “Not a good habit for a buccaneer. An enemy with a cutlass could approach from behind and slit your gullet.”

Rodrigo noticed that when she attempted to be serious, a crease appeared above her nose. He thought how easy it would be to smooth it away with his thumb.

“I admit, the thought of treasure quite blinded me to the danger of being ambushed,” he said.

“Well then, you should be glad I followed you, if only to be on the lookout for scavengers of the high seas. Why, you might have ended up in Davy Jones’s locker if left to your own devices.”

Meg’s teasing words elicited another chuckle. She had upon her head one of those strange bonnets British women wore, tied beneath her chin with pink ribbons. But in Meg’s case, the headpiece did little to control the hair that escaped and blew around her face.

Rodrigo caught one of the curls near her neck and rubbed the soft strands between his fingers. “How lucky I am to have such a lovely protector,” he murmured.

Meg’s gaze locked with his for a brief instant, and the joking sparkle left her eyes, only to be replaced by something else. Something deeper. Something that made Rodrigo’s heart compress and his breath catch in his throat.

She lowered her lashes, and a flush spread over her cheeks. He wondered what she had seen in *his* eyes.

Meg moved to rise from the bench. “I should go. I must practice the pianoforte before Lady Harrison’s musicale tomorrow. They will be missing me soon, but I couldn’t resist following when I saw you approaching the stable.”

Rodrigo released her curl and lowered his hand to her shoulder. "Please, remain just a moment longer. I do not want my adventure to end so quickly." He smiled in an attempt to put her at ease and return them to their former playfulness. If only he were the prince, he could command her to stay.

"But you already have the treasure."

"Yes, but now I am uneasy about the warning on the map. What sort of fate do you think one would face when a pirate discovers his treasure missing?"

"Perhaps the creator of the map just thought to make it authentic and believed a threat to be appropriate, although she may not have had a particular penalty in mind." Meg's lips quirked, and her eyes twinkled. "But now that you mention it, I think a penalty is entirely suitable. How would you like to take my place at Lady Harrison's musicale? You could play the pianoforte, and I have the perfect gown for you to wear. You should look lovely in apricot."

"A harsh penalty to be sure," Rodrigo said, rubbing his chin. "But for the turrón, it would be worth it." He turned his gaze back toward her. "I would not want to deprive the *ton* of the opportunity to be enchanted by you, Margarita."

Meg sighed. "I wish I didn't have to perform. I play dreadfully." Her shoulders slumped.

"And you cannot simply tell them that you do not wish to do it?"

Meg shook her head. The wayward curls shook with it, and Carlo's fingers itched to touch them again. He balled his hands into fists upon his legs.

"The young ladies who will be presented this year are expected to either sing or play an instrument. And neither is my strong suit." Her lips lifted in a sad smile. "If only it were a poetry recital." She stood and brushed at her skirts.

Rodrigo stood next to her. "If the purpose of the exposition is to show each young lady in her best light, you should do the thing that you are most comfortable with. And I know you will render the *ton* speechless." He tipped his head and leaned toward her until she met his gaze. "No matter the venue, I fully believe Margarita Burton will surpass every lady in question."

Meg did not respond. She wrung her fingers, and he could tell that the idea of performing still troubled her. "Perhaps we might take Patito and Bonnie for a ride later today?" Rodrigo suggested.

Meg shook her head. "The other ladies and I are meeting with a modiste this afternoon to plan our gowns for the masque."

The mention of the ball hit him like a blow. Was it truly in nine days? The event had seemed so far away when he had made his promise to the duke and Serena, but as it approached, he felt a mixture of excitement and apprehension. Meg would finally know the truth about him, but how would she react to his identity—and his deceit?

"I imagine choosing a disguise would be an activity pleasing to you, Margarita. You will select something extraordinary, no doubt. And the very idea of a masquerade must appeal to your adventurous spirit."

"I hope to at least be able to choose the color." Meg's eyes were alight, leaving him in no doubt of her eagerness to don a mysterious costume.

"Yes, your remarkable hair," Rodrigo muttered. "I hope the modiste appreciates how fortunate she is to work with such *belleza.* Such beauty." He glanced at the curls that rested on her neck and shoulders.

Meg smiled shyly, looking toward the pond. "I have been able to declare a small victory in that department." The corner of her lips pulled in a smile, and she glanced sideways at him. "The duchess told me she is to wear an apricot gown to the Harrisons' musicale, and it would be a disaster for the two of us to arrive together in the same colored dress." Meg's face grew thoughtful. "It was almost as if she knew how I felt about the gown . . ."

"It sounds like *un afortunado accidente*, a lucky coincidence." Rodrigo made a note to thank his sister. "I hear the prince promised Her Grace that he will attend the ball."

He watched her reaction closely, but Meg just shrugged her shoulders. "That is nice," she said, and he did not know whether to be offended or pleased with her reaction. "I really must go now." She dipped in a small curtsey. "Good day, Carlo."

Rodrigo took hold of her arm, turning her back toward him. "Thank you, Margarita. I do not express my feelings well or often, but today, I was happier than I have been since leaving Spain—or possibly since I can remember."

Meg's face softened into a gentle smile. "I am glad to hear you laugh. I'd not heard the sound before."

"I'd not had many reasons for it lately."

"That is what friends are for, Carlo."

Rodrigo stepped closer and brushed his knuckles over Meg's cheek. "And is that what we are? Friends?"

Meg studied him for a moment, and he wondered if she saw the vulnerability that he felt, exposing himself in this way. "You are more than a friend, Carlo." Her voice was soft, but she raised an eyebrow. "I consider you a partner in our quest for adventure, and that is much dearer."

Crooking his finger beneath her chin, he lifted her gaze to his. Her eyes were the golden brown of toffee, the lashes around them the same color. "*Compañeros de aventura.* I like that very much, Margarita." Meg's mouth opened the slightest bit, and his gaze moved to her lips.

"I—I will see you tomorrow." She turned and hurried down the path toward the castle. "Or perhaps the next day," she called over her shoulder.

Rodrigo leaned to the side until his shoulder rested on one of the gazebo pillars. He crossed his arms, shaking his head. He had been completely wrong about Meg Burton. The idea that she was like all the other young ladies was laughable. In truth, she was unlike anyone he had ever met. Her enthusiasm for life, her wide-eyed optimism, and combination of naiveté and intelligence enchanted him. Meg was passionate about the things she cared about, and she simply made him happy.

Her joy and playfulness had a way of spreading over him when she was near, and she chased away the darkness that had plagued him for so long.

Rodrigo's country was in uproar, his parents captured, and he was attempting to protect both his sister and himself from brutal enemies. But his greatest threat did not come from the French. If he was not careful, he would lose his heart to Miss Meg Burton.

Chapter 10

Meg hurried from the forest clearing. Her pulse and mind were racing. What was she doing? Carlo's words, his expressions, his touch had all left her flustered. Surely she was just affected by his reaction to the treasure hunt. But the memory of his laughter and the dimple in his cheek made her heart race even faster. Perhaps she was merely nervous for the musicale.

When she thought of Carlo's laughter, a warm tingling spread from her chest all the way down to her fingers, and she felt like skipping or singing—which wouldn't do at all. The treasure hunt had been a success, and she was glad she'd acted upon the idea, as silly as it had seemed.

She brushed aside the curls that blew into her face, and the memory of Carlo doing the same accelerated her heart rate again. She could still feel the heat where his fingers had touched her cheek, and she shook her head to extinguish the thought. She would do well to remember that Carlo was a servant, and it was extremely inappropriate, not to mention unkind, to lead him on like this. But the thought of spending the remainder of her time at Thornshire without the hope of seeing Carlo hurt, like her heart was being squeezed, and she couldn't bear the idea.

Carlo was the only reason her stay at Thornshire had been barely tolerable. The friendship was diverting and not in any way unseemly, she rationalized to herself. She and Carlo were simply like-minded people who enjoyed each other's company. They were both far from home in an unfamiliar environment. There was nothing wrong with having a friend, or even better, a *compañero de aventura*. She could not control the flip of her heart when she thought of Carlo saying the words with his deep, accented voice.

But that was all it was, a friendly association. Meg arrived at the front entrance to the castle and straightened her shoulders. It was time to be a lady. She would need to turn her thoughts to impressing Lord Featherstone and the other gentlemen of the *ton* and put any sort of thoughts of Carlo from her mind. Besides, if Carlo knew that Meg was in England to ensnare a rich man, he wouldn't want to have anything to do with her. She hated the thought of his disappointment, and her face burned again, this time in shame.

Meg stepped into the main hall and occupied herself with removing her bonnet and gloves. She allowed a servant to take her wrap.

"Miss Meg."

Meg looked up as the duchess approached from the dining room. She curtsied. "Good morning, Your Grace."

"Please, since you are my guest and my husband's relative, I would like you to call me Serena."

Meg smiled. "Only if you will call me Meg."

Serena nodded her head once, and Meg was again impressed by the dignity the duchess exhibited. If Meg did not know Serena was a Spanish *princesa*, her natural grace would have given it away. Compared to the duchess, Meg's manners felt awkward and inelegant, although she knew Serena would never intend for her to feel this way.

"You have already taken a walk. How I admire your ability to rise early. The exercise has brought color to your cheeks."

Meg did not correct her. She would allow Serena to think that the blush was a result of her morning constitutional. "Thank you again for your help yesterday, Your—Serena."

"The pleasure was all mine. I had a lovely time with you in the kitchen, and the sweets brought back such wonderful memories of España." Serena smiled, and Meg noticed her face was tinged with sadness, so much like Carlo's when he spoke of Spain.

Serena took a breath and let it out slowly, and her features returned to their typical pleasant expression. "I am so glad you enjoyed the turrón. Cook told me you were so pleased, you asked for an entire box."

Meg looked at Serena and did not see anything in the duchess's expression beside polite interest, but the question made her wary. She did not want to reveal anything that might cause a problem for Carlo. However she did not want to tell a falsehood to the woman she admired and who had treated her so kindly.

"I wanted to share the turrón with a friend," Meg said, her gaze slipping away from Serena's. She hoped the answer was both satisfying to the duchess and vague as to the actual recipient of the sweets. When she looked back at Serena, Meg thought there was a twinkle of something in her eyes. Meg assumed it to be amusement at the idea that she had such a taste for confectioneries or perhaps at her attempt to pronounce the word the same way Serena and Carlo did, rolling the "r" and making a simple treat sound like something so much more exotic. But the look was gone quickly, and Meg wondered if she had really seen it in the first place.

"Come, Meg. The modiste and her assistants will arrive soon, and I am eager to choose a costume." She linked her arm through Meg's, and the two began to climb the stairs. "I confess, I am a bit nervous. I have never been to a masquerade ball. Once I was old enough to attend something of that nature, España, she was in such disorder that . . ." Serena's voice cracked.

Meg squeezed Serena's arm. "I have never been to a costume party either. Unless you consider wearing a mask and jumping out from behind the sofa to frighten my brother. But I hardly think that is the same thing." Serena laughed, and Meg felt relieved she had been able to offer some cheer.

"I enjoy teasing my brother too." She glanced at Meg. "Although it is not the same when we are adults, is it?"

"Not at all," Meg said as she tried to imagine Serena donning a mask and frightening the fat prince. He would undoubtedly be annoyed she had disturbed him. Meg felt grateful to have a cheerful brother who teased and laughed, instead of an unpleasant one who avoided everyone, was cruel to his servants, and ignored his horse.

When they arrived in the upstairs drawing room, Lady Vernon, Lady Featherstone, Lucinda, and Helen were already looking through picture books of costume gowns.

A few moments later, the modiste and her staff of assistants arrived.

"Mother, I should love to dress as a wood nymph, Lucinda said, holding up a book and pointing to a picture of a fairy-like creature in a delicate flowing gown.

Lady Featherstone looked at the picture and nodded in her abrupt manner. "And what color gown would you choose?"

The modiste began to describe a light-green gossamer that should look perfect on Lucinda. The assistants started taking notes, sketching, and measuring.

Meg tapped her fingers on her knees. She was glad she was seated or she was sure she'd begin bouncing from foot to foot, so excited was she to wear a fanciful costume. She imagined a gown with layers of ethereal fabric. When she danced, the dress would float around her. Perhaps a Greek goddess or an Arabian princess. She wouldn't even mind wearing feathers in her hair.

She picked up the costume book and began to look at the pictures. An evil sorceress, a gypsy. Meg could feel her heartbeat in her fingers.

Serena decided upon a flamenco dancer, and Meg imagined how beautiful she would be with her flowing dark curls. It was the perfect costume for a Spanish princesa, Meg thought.

"I hear a rumor that your brother will attend the masque, Your Grace," Lucinda said.

Serena's gaze flicked to Meg, and Meg wondered if she had allowed her dislike of the prince to show on her face earlier. "Yes, he has promised he will attend." Serena stepped behind a screen to try on a skirt that the modiste had brought.

Lucinda's gaze had followed Serena's, and Meg looked away and pretended to be absorbed in the costume book. She would need to be more careful not to offend Serena by appearing disapproving of her brother

Helen was still undecided on her costume, and the women's attention turned to Meg.

"Unless we plan to cover up her hair, let us think of a famous redhead," Lady Vernon said.

"Cleopatra?" Meg offered.

"I have the perfect character," Lucinda said loudly from where she was standing. "Queen Elizabeth!"

"I love it," Lady Vernon said, clasping her hands.

"I have just the fabric," the modiste said.

"Good Queen Bess," Lady Featherstone mused, pursing her lips and nodding her head. "I can see it."

"Or there is Cleopatra," Meg said, but her words were drowned out by the modiste and her assistants pulling out fabric swatches and rustling papers as they sketched. Meg felt her shoulders slump but tried to keep a smile upon her face as they took measurements. She had lost control once again, this time of the thing she was most excited about.

Lady Vernon hurried from the room and returned with a large volume, setting it upon the table and turning the pages until she found the one she was looking for. She lifted the book and pointed to the picture with a triumphant grin.

Meg's stomach sank. Queen Elizabeth was a white-faced stern-looking woman who wore a large dress that looked as though it were made of drapes with a high collar and oversized ruff.

"You will be magnificent, Meg," Lady Vernon said. "We shall need a tiara, and look at the pearls along the trim of the bodice."

"I will use pearl-colored beads," the modiste said. "If we use this tapestry, the gown . . ."

But Meg did not hear the rest of the discussion. She stared at the picture of Queen Elizabeth and tried to hold back the tears that threatened to spill over. Her hopes of looking beautiful and exotic had been dashed, and she would make her first impression upon society as a stuffy Tudor monarch wearing yards of heavy fabric and a collar that looked as though it belonged on a cake or around William Shakespeare's neck.

Finally the modiste had all the measurements and orders. Helen decided to dress as Cleopatra, and the countesses both chose Greek goddesses.

Once the party disbanded, Meg dashed straight for her window seat in the library, closing the curtains. For the second time in just a few days, her tears overflowed, but this time she did not even attempt to stop them. Her stomach felt as though it had turned to lead. She had never felt so frustrated or helpless. She'd not made one decision for herself since arriving in England. Well, except for the treasure map and the turrón and the ride with Bonnie and Patito. She tried to smile through a sob. The only things that had brought her any happiness had involved Carlo. And what would he tell her to do?

She could allow herself to be led around, each move she made carefully controlled, and every choice made by another. Or she could make her own decision. She remembered what Carlo had said in the gazebo, "You should do the thing that you are most comfortable with. And I know you will render the *ton* speechless." Even though he was most likely trying to reassure her, his words had the opposite effect. They penetrated through her despair and provoked her to action.

When she'd had a good cry and her tears had stopped, she smoothed her skirts over her knees and took stock of her situation. She was not a child, but a woman. An educated woman, and she was perfectly capable of choosing her performance for the musicale.

She grabbed her favorite poetry book and pushed aside the drapes. Standing, she lifted her chin and squared her shoulders. There was not much she could control in England, but this was one thing. Now, all she needed was the nerve to actually see it through.

Chapter 11

Rodrigo left the castle through a back entrance, discouraged that another meeting with Colonel Stackhouse had been no more productive than the first, though he was coming to enjoy visiting with the gruff veteran. While he had a high regard for the man—truly, the colonel and the duke were two of the most levelheaded men he'd met in England—it was disheartening that even the colonel's resources had uncovered nothing concerning the whereabouts of Rodrigo and Serena's parents.

Rodrigo pushed out a breath and raked his fingers through his hair. He started toward the stables, looking forward to a hard run with Patito to tire them both and ease some of his tension, but he stopped and stepped into the shadows when he saw Meg leaving the castle.

She held a book in her arm and looked over her shoulders as she closed the door, as if she did not want to be seen. What was she up to now?

Rodrigo's mood instantly lifted.

Meg hurried down the pathway behind the castle toward the duke's greenhouse. She glanced behind her once more before opening the door and slipping through.

Rodrigo waited a few moments and strode up the path himself. He cracked the greenhouse door and peeked inside. The light filtered strangely through the glass and plants, casting flickering shadows over the room. The smell of the flowers, vegetables, mulch, and soil was heady and reminded him so much of the gardens in Spain that he stopped for a moment and allowed the memories to wash over him.

Meg paced back and forth between rows of hanging plants and raised flowerbeds, muttering to herself and occasionally stopping to look in her book. She was so intent that she didn't notice him. He stepped inside, closing the door behind him, and leaned his shoulder against the doorframe.

She paced between the rows, apparently committing the words of the book to memory. From her cadence, he assumed it was a poem that she was learning. He noticed that she furrowed her eyebrows and a line appeared above her nose when she had to stop and look in the book. Occasionally the tip of her tongue poked out of her mouth as she read. Her nose wrinkled, and she muttered, shaking her head. Then she would resume her pacing, the inflection in her tone rising and dropping. Rodrigo thought he could watch this same sight for hours.

Meg passed between a cluster of hanging vines and froze, then she turned quickly toward him, and their eyes locked.

Rodrigo realized that he was standing with his head tipped and an idiotic smile upon his face. He straightened up and began to construct an apology, just now realizing how bad-mannered it was to sneak upon a lady and watch her without her knowledge; but Meg's expression stopped him.

Her face relaxed into a relieved expression. "Carlo, I am so glad you are here."

He raised his brows and allowed his mouth to curve into a smile. He'd not expected that.

"I am attempting to memorize a poem to perform tomorrow. I thought I knew it better than I do." The crease appeared above her nose, and she looked up at him with large eyes. "Will you help me?"

She had no idea of the power in her expression. He would have done anything she asked when she looked at him that way.

"Of course." He held out his hand for the book.

She opened it to the page her finger had been marking and handed it to him.

Rodrigo read the poem's title. "Christabel?"

"Do you know it?" she asked.

"I am afraid I do not know very much English poetry. But this Christabel, she is Spanish?"

Meg shook her head. "Coleridge left her nationality deliberately ambiguous, I think."

"And it is very lengthy," Rodrigo said, turning the pages. "How much of it are you planning to learn?"

"Part the first," she said.

He found the passage, and he couldn't help but be surprised at the length of the section.

"I think I know most of it. Can I start at the beginning?"

Rodrigo turned back to the first page of the poem. He sat upon a bench and nodded to indicate that he was ready.

Meg took a deep breath, relaxed her shoulders and began.

"'Tis the middle of the night by the castle clock,

And the owls have awakened the crowing cock;

Tu-whit! Tu-woo!

And hark, again . . ."

Rodrigo listened, enthralled as Meg recited the poem. He occasionally prompted her with a word she had forgotten, but she remembered the majority of it. And her delivery was fascinating.

She told the story of Christabel as if the words were her own. They flowed naturally from her. Her stance was confident, her voice rising and falling with the narration. Her love of poetry and her understanding of the tale was evident as her face shone.

Rodrigo could not believe an English Gothic narrative poem could make his heart start racing and his throat go dry. But he knew it was not the words that had such an effect on him; it was the young lady who said them and the passion she put into her delivery.

When Meg finished, Rodrigo was completely tongue-tied, too caught up in her performance to speak. Meg stood, waiting for his appraisal, and her confidence appeared to shrink when he did not say anything.

He stood and rushed to reassure her. "Margarita, it was . . . I do not have the words. You were *maravillosa.* I do not think you have anything to worry about tomorrow. You will be the sensation of the musicale."

"Truly?" Meg bit her lip uncertainly. "Do you think Christabel was a good selection?"

"Truly." He took her hand. "The story is wonderful, especially when it is you telling it. I cannot believe you have committed the entire thing to memory." He tightened his fingers around hers, pulling her closer. "Although, I still think Christabel is Spanish."

She smiled and tipped her head. "Poetry is meant to be interpreted by the reader. If you would like Christabel to be Spanish, I do not think Mr. Samuel Coleridge would begrudge your analysis." Meg's eyes glinted in a way he had come to recognize as an indication that she was teasing. She pulled her hand from his and tapped her finger on her chin. "I certainly could believe Geraldine to be Spanish."

"The wicked one?" Rodrigo placed his palm over his heart as if he were wounded. "How could you say such a thing?"

"Is she wicked?" Meg pursed her lips. "I think just misunderstood."

Rodrigo cupped his hand beneath her elbow and led her toward the bench. He pulled her down to sit next to him. "Joking aside, why did you choose this poem?"

Meg's face turned serious, and the little crease appeared above her nose. "I suppose I relate to the two women." She shrugged. "I think every person strives to be perfect like Christabel, but we fall short. I believe Geraldine wants to be virtuous. She wears a white robe to hide her blemish; she tries to behave like Christabel. Maybe because she wants to please everyone else." Her eyes moved from his to the stones of the greenhouse floor. "It is difficult to hide oneself beneath the expectations everyone else creates."

"And this is why you chose to recite a poem at the musicale."

Meg nodded, folding her arms. "I only hope when the time comes that I am brave enough to go through with it."

"Are you suggesting that *mi compañera de aventura* lacks courage? I do not believe it."

Meg sighed. "I just wish you could come tomorrow. I wouldn't be so nervous if you were there." The moment the words left her mouth, Meg's face paled and then filled with color. "I am sorry, Carlo. I did not mean . . ." She rubbed her hand up and down her arm.

He squinted his eyes in confusion. What had upset her?

Meg looked up at him through her lashes. "I spoke without thinking. I really did not mean to say something so rude or to imply . . ."

At once he understood. He had forgotten she thought he was a servant. Of course she had considered it an insult to remind him that he was not welcome among the *ton*. And knowing that this distressed her touched him. He was again surprised at the effect Meg's concern had on him.

Meg reached over and pressed her palm on his cheek. "Please do not allow my words to upset you."

Rodrigo was finding it difficult to hold any thought in his head as Meg's soft skin pressing against his face seemed to be the most important thing currently happening in the world. "Do not worry yourself, Margarita. I have no wish to mingle with the aristocracy." He certainly did not misrepresent himself in that statement. "I am not offended—quite the opposite, in fact." He took her hand and held it in both of his. "I find it very pleasing to know that you desire my company."

Meg looked up at him, and for a moment he thought she might say something. Finally she glanced at the greenhouse windows. "I suppose I should dress for supper before I am missed." She pulled her hand from his grasp and stood.

He stood with her and caught her hand again. Lifting it to his lips, he brushed a kiss over her fingers and heard Meg's swift intake of breath. "I wish you *buena suerte*, good luck, tomorrow."

"Thank you, Carlo." Meg kept her eyes lowered as she turned and hurried from the greenhouse. The enchanting blush had returned to her cheeks. And Rodrigo felt immense satisfaction that his action had put it there.

He was still smiling a moment later as he left the greenhouse and walked toward the stable. But a sight stopped him short.

Meg was walking up the path to the front entrance to the castle, and Lord Featherstone approached her. She curtsied, and he nodded his head slightly. Although Rodrigo could not hear them, he could tell they were exchanging pleasantries. Lord Featherstone gestured toward the book Meg held, and she hesitated briefly before extending it toward him.

The earl took the book of poetry and glanced at it. Even from a distance, Rodrigo could see the man's disapproval as he returned it to Meg and then offered his arm. She took the book, slipped her hand into the crook of his elbow, and walked toward the castle.

It was only a short walk, but Lord Featherstone did not give Meg a chance to speak the entire distance. Rodrigo could see that she nodded and maintained a pleasant countenance, but her shoulders drooped slightly and she seemed to withdraw into herself.

Rodrigo's heart dropped. He could not help but think of the light in Meg's eyes and the confident way she had delivered her poem. Her entire being had appeared more alive and vibrant. But as he'd seen Lord Featherstone speak to her, undoubtedly demeaning her love of poetry and reading, Meg had appeared to wilt. It surprised Rodrigo how the sight pained him, and he could think of nothing more important than figuring out how to ensure that she never lost the enthusiasm he had seen in the greenhouse. Without it, he feared the Meg he had grown so fond of would fade away completely.

He gritted his teeth, wishing he could ensure that Meg never lost what made her Meg, but he felt as powerless to help her as he was to help himself.

Chapter 12

Meg's hand tightened on Daniel's arm, and she gasped as they entered the Harrisons' ballroom. The room was filled with people. She had not imagined so many ladies and gentlemen lived in Southampton.

"You will be splendid," Daniel murmured to her, even though his eyes were roaming the room, no doubt assessing the attractive young ladies.

On one end of the ballroom, a raised stage held a pianoforte and a harp. Rows of chairs faced the stage. Daniel followed the Poulters down the aisle, seating Meg next to Lady Vernon.

The countess must have seen the worry on Meg's face. She patted her arm. "Don't worry, you look lovely, dear. And your music . . . ah, well, you have prepared as well as you could, so do not be dismayed on that account."

Meg did agree with Lady Vernon on one point. She felt beautiful. She completely adored her gown. Thanks to the urgent change of wardrobe brought about by Serena's apricot dress, Meg wore a white silk gown with gathered lace at the elbows and long white gloves. A honey-colored sash tied around her waist matched perfectly with the amber pendant at her throat.

She was especially pleased with the way Bessie had arranged her hair. The majority of her locks were twisted and fastened atop her head, with cascades of loose curls escaping to hang at her neck and on her shoulders.

Daniel stood at the end of the row of chairs, waiting for Helen and Lucinda to be seated, but before he could take his place, Lord Featherstone sat in the seat next to Meg.

Daniel smiled at her, raising his brows.

Meg looked at her brother with an even gaze until he looked away, shaking his head.

"Miss Margaret," Lord Featherstone said, fixing his brilliant blue eyes on her. "Have I told you how extremely beautiful you look this evening?"

"Thank you, my lord. And yes, you did tell me, before we left the castle, and once in the carriage, and—"

"But a lady does not tire of flattering remarks, does she?" he said smugly, stroking his whiskery lip and adjusting the lace cuffs that splayed elegantly from his jacket sleeves.

Meg wouldn't have thought that a lady would tire of compliments about her appearance until Lord Featherstone had spoken them so often that they had lost their sincerity. Was it too much to ask for him to occasionally notice her character or intelligence? She shuffled the pages of sheet music around on her lap.

"Do not make yourself uneasy about your deficiency of musical skill," the earl said. "My sisters have warned me it is not your strong suit."

"My lord, if you are trying to set me at ease—"

"Just remember that your appearance is every bit as important as any talent, and you are not lacking where that is concerned." He shook his head affectionately, and Meg employed every bit of self-control she possessed to manage a small smile, though she could not convince her eyes to participate in the expression.

She turned toward Lady Vernon, hoping that she might at least be saved from Lord Featherstone's condescension by entering into conversation with the countess, but Lady Vernon was laughing with Lady Featherstone. After spending over a week with the two women, Meg knew there would be no chance of intruding on their discussion.

Meg straightened the papers in her lap once again as she looked around the room. What had she been thinking? These people were all elegant and refined. She didn't fit among them, and she certainly would not impress the *ton* with her nonconformist exhibition. Why had she ever thought it would be a good idea?

The performances began, and Meg's despair grew. Each young lady seemed to be more talented than the one before. They were graceful and sophisticated, and every one played or sang beautifully.

Meg wondered if she should feign a stomachache to be spared what would certainly be a humiliation not only to her but to Lady Vernon and the duke as well. It would not take much effort to pull it off, since she was very close to losing what little bit of supper she had managed to swallow.

Another young lady stepped onto the stage and sat, arranging her skirts and then pulling the harp to her shoulder. She began to play, and Meg's eyes moved around the ballroom. She sat up, just now becoming aware of the other spectators. She had been so concerned with her upcoming debacle that she had not noticed that most of the audience was not paying any attention to the performance. They whispered to each other or looked around the room. Was everybody bored?

She was still pondering the implications of her discovery when Helen's name was announced. As her friend scooted past, Meg squeezed her hand and then watched the crowd. While Helen made her way to the stage, the entire room was silent and every eye was on her. Ladies craned their necks to get a better view, and gentlemen sat taller in their seats, studying her, but as soon as she began to play, conversations resumed and attentions turned away from the stage. Meg could not believe it. Helen was the most gifted performer of the night, and if *she* could not keep the interest of the audience, then Meg didn't have anything to worry about. She didn't need to impress these people with her talent. She would give a completely unremarkable musical performance, and it would not matter in the least.

Meg felt as if an enormous weight had been lifted from her shoulder. An albatross, just like in *The Rime of the Ancient Mariner*. But the thought stopped her as the poem came to her mind. Her heart began to pound again. She had been so certain yesterday when she had rehearsed with Carlo. But Lord Featherstone's manner as he dismissed her poetry as trivial had opened the door to doubt. And now she possessed the knowledge that she could do the safe thing, banging out a few chords and melodies that nobody would notice, and then escape, leaving none the wiser as to her abandoned radical plan.

It was the coward's way, of course, and the guilt she felt at her lack of courage was magnified at the thought of Carlo's disappointment when she told him she had not gone through with it. But he wasn't here. He didn't have to mingle with these people for the next few months and live with their judgments.

Her rationalization was unable to chase away the feeling of disappointment in herself. She was doing precisely what she had been told, in order to be the person others wanted her to be. When had she become so disloyal to herself?

When Helen finished, the audience applauded politely, and Meg's name was announced. She stood and walked to the stage aware of hundreds of eyes assessing everything about her from her hairstyle to her clothing to her posture. The feeling of disappointment in herself grew as she stepped to the pianoforte and placed the sheet music upon it.

She sat and took one last glance at the audience. Lord Featherstone's bright eyes stood out in the crowd as he watched her approvingly, Lady Vernon nodded her head, Daniel gave a reassuring smile, Colonel Stackhouse looked as if he wished he were anywhere else. She turned back toward the instrument, but from the corner of her eye, she saw movement. Her gaze snapped to the back of the room, where Carlo had just entered.

Every other person in the room disappeared as she met his eyes. He was dressed in a dark coat, his cravat tied perfectly, looking every bit the gentleman. Tears stung in Meg's eyes as she realized what he must have gone through to be here, and if he was discovered, she did not know what would happen. But he had certainly done it for her. *He* had not taken the coward's path but seemed to realize she was considering it herself.

Carlo's brows raised, and he gave a slight nod.

Meg felt a surge of confidence rise inside her. She lifted her chin, stood, and walked to the front of the stage. The whispering in the room instantly quieted as the audience watched her, wondering what she was doing.

Her heart pounded in her ears, and her mind completely emptied until she met Carlo's gaze again. The corners of his lips lifted in the slightest smile, and she was calmed. She straightened her shoulders, took a breath, and began.

As Meg spoke the words of the poem, she gazed around the ballroom. The audience had not returned to their conversations. Each person's face was turned to her, and she saw a multitude of reactions in their expressions.

Lady Vernon's fingers were in front of her open mouth. Colonel Stackhouse had sat up straight in his chair, obviously relieved that something out of the normal was happening. Lord Featherstone looked as if he had been served a plate of leeches, so great was his disgust, but Meg did not care one fig.

When she reached the part of the poem when Geraldine's robe drops open to expose the blemish on her skin, Meg heard gasps round the room, the loudest, she thought, from Lord Featherstone. Carlo continued to watch her, his expression unchanging, and Meg drew courage from his steadiness.

She reached the conclusion, telling of Christabel's "vision sweet," and the room was silent. Meg dipped in a curtsey, and the audience burst into applause. Meg's muscles relaxed, and her chest filled. She curtseyed again, unable to stop the smile that spread over her face.

Some of the gentlemen rose to their feet. Meg lost sight of Carlo in the commotion and felt a tinge of panic as her eyes scanned the ballroom.

She breathed a sigh when the crowd parted, and she saw him. Carlo pressed his fingers to his lips and then lifted his hand away; his small gesture touched her more than any accolades, and Meg's heart began to race again, but this time it had nothing to do with her performance. She breathed deeply to get her emotions under control as she took the footman's hand and walked down the stage steps on shaking legs to return to her seat.

As she passed between the rows, she glanced back once to where Carlo had stood, but he was gone.

Meg had assumed she would receive a cold reception from Lord Featherstone and Lady Vernon, but it was not the case. Lady Vernon clasped Meg's hand. "That was simply wonderful, my dear. And such a surprise. You nearly stopped my heart when you . . ." She moved her hand back and forth pointing between the stage and the pianoforte. "But you carried it off magnificently."

"Thank you," Meg whispered, since the next number had begun.

Lord Featherstone leaned toward Meg, all traces of disgust gone from his face. "I am completely astonished." His leg pressed against hers in a most improper manner, and Meg scooted closer to Lady Vernon. The earl did not move his leg, however, and Meg felt uneasy at his closeness. "Your passion as you performed is . . . stimulating," he said, his mouth entirely too close to her ear.

"Thank you, my lord," Meg whispered and leaned forward in her chair, attempting to look as if she were interested in the musical number.

The whispering in the audience had not only continued, but it had intensified. Meg noticed a number of heads turn in her direction, and she did her best not to allow it to unnerve her. She had known her actions would have repercussions, and she would have to live with the consequences.

When the final performance ended, Meg found herself the center of attention. Gentlemen and ladies alike asked to be introduced to her, and she found it quite annoying that Lord Featherstone remained nearly attached to her side as she was attempting to become acquainted with the other guests. The earl's manners had shifted quite decidedly in a direction that made Meg's scalp prickle, and she moved away, standing next to Serena.

A few of the young men she spoke to asked if they might call on her. One even reserved a dance at the masque. Meg was surprised that her performance had elicited such a positive response, but as one Mr. Newton confided to her in a low voice, "The musicale is one of the most tedious events of the year, and most of us dread it. But you managed to liven it up and make the night interesting."

Meg smiled at this, proud of her performance and glad, not to mention relieved, that it had been so well received.

After a few more hours of refreshments and conversation, the party left to return to Thornshire. Lord Featherstone sat next to Meg in the carriage and hurried to alight before her in order to assist her as she stepped down.

He kept hold of her hand, tucking it beneath his arm as he led her into the castle. The others in the party dispersed in the main hall, but Lord Featherstone retained his grip on Meg's hand. Once she had finally managed to pry it away and make her farewells, she hurried up the stairs, hoping to put as much distance between the earl and herself as possible. She did not know what had changed in his attitude toward her this evening, but where the earl had merely been annoying before, now Meg felt positively ill at ease around him.

Bessie helped her undress, and once Meg had crawled beneath the blankets, her mind returned to the events of the evening—one in particular, Carlo's simple gesture of blowing a kiss. The melting of her heart that the memory elicited sent her to sleep with a sigh and a smile on her face.

Chapter 13

Rodrigo leaned against the windowpane in the attic room. He'd found that this particular spot in the dower house afforded a view of Meg's bedchamber window, though he had to stand upon a chair and crane his neck awkwardly to see it. He'd climbed the stairs to this forgotten part of the house so many times in the last few evenings that he had lost count.

As he watched, the window at last went dark, and Rodrigo stepped down, brushing the dust from his jacket. He knew he should feel ridiculous checking every half hour to see if Meg had gone safely to sleep, but after two nights of reprimanding himself, he'd finally accepted that he'd get no rest otherwise and continued his nightly watch.

He'd not spoken to Meg since their practice session a few days earlier in the greenhouse, but he'd seen her often enough, taking carriage rides and strolls with the gentlemen who had begun calling at the castle following her performance. Meg's recitation had apparently impressed society far more than she'd expected. The sight of her with these other men made his stomach burn. He hated the thought of Meg spending time with them, and even more when he imagined her laughing and looking at them through her lashes in the way he considered so utterly charming. Did any of the gentlemen touch her soft curls or notice the crease above her nose when she was lost in thought?

He hated everything about this situation. And it was all the more frustrating because it was of his own making. He would have never imagined it would go so wrong.

All it would take for him to join Meg's throngs of admirers would be to simply reveal himself as Prince Rodrigo. But then, that is what he would be, only one of many. He uttered an oath that would have burned a priest's ears. His friendship with Meg was unique, and he wanted it to remain that way. So he resigned himself to wait and hope that he would happen upon Meg in the stables or the gardens or see her in the library window—which he also checked multiple times daily.

A smile curled his mouth, and he patted the lump in his jacket pocket. He'd finally come up with something, a way to see Meg and watch excitement light up her eyes again. This simple object gave him the advantage over all her other admirers.

He set the candle on the desk in the study and sat in the soft chair. Pulling out a clean piece of paper, he dipped a quill into the ink and thought for a moment before writing.

Dear Miss Margarita Burton,

I have discovered an object I think will be of some interest to you, as you have a fondness for anything that is potentially terrifying, and I am seeking a compañera de aventura.

If you are feeling particularly daring and willing to risk all for an unknown quest, please meet me in the Oriental drawing room at 7:00 tomorrow evening.

Your mysterious friend

When he was finished, he leaned back and allowed the smile to spread wide across his face as he imagined Meg's reaction to the note. If that didn't pique her curiosity, nothing would. He read over it once more, and a roil of unease moved through him. He had talked to Serena about the household's schedule, and she had told him that they had been invited to dine at the Newtons' tomorrow. Meg would have to invent an excuse to forego the dinner party. Would she be willing to miss out on the gathering for him?

Rodrigo prepared for bed, but he could not fall asleep. He attempted to distract himself by reading from a volume of romantic poetry that he had borrowed from the duke's library, but the verses did not hold his attention the way they had when Meg had spoken them, and he gave up the effort, tossing the book onto a table and blowing out the candle.

He spent a long restless night and was groggy and agitated in the morning when he sent the message to Meg, along with another to Serena, explaining his plan. By midafternoon, a note arrived from his sister. Meg would not be joining them for dinner at the Newtons'. She had apparently come down with a headache and decided to retire early.

Rodrigo's chest swelled. He should never have doubted Meg. Or at least her taste for adventure.

***

Rodrigo watched from the library window as the carriages departed for the Newtons', then he made his way to the Oriental drawing room to wait. He thought this room, with its carved Chinese furniture and samurai swords hanging on the walls, was especially suitable for the launch of an escapade.

It was exactly seven o'clock when Meg entered. When her gaze met Rodrigo's, her face lit up. She rushed across the room, grasping onto his hand with both of hers. "Carlo, I have missed you. And I've not had an opportunity to thank you for attending the musicale."

Any worries that she might have been hesitant about joining him fled, and the tension in his neck relaxed. "I could not have allowed an opportunity to hear about Christabel pass by."

She tugged on his hand, shaking her head. "You're being too gracious. I do not know what pains you took to be there, but it touched me that you would come. I was not brave enough to follow through with my plan until I saw you."

The only pains Rodrigo had endured were from escaping Lord Harrison, who, as soon as he saw that the prince was at the musicale, did not want him to leave. Rodrigo had finally resorted to acting as if he'd eaten something that disagreed with him and slipped out while the earl went in search of a servant to bring a cup of tea. But in Meg's eyes, he had done something much more noble, and he did not mind her assumption.

"So, tell me, what is our adventure? And the mysterious object? I have wondered about it all day." Meg's eyes shone, and the sight delighted him.

"Before any mysterious objects are revealed, you shall need this." He bent down behind the couch and picked up a cloak.

"Are we to go outside? If I had known I would have—"

"Worn your bonnet and gloves?"

Meg nodded.

"That is why I did not tell you," Rodrigo said, squeezing her fingers. He pushed her loose curls aside as he wrapped the cloak around her.

Meg's mouth opened, and her eyes widened in shock, but she did not reprimand him for his forward behavior as she was apparently distracted by Rodrigo's efforts to straighten the wrap on her shoulders. She ran her fingers over the soft material. "This isn't my cloak, Carlo. Where did you find it?"

"It is your cloak now, but you must hold still while I fasten it." He tied the ribbons beneath her chin, delighted that the duke's steward had managed to procure a cloak so close in design to the picture Rodrigo had seen in Meg's sketchbook.

Meg spread her arms out, allowing the lightweight fabric to billow around her. "It is beautiful, but I cannot accept this gift. I . . . you . . . it must have been very costly." She winced uneasily.

"Now is not the time to discuss a man's salary or what he chooses to do with it. We have much more important matters to attend to." Rodrigo held up an old key that hung from an iron ring.

Meg's crease appeared above her nose, and she squinted, tipping her head in confusion. "A key? A key to what?"

Rodrigo moved the key closer, dangling it in front of her.

Meg took it, turning it over in her hands, then looked up at him.

He lifted his shoulders and studied his fingernails. "I was told by the duke's housekeeper that it opens the door to the west tower. But I cannot imagine that being of any interest to you—"

"The tower!" Meg gasped, and her gaze moved to the French doors that led to a large patio. One could follow the steps from the patio down to the duke's gardens. But there was another staircase that led up to the battlements that ran across the top of the castle wall. "I should love to explore the tower."

Meg moved toward the doors, but Carlo stopped her. "One moment please." He reached behind the sofa again, swinging a cape-like cloak around his own shoulders and buckling a scabbard around his waist.

"Why are you bringing a sword?" Meg asked, her eyes widening.

"One cannot be too prepared. Who knows what enemies to the kingdom we will meet in the tower?"

She giggled and clasped her hands together excitedly.

Rodrigo lifted a basket the cook had prepared for him and strode toward the door, opening it and then following Meg outside.

Meg stopped at the bottom of the staircase, but Rodrigo indicated for her to precede him. It was highly improper for a gentleman to follow a lady up the stairs, but this was Meg's adventure. She should lead the way. And Rodrigo would not admit to her, but he wanted to remain close behind her in case she should trip on the steep steps. There was no railing.

The staircase ran next to the castle wall, and when they emerged onto the battlements, Rodrigo saw that his orders had been followed, and torches had been lit at intervals, illuminating the walkway.

Once they reached the door to the tower, Meg inserted the key into the old lock and tried to turn it, but it wouldn't move. She jiggled it and twisted it and then stepped aside to allow him to try. It took a bit of work, but the key finally turned with a screech of metal, and Meg pulled on the iron ring that served as a door handle. The heavy wooden door creaked open, and a gust of mildewy-smelling cold air rushed out.

Anticipation shone in Meg's eyes. "What do you suppose we will find?"

Rodrigo looked up, tapping his finger on his chin. "Perhaps a dragon's lair or the ghosts of brave knights or a smuggler's hoard."

Meg's smile grew. "Then what are we waiting for?"

"After you, Margarita." He pulled a torch from its holder in the balustrade and handed it to her.

She poked the light into the tower, exposing a curving stone staircase. Meg grabbed Rodrigo's hand, squeezing it tightly. He knew she would never admit to being nervous, but the coldness of her hand, and the slight trembling gave her away.

Meg began her ascent. The torchlight illuminated a small sphere around them, exposing the ancient stone walls and steep stairs, but the rest of the tower was eerily dark. The firelight played over Meg's hair, and Rodrigo stayed close behind in case she slipped or the old stones crumbled.

The narrow staircase curved around to the right. Meg held the torch with her right hand and his hand with her left.

"It is difficult to climb like this. I feel as though I am walking backward," she said.

"This way, the attacker will automatically find himself at a disadvantage. If you were coming down, protecting the tower, it would be much easier. Your sword hand would not be in such an awkward position. Tower stairs were specifically built with defense in mind."

"And how did you become such an expert in medieval tower construction?" Meg asked, and from her voice, he could tell she was smiling.

"I am an expert in a good many things, *querida*."

Meg let out a huff of air through her nose. The noise sounded like a blend of laughter and exasperation.

Rodrigo smiled. Even though he could not see her face, he could imagine the exact expression upon it.

When they reached one of the tall, thin windows, Meg stopped. She released her hold on him and passed the torch in front of her to her other hand, shaking her arm to restore the blood flow as she looked out of the window. "I didn't realize we had climbed so high already." Meg began to transfer the torch back to her other hand but stopped, tilting her head.

"Do you hear that noise?" she whispered. "It sounds as if something is ahead of us.

Rodrigo listened and heard a soft fluttering. "It is only bats."

"Bats?" Meg's gaze darted upward, but she could only see the underside of the stone stairs above their heads.

Since she was on the step above him, they were the same height. Rodrigo leaned toward her until their faces were merely inches apart. He raised his eyebrows. "Bats."

Meg flinched and glanced upward again.

Rodrigo chuckled. "I would have thought you possessed more fortitude than that. Do not tell me my fearless partner is afraid of small flying rodents."

She grimaced. "Please do not say that word."

"Rodents?"

"I told you not to say it."

"Margarita, bats are harmless."

She nodded, but her eyes narrowed warily.

"Unless . . ." he muttered, pursing his lips.

Meg's eyes widened. "Unless what?"

"Unless these particular bats are under the control of a malevolent vampire. Then you must beware that they do not carry you away to their evil master."

Meg's face relaxed, and a small smile lifted one corner of her mouth. She swatted at him with her free hand. "You're right. I am in a much better position to attack from up here. You should remember that when you decide to tease." She grasped his hand again. "Shall we face the minions of darkness then?"

They passed another window, and after a moment longer, the firelight lit up the ceiling. Rodrigo moved onto the step next to her, handing her the basket and using both hands to push open the heavy wooden trapdoor. He climbed out and helped Meg step up onto the landing, closing the trapdoor behind. A low wall encircled the tower, and Meg stepped toward it.

Rodrigo joined her and took the torch, wedging it into a gap between the stones. Even though it was dark, moonlight bathed the land around them in silver.

A gust of wind blew Meg's hair and billowed out her cloak. She wrapped it closer around her and turned toward him. "It is breathtaking.

I have never seen a view like this." She placed her hands on the wall and leaned forward, looking straight down at the duke's gardens below.

Rodrigo's heart jerked. He stepped closer and put a hand on her arm, pulling her back. "*Cuidado*," he said. "Be careful. The mortar is old, and it is a long way to fall."

Meg turned to him, her eyes twinkling in the moonlight. "Carlo, does such a lofty height frighten you?" She shrugged playfully. "Then perhaps you should not have teased me about my fear of bats. I may have to repay the favor."

He truthfully had never feared heights until he had seen Meg lean over the edge. The idea of her falling was terrifying. "I simply thought you might be hungry," he said. "Come, help me spread the blanket for a picnic."

They opened the blanket and sat upon it. Meg arranged her skirts and cloak, and Rodrigo leaned back against the wall, facing her. He handed her a plate with some small sandwiches on it. "I am sorry the food is so simple," he said.

Meg shook her head. "It looks wonderful. I am so tired of fancy meals I could—"

"Throw rocks into an icy pond?" Rodrigo suggested.

"Yes." Meg laughed. "I do not know how people do it every day, waking up to a grand breakfast, then a luncheon, and in the evening, dressing for an elaborate feast. I'm used to an occasional dinner party, but by far, the majority of our meals in Charleston we prepare ourselves." Meg broke off a piece of bread and put it into her mouth. As she chewed, she looked up toward the sky. Moonlight lit her face and shined in her eyes.

Carlo's breath caught in his throat.

"This is delightful, Carlo. A picnic by moonlight on top of a castle tower." Meg sighed. "I cannot imagine anything more perfect." She closed her eyes. "The moon shines bright. In such a night as this, when the sweet wind did gently kiss the trees . . ."

"I cannot imagine anything more perfect than hearing you recite poetry," Rodrigo said. *Especially when the poem involves a kiss.*

"I am sure it becomes tiring for others, but sometimes I feel that it is the language of my soul, and I do not want to subdue it." She smiled shyly. "Does that make sense to you?"

"Yes. And when your soul speaks, it touches other souls, no?"

"I like to believe that."

They remained silent for a moment, and Rodrigo took the opportunity to study Meg again. Her fair skin glowed in the silver light and her eyes were wide and shining. Heat spread from his chest as he watched her admiring the night sky. Why was this woman not Spanish?

"Carlo, I have spoken so often of myself and gowns and poetry, but I have hardly asked about you or your family. You must worry dreadfully about them."

Rodrigo felt the familiar ache in his chest. "Yes. I worry about them. There is nothing so terrible as war."

"And did you experience it yourself?"

He shifted his position, stretching his legs in front of him and crossing one ankle over the other. "When I was younger, I was very sheltered from the situation, though Spain had been in turmoil for many years before the French invasion. It did not seem as if any of it would affect me, and I continued to enjoy myself with my friends and ignore the reports from the other parts of the country. But there was one terrible day I will never forget. And since then, my life has not been the same."

Meg scooted closer to his outstretched legs, leaning toward him to listen.

He rubbed his eyes, frustrated with the burning behind them. "Napoleon's Grande Armée took over Madrid, and in defiance of Pope Pius VII, he forbade the Spanish people to inter their dead in churchyards; instead, they were buried in masses in municipal graveyards. You can imagine how this upset the Spaniards, who believe their loved ones will not find peace unless they rest in sacred ground. One rainy night, I was returning home late. When I passed by, I saw people stealing into the cemetery to retrieve bodies. And while they were digging or carrying remains, French soldiers arrived and began to arrest them.

"I did not know what to do. I was frightened, and I hid behind a wall, watching as fighting began. Some people were killed; others were taken to prison. The people, they did not have weapons like the soldiers, and they did not stand a chance. Women were screaming and weeping and begging the soldiers to allow them to take their family members to the churchyard, but they were beaten or dragged away. I will never forget the sight of the cemetery in the rain with bodies—some old and some new—lying in the mud, nor the feeling of utter helplessness as I realized the people were outnumbered, and I was useless to help them."

"I am sorry, Carlo. It must have been terrible."

"The most terrible part of it was that, until then, the war seemed so far away. It did not seem real, and as a foolish young man, I did not allow it to concern me. I did not care." Rodrigo's stomach hardened, and his jaw clenched.

"I did not know that—about the cemeteries. I have only read reports in the periodicals and Lord Byron's account in *Childe Harold's Pilgrimage*."

In spite of his frustration, Rodrigo smiled, shaking his head. "Do you have a poem for every occasion?"

"Yes." Meg laughed softly. "Some women have the perfect hairstyle or gown, but I find a verse to suit any situation." Her expression turned serious, and she moved to the other side of the blanket, sitting next to him with her back against the wall.

She pulled her knees up and wrapped the cloak around her legs. "In Charleston, there are three forts guarding the entrance to the harbor. Fort Moultrie, Fort Johnson, and Castle Pickney. The entire city has sunk into an economic depression because so many funds have been used to build up the defense after the Federal Embargo Act made Britain and America enemies once again. It has become fashionable for young men to purchase their own uniforms and meet together as volunteer militia companies to train and drill. My brother, Daniel, is a member of the Charleston Fencibles." She twisted her fingers together.

"At the theaters and even at garden parties, 'The South Carolina Hymn' is sung before every performance to arouse patriotism and martial spirit. It is as if everyone is playing a game, and the idea of war seems so romantic and exciting.

"But people forget that war is not simply about regimentals and anthems and brave soldiers. It is also about heartbreak and death and real people. I am glad you told me your story, Carlo, even though it was difficult." She lifted his hand and interlaced their fingers.

They sat for a moment, each lost in thought before Meg spoke again. "Were you near Madrid when the royal family was taken?"

Rodrigo's heart stuttered at the abruptness of the question. "No. I was traveling in Italy."

"With the prince?" Meg asked.

He looked sideways at her. "Yes."

"I imagine it was horrible for him. And though Serena does not speak of it, there are times when I see pain in her eyes. I am sorry for them. How they must be hurting."

Rodrigo nodded. He did not trust his voice to speak.

Meg lifted their intertwined hands and ran the pad of her thumb over his finger. She tipped her head forward to catch his eye. "Carlo, I know you wish to be in Spain helping your people, but I am very glad you are safe here, with me, on a haunted castle tower. Perhaps it is selfish for me to think so, but I am glad you are away from danger."

By the torchlight, he could see the blush that colored her face and felt as if the heat spread directly to his heart. But the warmth did not remain as he realized that leaving England to rescue his parents would cause not only Serena to worry for him. If the opportunity arose, and he departed on a rescue mission, he worried it would result not only in his own peril but could also break a young lady's heart.

Chapter 14

MEG LEANED HER HEAD ONTO Carlo's shoulder and squeezed his hand, wanting him to feel comforted. He seemed so sad when he spoke of Spain. She could hear the pain in his voice and wished she knew what to say to make things better.

The night had been exactly ideal. In the moonlight, the top of the tower seemed magical. A gentle wind blew, but at this height there was no noise from the castle below. It was as if she and Carlo were alone in the world.

She pulled her cloak closer around her with one arm. Meg loved this cloak. The price must have been very dear, especially for a servant, and it touched her that he would know how much she would appreciate a swirling cloak as she stood on top of a castle tower. She worried at his level of sacrifice. What would such a gift mean to a servant's livelihood?

Carlo had planned the evening to perfection, choosing the exact things that Meg loved. He made her feel as if her romantic fantasies were important instead of laughable. He liked that she read poetry. He was the first to believe in her when she wanted to recite at the musicale and did not wait to see how her performance was received before applauding her. Carlo was her champion.

She could not imagine being more comfortable in anyone's company, since she did not have to pretend to be anyone other than Meg Burton around him. When Carlo was near, she didn't even feel homesick. He cared about what would make her happy and planned a special adventure instead of taking her for a turn about the grounds or visiting in the drawing room. Her stomach shifted uncomfortably as she realized that as a stable hand, it would be unacceptable for him to do either of those things. And she began to worry that the relationship had already progressed too far.

"Are you going to tell me?" he asked, breaking the silence.

Meg lifted her head. "Tell you . . . ?"

"The poem. *Childe Harold's Pilgrimage*. Are you going to tell me what it says?"

"No." She leaned forward, turning her face to the side to look at him.

Carlo raised his brows incredulously. "You are declining an opportunity to quote poetry?"

"I fear it will make you sad."

"It does not make me sad when your soul speaks to mine, Margarita." He turned his shoulders to face her more fully but did not release her hand, which had somehow become so warm she thought it could melt butter.

"Very well." She squinted her eyes, gazing across the tower at nothing for a moment while she collected her thoughts. "But first I will set the stage. Childe Harold is a bored young man who has grown weary of the life of debauchery he leads. The one woman he loves is unattainable, and Childe Harold leaves his home in England in search of change. He describes his travels over the rough sea, nearly regretting his decision to go abroad. He sees Portugal from a distance and marvels at the green lush land, but when he arrives, he finds it a ravaged nation. The people are impoverished, and everywhere he looks are crosses marking graves. Even a man as wicked as he feels pity and sees the injustice in war.

"After a moment of introspection, Childe Harold spurs his horse onward to Spain. And that is where I will begin." Meg tightened her grasp on Carlo's hand. She closed her eyes and blew out a breath, then opened them.

"Oh lovely Spain! Renowned, romantic land!

Where is that standard which Pelagio bore . . ."

As Meg continued through the stanzas, Carlo's gaze seemed to look through her. Emotions flickered over his face. She stopped once, but he asked her to continue.

Meg resumed, telling of Lord Byron's view of the battles fought and the devastation left behind and his admiration for the bravery of the Spanish people.

When she finished, Carlo remained quiet, staring past her.

"I knew it would make you sad," she said quietly, aching inside as she watched him.

He slowly turned his gaze to her and appeared to come out of whatever memory he had been lost in. "It is very beautiful and very true. Thank you, Margarita. I told you, it does not make me sad when your soul speaks to mine." He lifted their entwined hands, brushing her knuckles across his lips.

At the intimacy of the gesture Meg's heart came to a standstill.

"Although, I wish your soul did not always prefer to speak in English."

She could not bring her mind to work while her heart was pounding so loudly in her ears. Meg didn't look at Carlo as she gently pulled her hand away and tried to calm herself by cleaning up the dishes and food, placing their picnic back into the basket, and looking anywhere but at him. "I have only read a bit of Spanish poetry, and even then, it was a translation, of course. I would like to read more, but I only know a handful of Spanish words—and one of them is 'ducky.' I do not think Quintana ever mentions ducks."

Carlo took the basket from her.

Meg stood, walking toward the wall, trying to create distance between them to quell the growing attraction she felt and the fear it spurred. "Manuel José Quintana, perhaps you have heard of him. He wrote *El Duque de Viseo*, but now he serves as the secretary to the Cortes Parliament in Cádiz." Meg knew she was babbling, attempting to cover her nervousness.

"Yes, I know Señor Quintana." Carlo came to stand next to her. He looked at her strangely.

Of course he knew of Manuel Quintana. Certainly every person in Spain did. Meg's mind was racing, and she took a deep breath. She needed to stop rambling on like a ninny.

"I . . ." Meg didn't know what to say. Her mind was in chaos, and she did not understand what she was feeling. Part of her wanted to run away, and another part could not bear the idea of leaving. She looked across the duke's forest and pulled her cloak around her shoulders.

She felt Carlo's eyes on her, but when she looked at him, she found she could not raise her gaze above his collar. She was afraid of what she would see in his eyes but, more than that, afraid of what he might see in hers.

Carlo turned her to face him and with a finger lifted her chin. He studied her intently, but she was not afraid; rather she was comforted by his gentle expression.

He was the same man. Whatever she had felt when he'd touched his lips to her fingers had not changed their friendship. Her chest relaxed, and she breathed freely, relieved. She did not know what had come over her, but she wouldn't allow it to cause discomfort between them.

Carlo took a pocket watch from his vest pocket and glanced down before replacing it.

Meg couldn't help but wonder where the timepiece had come from. She realized it must have been one of the prince's castoffs. The idea bothered her. She wished Carlo didn't have to depend on that man for his livelihood.

"The hour grows late. We should return," he said.

Meg nodded. She helped him fold the blanket, which he replaced in the basket.

Then he offered her the torch, but before she took it, he leaned close and tapped his finger on her nose. His brow lifted. "Beware, Margarita. I do not know if we shall escape this tower unscathed."

Meg's lips lifted in a smile. She took the torch, noting with satisfaction how her cloak fell back from her shoulder in waves as she raised her arm. "I am glad to have a brave knight to protect me."

She took his hand again, feeling the instant reassurance of his closeness. Meg did not hear any fluttering and was glad that the bats had abandoned the tower for the night. It was much easier descending the steps, likely because they were not cautiously venturing into the unknown. They stepped out the door, and Carlo swung it closed, locked it, then took the torch from her, returning it to its brace on the balustrade.

Carlo offered his arm, and Meg slipped her hand beneath his elbow. They walked between the rows of torches on the battlements.

"Do you think Patito and Bonnie might want to go for a ride tomorrow?" she said, feeling a bit shy. "If—"

But her words froze in her mouth when she saw men moving along the top of the wall toward them. Armed men.

Carlo pushed her behind him. He pulled the sword from its sheath with a hiss of metal. "Margarita, I fear we are under attack!"

Tremors began in Meg's hands and fingers. She clung to Carlo's arm, and he led her to the side of the walkway. "Carlo, what do we do?" She pressed a hand over her mouth, holding back the scream that was fighting its way out.

"Do not fear, fair maiden. I will protect you."

Even though her pulse was thrashing painfully, she paused at his words. It did not sound like something Carlo would say if it were truly villainous men coming for them.

Carlo stepped to the first man, his sword raised. "*En garde*, villain." He flung back the cape from his shoulder with a flourish.

The man in front of him seemed to hesitate. He and Carlo stared at each other, and Carlo nodded his head slightly, lifting his brows.

"We will conquer this castle and take the fair maiden to our hideaway." The man's voice was monotone, and he shuffled his feet. He spoke with a thick accent, and Meg's fear began to abate as she realized the man was Spanish.

"Never!" Carlo cried and leapt toward the man, bringing his sword down. The man lifted his own weapon, blocking the strike. Carlo spun around with his cape flying, as he executed some moves that his opponent seemed to anticipate perfectly and block; although the man lacked any enthusiasm and appeared rather humiliated by the entire experience.

The attacker let out a pitiful groan, and holding his chest—which Meg noticed had not been injured in the least—he ran off.

Carlo turned to the next man. "And now, you black-hearted wretch, let us see if you've a taste for blood!" He charged at the man, who appeared to have more skill than his comrade. He put up a good fight before running off, cradling his own nonexistent injury.

Meg realized her hands were still covering her mouth, but instead of holding back a scream, she was completely delighted. Carlo must have practiced and choreographed his fight with these men. Were they the prince's guards? And though she had long since realized the performance was for her benefit, she also recognized that Carlo was an exceptionally talented swordsman.

He blocked, thrust, and parried, all the while maintaining his ridiculous banter. Meg was mesmerized as she watched him fight with a combination of grace and strength. In merely a few moments, each of the enemies was defeated and ran off to nurse their wounds—or more likely their pride.

Meg pressed her palm to her chest, and the back of her hand to her forehead, as if she would swoon. "Oh, you have rescued me, brave hero." She giggled.

"Do not return, you lecherous cads!" Carlo called after the retreating men as he returned his sword to its scabbard. His cape waved behind him when he turned toward Meg, breathing heavily, and wiped the sheen of perspiration from his forehead. His eyes were alive with excitement, his face flushed, and before Meg knew what happened, he swept her into his arms and pressed his lips to hers.

The world around them disappeared, and Meg was aware of nothing but the softness of Carlo's lips, his strong arms encircling her, and his heart beating beneath her palms. Her blood surged and heated, and she was swept away on a sea of emotion that slowly abated as their lips parted and Carlo brushed his thumb along her neck.

His eyes bore into hers, and she saw within them a fire that both terrified and thrilled her.

"And Eden revives . . ." she murmured, leaning her head against his chest. She slowly emerged from her haze, blinking her eyes.

A shock jolted through her system. And her eyes snapped open. She realized that she clung to Carlo, her hands fisted in his cape. "No," she said, and then more forcefully, "No!" She pushed against him.

Carlo's face clouded in confusion. "Margarita?"

She should have never allowed this to happen. She had let her loneliness, her desire for friendship to dictate her actions, and now it had gone too far. Carlo was a servant. She could not form an attachment with him.

And what if they had been seen? Such a thing would lead to her disgrace, and for him—her stomach lurched. Daniel or the duke would have to call him out to defend her honor. He would be transported—or worse.

Tears began to fill her eyes, and her throat constricted. "Carlo, we cannot. If we are discovered . . ." Her words choked on a sob, and she turned, covering her face with her hands.

Carlo turned her back to him, pulling down on her arms.

"There is nothing to fear."

"Don't you understand?" Meg's voice rose. And she was shaking. "You are a servant. You will be punished or . . ."

He shook his head. His expression held none of the fear it should. "No, Margarita, listen to me."

Meg wanted to put her hands over her ears. She could not listen anymore. Not when she cared for Carlo more deeply with every word that he said. She pulled her arms from his grasp and ran blindly away. Carlo called her name, but she did not stop.

At last, Meg stumbled through the doorway of her bedchamber. She did not remember by what route she had arrived. It seemed as though her mind had been replaced by mist. Her head ached, her heart ached, and she could no longer hold back her sobs. She lay down upon her bed fully dressed and allowed her tears to soak her pillow.

Why had she done this? Why had she not done what she should and attended dinner at the Newtons' with her hosts and the rest of the guests?

She had known as soon as Daniel had explained their situation and her duty to marry a man of means that she was not destined for a love match. But to fall in love with another, one who she would never be able to be with? It would have been better to have remained ignorant than to know what she would lose.

Meg gasped as the ache in her heart turned painful. She had fallen in love with Carlo. And had he fallen in love with her? Why did she allow this to happen? Not only was it out of the question for her to love a servant, but if the truth were known to anyone, it would disgrace not only her, but the duke and Serena. She could not allow this to continue.

She would put her feelings aside and turn her attentions to other gentlemen, those who could help her family out of their predicament. And it would not do to maintain a friendship with Carlo. The only course would be to sever all contact with him. It would be better for both of them. The very idea hurt so enormously that Meg gasped again, wrapping her arms around her chest to try to stop the aching. She wept until no tears remained and fell asleep wrapped in a soft billowy cloak, her heart shattered.

Chapter 15

RODRIGO SANK INTO A CHAIR next to the fireplace in his sitting room. He rubbed the back of his neck, bending his head from side to side, attempting to relieve the stiffness. His habit of balancing upon a chair while he stretched his neck to watch for the light in Meg's bedchamber window was beginning to take its toll on his muscles.

He had long since shed his cravat and jacket and rolled up his shirtsleeves, and now he waited impatiently for the valet to help him with his boots. Rodrigo rubbed his eyes. It had been three days since Meg had left him on the castle wall. Three days since he'd kissed her. He had thought of little else.

What had started as an interesting diversion for him—concealing his identity—had gone too far. And Meg had been hurt. He'd seen in her eyes the precise moment she'd realized that, as a servant, his very livelihood—and perhaps even his life—was in jeopardy if he was discovered. Her look of utter anguish tore at his heart, and he despised himself for being the one to cause it. And to cause it through deception.

How could he have been so cruel? And so blind? He'd had an unfair advantage over her all along. He had been free to develop feelings for Meg, and with every interaction, she had been conflicted as she'd worried about disappointing her family and causing Rodrigo harm. His stomach twisted painfully as he thought of the guilt she must have felt. And how unnecessary it was. If only he had been honest from the start.

But would she have loved him? A small voice in the back of his mind tormented him with the thought. If he had not carried out this charade, they may never have become friends. The two of them would certainly never been so free to learn of one another. They may have been introduced in a formal setting, but he avoided the young ladies of society so completely that if their relationship had not developed under such unique circumstances, it would never have had a chance, especially since he'd had no intentions of forming an attachment.

The thought that his pride and narrow-mindedness could have meant he'd never have found Meg made him ashamed. What else had he missed while he had been too caught up in himself?

His valet finally arrived, and Rodrigo was glad to be rid of his boots. The housekeeper brought his nightly glass of sherry, and he thanked her, not failing to notice her look of forbearance at his aversion to the drinks the British men preferred, such as gin or port or that dreadful watery tea that nobody on this island could seem to drink enough of. After assuring the servants that he did not require anything further, they withdrew.

Once he was alone again, Rodrigo's mind returned to Meg. Attempts to find her, to explain himself, had been hugely unsuccessful. He'd spent countless hours at the gazebo in the forest or watching the library window. He'd even sent her a note directly but had heard nothing in return. It was all he could do not to storm into the castle and search every room.

Rodrigo opened the book of poetry, finding the pages he'd read so often the past few days. *Childe Harold's Pilgrimage*. The words were not exactly soothing, but somehow the sorrow as well as the pride the poem evoked made him feel as if he were still part of the conflict. That he had not abandoned Spain. He did not want to forget the pain of the people, and the verses—his lips twisted in a smile—the verses spoke to his soul.

He would have never guessed that British Romantic poetry would help him feel a sense of Spanish patriotism. The smile remained on his face as he thought of Meg reciting the verses on the moonlit tower. She'd been right when she said there was a poem for every occasion.

Rodrigo was restless. He flipped casually through the book, hoping to calm his mind so he could retire for the night. As he skimmed a page, a particular phrase leapt out at him. "And Eden revives . . ." It was what Meg had whispered after he had kissed her.

He sat up and looked more closely at the words.

Oh! Cease to affirm that man, since his birth,
From Adam, till now, has with wretchedness strove;
Some portion of Paradise still is on earth,
And Eden revives, in the first kiss of love.

Rodrigo read the words again and again, and a lump formed in his throat. Somewhere inside him an arrogant prince sneered at the love-besotted fool who was becoming teary over a verse of poetry. Lowering the book to his lap, the love-besotted fool leaned his head against the back of the chair, closed his eyes, and allowed his heart to swell as he remembered every detail of that moment, when there was no prince in disguise or need to find a rich gentleman, no pressures of society, apricot gowns, or even nations suffering from war. There was only Meg and Rodrigo, and however briefly, it had truly been a paradise on earth.

***

"What have you done?"

Rodrigo cracked his eyes open and looked around groggily. He would recognize his sister's voice anywhere, but what was she doing in the dower house in the middle of the night? He blinked and then sat up when he saw the sun pouring through the windows. How long had he slept? From the way his back and shoulders seized, he figured it was well past time to rise. He leaned forward, attempting to stretch his cramped muscles. Only then did he remember what had awakened him.

Serena stood directly in front of him, her hands upon her hips and her expression furious. "What have you done to my houseguest?"

Rodrigo didn't even bother to pretend he did not understand. He slumped back in the chair and rubbed his hands over his face. "I kissed her."

He did not think Serena could have looked angrier, but he was wrong. Her face turned red, and her eyes bulged. Rodrigo was amazed that his sister could appear so much like their mother when he'd been caught at mischief. He winced.

Serena's words were a screeching tirade. "How could you do such a thing? How could you toy with this girl's heart? This is why she wanders the castle like a ghost. Why her smile is gone and her eyes are red. How dare you treat my husband's cousin as a conquest and toss her aside!"

She swatted his legs off the ottoman and picked up the book on his lap, glancing at it and turning as if to toss it aside. She drew a breath that Rodrigo was sure was in preparation for another battery of words. But then Serena froze, looking at the book again. Her gaze lifted to meet his, and she let out her breath and sat upon the ottoman. Serena's expression softened as she regarded him. "You are in love with her."

Rodrigo nodded. He rubbed his eyes.

"But she is American. What of your planned marriage? Has your decision changed, *hermano*?"

"I do not know."

"And you did not tell her who you truly are?"

"I tried, but she would not listen, and she has avoided me ever since."

Serena ran her hand over the book cover. "*Pobrecita.* Poor Meg." She looked back at Rodrigo. "But you must tell her the truth."

He nodded. "I am seeking the perfect opportunity. I do not want her to feel embarrassed or that she has been made a fool of. I need to speak to Meg alone, and hope—"

Serena squinted her eyes and rubbed her hand over the book. "Yes, you must approach the situation gently. Her feelings could be injured beyond repair."

He pushed his fingers through his hair and rested his elbows on his knees. "How does one say, 'I'm sorry I have deceived you for the past two weeks, but I had a good reason for it. But now I am in love with you, and I hope you will forgive me and trust me hereafter?"

Serena shook her head. "Rodrigo, why ever did you get yourself into such a circumstance?"

He did not answer, holding his head in his hands.

"There is to be a picnic this afternoon in the meadow behind the castle. Perhaps you could find an opportunity to speak to Meg then?"

"It is a good idea. I will try."

"The masque is tomorrow, you know. And we leave for London in two days, and . . . *hermano*, what are you going to do?"

"I do not know. Perhaps I will change my mind about accompanying you to the city. I do not want to lose Meg." Rodrigo let out a heavy breath. "Serena, am I betraying España?" His voice dropped. "Am I betraying *mamá y papá*?"

"By loving an American woman? Hermano, the world is uncertain. España, she is uncertain too. Our lives will never be the same, no matter who triumphs in this war. And our parents, they would want your happiness."

Serena wrapped her arms around him—rather awkwardly in the chair—and kissed his cheek.

He would never understand how Spanish women could have such extreme changes in mood. *Or maybe it is all women*, he thought, remembering how Meg had transformed after their kiss.

"You have made no promise to Evangelina. I know you will do the right thing, hermano. I am glad you have found someone who makes you happy. Not all of us are destined to marry Spaniards."

"*Gracias*, crazy woman." He smiled and shook his head. "And now, if you will excuse me, I need to dress, and I do not think you want to remain here for that."

Serena handed him the book of poetry and left.

Rodrigo ate a quick breakfast and hurriedly prepared for the day. He hoped Meg would tire of the company at the picnic and wander away from the group long enough to give him an opportunity to speak with her privately. His stomach sank as he considered the various reactions Meg might have to his confession. Knowing this woman, she would not make it easy on him, but it would be worth any reprimand or penance if only Meg would forgive him.

Chapter 16

Meg leaned to the side as a servant removed her plate. Pheasant, roast beef, Yorkshire pudding, sausage, potatoes, soup, scones, fruit, pastries . . . she sighed. *Picnic indeed.* The only difference between this meal and every other served at the castle was that this one was served outside. Tables with long tablecloths and floral centerpieces were clustered in the sunniest spot on the grounds behind the castle. The setting and the weather were ideal, but the formal nature of the meal made it seem like a great deal of extra work for the servants just so that the household and their guests could have a change of scenery. And she did not particularly enjoy eating while wearing gloves and a bonnet.

She could not help but compare this outdoor luncheon to the picnic she and Carlo had shared. Though the events bore the same name, she would not categorize them at all alike. The picnic on the tower had been casual and romantic and completely lovely.

Meg wished that everything did not remind her of Carlo. The hallway outside her bedchamber brought back the memory of his attempt to haunt the castle. Her window bench in the library reminded her of the day he had beckoned to her to join him for a horseback ride. Even her books and poetry brought him to mind. She did not walk to the gazebo in the woods any longer, not only because the memories of their meetings there were so strong but also because she worried she might chance upon him and did not think she could bear it.

"How did you like your pheasant, Miss Margaret?" Lord Featherstone asked, leaning toward her and brushing her arm with his. He was, of course, sitting next to her. She'd hardly had a moment to herself without the earl dogging her steps. The more she became acquainted with Lord Featherstone, the more uneasy she felt in his presence.

"It was very good, my lord," she said, scooting to the other edge of her chair since Lord Featherstone had made it a habit to press his thigh or arm or shoulder against her or to find an opportunity to *accidentally* touch her.

"I am glad you enjoyed it. It was a particularly successful hunting trip yesterday."

Meg smiled and nodded at the earl then turned to her other side, where Helen and Lucinda were discussing the ball.

"Mr. Newton will certainly wish to dance with me," Lucinda said. "He has paid me particular attention ever since his mother's dinner party."

Helen gazed across the table at Daniel, who leaned back in his chair, laughing at something the duke had said. Meg recognized the sorrow in her friend's eyes and felt the strongest urge to throttle her fickle brother. Meg had known it would only be a matter of time before he turned his attention to another young lady, and she was angry Daniel had hurt Helen.

Lord Featherstone leaned forward, apparently intent upon the flowers in the center of the table. He reached for the arrangement, turning it slightly, and in the motion, grazed his arm over Meg's shoulder.

She leaned closer to Helen.

Lord Featherstone sat back in his chair, turning to face Meg and moving his knee to touch hers. "Miss Margaret, the grounds are so lovely today. I would be very pleased if you agreed to take a turn with me."

Meg intended to form an excuse, but she caught Daniel's eye, and his encouraging look persuaded her. She didn't want to have to explain to her brother later her reasons for turning down Lord Featherstone. It was easier to simply nod and agree.

"Thank you, my lord. I would enjoy a bit of exercise."

Lord Featherstone offered his hand, and as she stood, she saw Daniel pulling gently at his cheek with his finger, reminding her to smile. She shot him a look and turned her attention to the earl, who tucked her hand beneath his elbow, squeezing her arm against his side.

They walked past the greenhouse, and the familiar lump rose in Meg's throat. If only she could return to that day when she had recited the poem to Carlo, when she had been so happy. Would she have done anything differently if she'd known that a week later, her heart would ache so badly? She looked in the other direction at the path where they had ridden Patito and Bonnie. Carlo had seen her frustration in the stables that day and known exactly how to cheer her.

"You are very quiet, Miss Margaret."

"I am just pensive today, my lord." Meg did not look at Lord Featherstone's face. She didn't have the energy to smile and laugh and pretend to be interested in his dull conversation.

He led her along the path into the forest and over the small bridge.

Meg pulled her hand from his arm and held onto the rail as she leaned forward, watching the springtime rush of water flow beneath them.

"You have been pensive much more often as of late. It is a refreshing change to see you act in a manner more suited to a lady." Lord Featherstone placed a hand on the rail next to hers. A bit too closely, she thought. "Although I do miss your passion." His voice was much too near her ear.

Just as Meg started to move away, Lord Featherstone's other hand clamped down on the railing on her opposite side, his arms trapping her.

Meg twisted around but quickly wished she hadn't. Lord Featherstone's face was so near to hers that all she could see were bright blue eyes and scrubby upper-lip whiskers moving toward her. Luckily the brim of her bonnet was stiff, and she used it to block the earl's advances by turning her head. "You are much too close, my lord." She pushed against his chest. But he did not move.

His heart beat beneath her palms just as Carlo's had. This time, however, instead of feeling loved and secure, Lord Featherstone's embrace filled her with panic. "I demand that you step back, sir."

The earl tightened his arms around her.

Meg tried to keep her voice calm as she struggled against him. "Lord Featherstone, if you do not unhand me, I will scream."

She heard footsteps on the bridge. "The lady asked you to stop."

Meg's muscles relaxed, and she felt a warm glow at the sound of Carlo's voice. She wanted nothing more than to run into his embrace.

Lord Featherstone released her and stepped back. Meg turned toward Carlo in relief, but the look of fury he directed toward the earl shocked her, and the warmth she'd felt was doused by cold dread. If a servant should strike a nobleman, he would be hanged. Already he had taken a risk coming to her aid.

Meg stepped between the two men. She could not allow the earl to know that she had an association with Carlo. And she definitely could not allow Carlo to challenge him. She did not believe Lord Featherstone would stoop so low as to duel with a commoner.

"Sir, you misunderstand Lord Featherstone's attentions. He was simply bidding me farewell." She turned to the earl. "Is that not right, my lord?"

"Quite, miss," Lord Featherstone said.

Meg was surprised at the earl's expression. He looked at Carlo with fear instead of the arrogance she would have expected as he certainly had the upper hand in the situation.

Carlo did not take his eyes off the earl. His jaw was set and his eyes cold.

Lord Featherstone turned to Meg, bowing his head. "If you will excuse me, miss. I thank you for the pleasant walk." His voice was stiff.

"Of course, my lord," she said, but she did not think the earl heard her. He was already off the bridge and well on his way back to join the rest of the company.

She turned toward Carlo and just as quickly was in his arms, despite knowing how wrong it was for her to be there. She leaned against him, holding on tightly as she trembled and tried to restrain her tears.

"Did he hurt you, Margarita?" Carlo's voice was low. He pulled away and cupped her chin, lifting her face. The anger was still in his eyes, simmering beneath the surface, but it was tempered with concern.

"No. He didn't hurt me." Meg's stomach quivered at the memory of the earl's advances, but she firmed her resolve and clamped down on the tears that threatened to surface. "Carlo, you should not have interfered."

"You would rather I allowed that man to—" He clenched his teeth together, his eyes darting toward the trees where the earl had gone.

"I would rather you did not hang." Meg laid her hand on Carlo's cheek, her voice cracked as she spoke. "Do you not realize what would have happened if the earl had not fled? He may even now be speaking to the duke or the prince. And you will be punished."

"No, Margarita. I will not."

"Carlo, you are not invincible. I do not know how it is in Spain, but in England, you—and I for that matter—we are at a disadvantage. We are not considered equals by the aristocracy, and it is best to avoid their displeasure." She lifted her other hand to frame his face. "I could not bear it if you were punished because of me."

Carlo tightened his arms around her waist, and she slid her hands down the sides of his neck, onto his shoulders. The bonnet she had been so grateful for a few moments earlier now seemed a hindrance.

"Margarita, I have something I must tell you."

His eyes burned, but it was not with anger as it had been when he'd glared at Lord Featherstone. The intensity she saw within them stole her breath. She knew what he would say. He was going to declare his love for her. She didn't think she could bear to hear the words. Not when the sound of his voice speaking them would remain in her memory, haunting her forever.

"Do not say it, Carlo."

He blinked and confusion clouded his features, but Meg was spared the heartache of rejecting him again when they heard her name called.

She recognized Helen's voice and pushed Carlo away. "I must go." Meg turned and hurried across the bridge and through the trees, toward the meadow. She didn't look back.

Helen waved when she appeared. "I saw my brother return alone. I wondered if everything was all right."

"Of course." Meg smiled and linked her arm through Helen's. "I wished for some time alone with my thoughts, and he kindly obliged me."

"I am relieved. I do not like the idea of you alone in the forest. Any number of dangers could lurk within."

None more dangerous than Lord Featherstone, Meg thought.

Meg did not return to the picnic, claiming that her walk had quite worn her out. It was not a lie, her emotions had been strained nearly to the breaking point, and she feared that if she did not retreat, she would unravel.

Bidding Helen farewell, Meg walked slowly through the castle entrance, stopping only long enough to allow a maid to take her bonnet and gloves. She proceeded up the grand staircase and directly to the library. Any solace she might have found in her books was long gone since she had packed them away in the bottom of her trunk a few days earlier. She avoided the window bench, instead making her way to the wingback chairs near the fireplace.

Since no one was around to be displeased with her lack of comportment, Meg slumped into the chair and pulled her feet onto the seat, wrapping her arms around her knees. She didn't know if she could endure another meeting with Carlo and the battle of emotions he produced. If her heart was abused many more times, she wondered if it would survive.

"I thought I might find you here, miss," Colonel Stackhouse said when he entered the room.

Meg jolted, sitting up straight and smoothing down her skirts. "You startled me, sir."

Jim sat in the seat across from her. "It has been quite some time since I've seen you in the library—nearly a week, I'd guess."

"I suppose I have not had much time for reading."

Jim pinched his bottom lip thoughtfully, and Meg's eyes were drawn to his face. His expression was much easier, less critical. He looked content—she would not go so far as to say he looked agreeable—and she was surprised to see that without his annoyed frown, the man was almost . . . handsome. "Miss Meg, I hope you will not resent me for speaking plainly."

"I would expect nothing less from you, Colonel." Meg allowed a small smile, though she felt uneasy at what he might say.

The colonel nodded. "Yes, I am not one to mince words, as you are well aware. So I will get right to the point."

Meg did not know what to expect. To say that he made her nervous was an understatement, but she believed she could trust him.

"Do you remember the advice I gave you when we last sat in these chairs?"

Meg remembered the day well, and she'd thought of his words often. "I remember, sir."

"Yes, I did not think you were the type to forget anything. I would wager you could quote my words back to me verbatim. And I am left to wonder why you choose not to follow the counsel I gave."

Meg lowered her eyes. Her stomach rolled in shame. "It is not my choice, sir."

"In that you are mistaken. The young lady who braved the disapproval of the *ton* by quoting a scandalous poem—and providing the best entertainment I've had in years, I might add—*that* young lady is not so foolish as to believe that her actions are not a result of her own choices."

Meg crossed her arms in front of her. "If you will remember, I told you that same day that I do not have the luxury of choosing my situation."

"And excuse me if I disagree with you. I believe there is always a choice."

Meg did not respond. Her eyes burned, and she could not lift them to meet the colonel's gaze, which she was certain held disappointment. She certainly felt disappointment in herself.

"Miss, I'll admit I've grown fond of ya." When Colonel Stackhouse spoke, his voice had gentled, and the sound was so surprising that Meg looked up. "And I hate to see you lose your enthusiasm for everything important to you in order to be agreeable to particular gentlemen. I noticed you've put away your books, you've taken to acting subdued and compliant, even when the things others have said should be riling you up in outrage.

I believe I even heard you discussing the number of drawing rooms in Lord Featherstone's country home with apparent interest. Frankly, you've become quite dull."

Meg nodded, hating that his words were true.

"This is exactly what I am talking about," Colonel Stackhouse said. "You're not even chastising me for a direct offense."

"I am sorry, sir. I suppose—"

"You're wilting, Miss Meg," he said in a soft voice.

Meg's tears spilled over, and she swallowed hard.

"Oh, by all the saints. Must you start weeping?" He handed her a handkerchief. "I will take it as a sign that my words made an impact." He studied Meg for a moment as she wiped her eyes and tried to regain her composure.

"Miss, if I may ask, does this change in your demeanor have anything to do with the confidence you entrusted me with, in regards to a certain riding companion?"

She nodded, and the colonel leaned back in his seat, breathing in and out as he stretched his hands on the arms of the chair. "Very well, then I will amend the advice I gave to you." He leaned forward, waiting until Meg met his gaze before he spoke. "Do not let logic or duty override matters of the heart."

Meg must have looked flabbergasted because the colonel's expression transformed into a sheepish smile. "I maintain the importance of the correct associations, Miss Meg." He cleared his throat. "I have learned both of these lessons myself these past weeks."

Meg did not have an opportunity to respond since the colonel stood and gave a small bow. "And that calls to mind a promise I made to accompany a particular person on a carriage ride before supper." His face colored the slightest bit, and a hint of a smile turned his mouth. "If you will excuse me."

Meg returned his handkerchief, bewildered by the unexpected change in the colonel's mannerisms. She thought about his transformed conduct and softened appearance. Was he relaxing and enjoying relative safety away from the war? Did he appreciate his increase in society? Or was Colonel Jim Stackhouse in love? The idea made her smile. It seemed a logical explanation for his sentiments, but if such was the case, with whom?

She thought back on the advice he had given more than a week earlier. He was correct; she could have quoted him verbatim, having repeated the words so often in her mind. "The correct relationship will make a person bloom. He becomes more himself, his talents deepen, his personality grows, and he thrives. But the wrong relationship will produce the opposite. The things that were once so vital no longer matter. His talents disappear, his individuality fades, and he wilts."

Meg pulled her feet back up into her chair, hugging her knees. She had no doubt that Carlo brought out the best in her, and she hoped she did the same for him. Meg thought of the colonel's latest advice. "Do not let logic or duty override matters of the heart." It was beautiful and exactly what she hoped for, but the colonel was blind if he did not understand that a future for Meg and Carlo was impossible.

Chapter 17

Meg stood in front of the tall mirror in her bedchamber as the modiste adjusted her gown. While she did not care for the enormous ruffled collar or wrist cuffs, Meg was quite pleased with the rest of the costume. She wore a full corset beneath, and the modiste's assistants had spent a fair amount of time tightening and cinching her waist until she thought she would pass out from lack of air, but when they assisted her into the dress, she was amazed at the effect. The stuffed sleeves and gathered skirts accentuated the silhouette of a petite waist. Rows of pearl beading crisscrossed over the tight bodice. The tapestry fabric was heavy, but the dress was crafted in such a fashion that it did not weigh her down, and there was even a bit of a train that Meg considered particularly wonderful though thoroughly impractical.

Bessie had already styled her hair, pulling the curls back and loosely arranging them. A beaded crown was settled into her tresses, and Bessie adjusted it to allow soft waves to frame Meg's forehead.

Meg held the mask to her face, studying the effect in the mirror. She could not help the thrill that tingled through her at the sight. The mask was made of the same tapestry as her gown and shaped to fit over her eyes and nose. Pearl beads outlined the edges and the eye openings, and ribbons hung from the sides to secure it to her head while she danced. She looked decidedly mysterious.

Meg lowered the mask and studied her face. She attempted a smile, but it fell flat. The melancholy that she could not seem to be rid of still cast its shadow over her features She hoped her mask would conceal that shortcoming because try as she might, it was impossible to reclaim the joy that had once been such a part of her.

Meg pinched her cheeks. The ball was the first official event of her Season, and she was resolved to make it a success. In time, her heartache would lessen, she was certain of it. And once she was away from the castle and in London, it would be easier. But for now, she would take advantage of this fortunate opportunity and enjoy herself at the party.

She lifted her chin and straightened her shoulders, wishing she could completely dispel the gloom that seemed ever present when Carlo was not. Meg shook her head. She could not allow her mind to travel down that path again. Not if she had any intentions of a pleasant evening.

She met the other ladies in the conservatory. Lucinda looked beautiful and ethereal in her green wood nymph gown, with flowers and twigs artfully woven into her hair. When she saw Meg, her bright eyes narrowed, and Meg felt a small thrill of victory. Although she had suspected it at the time, Lucinda's expression confirmed that her suggestion for Meg's costume had not been offered out of kindness, and she was disappointed to see that Meg did not look as dowdy as she'd hoped.

Helen was an enchanting Cleopatra. Her white gown was cinched at the waist with a gold belt, and a crown in the shape of a cobra wrapped around her light brown hair. She held an equally spectacular golden mask in her hand. When she saw Meg, Helen hurried toward her and took her hand. "Meg, you look stunning," she said. "You will certainly attract many gentlemen admirers."

"As will you, Helen. I believe the station of Queen of the Nile suits you."

Helen smiled shyly.

The countesses entered the room in flowing robes of Greek goddesses, with laurel leaves in their hair. Both women looked beautiful, but Meg was amazed at Lady Featherstone's transformation. She practically glowed.

Meg was so taken aback by the countess's newfound radiance that she was startled when Helen spoke. "Meg, did you hear Lucinda's question?"

"No." Meg turned toward the elder Poulter sister. "I'm sorry, Lady Lucinda. I am apparently very distracted tonight. Would you mind repeating yourself?"

Lucinda's sharp face retained its pleasant expression, but her eyes squinted slightly in a look of irritation. "I asked if you had heard Mr. Newton declare that he would claim my hand for the first dance? He is partial to me, you know. But, I shall of course reserve a dance or two for the prince."

"How fortunate for both gentlemen," Meg said, determined not to allow Lucinda's words to bother her. The prince surely deserved to dance with Lucinda after the rude way he'd been avoiding them.

"And I do hope the two of you have your share of dances," Lucinda said to Meg and Helen, though her attention was on her own reflection as she turned to study her figure in the window behind them. "It would be a very hard thing for you to be overlooked."

Before Meg could think of a reply, Serena entered the room. She was breathtaking in her red and black ruffled dress with a veil of lace held in her hair by a red mantilla comb. She already wore her black mask, and the red ribbons that hung from it curled into her thick dark hair.

"Oh," she said, clapping her hands. "*Todos se ven perfecto!* You all look perfect!" She admired each lady in turn, complimenting their costumes and tying a dance card to their wrist.

When she turned to Meg, Serena reached for her arm. She tied the silken cord to attach the dance card and a small charcoal pencil to Meg's wrist—beneath the ruffled cuffs of Meg's costume.

Meg lifted her arm, admiring the booklet. An elegant eye mask was drawn on the cover beneath beautiful calligraphy wording.

Charles Benton Bramwell, Duke of Southampton, and
Princesa Serena Antoinetta Bramwell, Duchess of Southampton,
welcome you to the Masquerade Ball.
Thornshire Castle,
Monday, March 30, 1812.

Meg started to open the cover, getting only a glimpse inside before Serena took her hand and reclaimed her attention.

"Meg, you are so beautiful, but your smile, it is missing."

"I must be more nervous than I realized," Meg said and attempted to lift her lips into what she hoped resembled a cheerful expression. If only Serena's accent did not sound so much like Carlo's.

"I know you will have a special night," Serena said and kissed Meg's cheek.

She turned to the group. "But I must meet my husband and welcome our guests."

"And your brother?" Lucinda said. "The prince still plans to attend?"

"Yes, Rodrigo, he will attend tonight." She squeezed Meg's hand once again and departed, walking with her chin raised and back straight and leaving Meg in awe of Serena's beauty and grace. She was the perfect hostess.

Lady Featherstone and Lady Vernon helped the young ladies fasten their masks, and the group descended a back staircase to meet the gentlemen in the great hall. When they arrived, there was such a crowd of people, and all of them with their faces concealed, that Meg could not immediately locate Daniel.

Meg kept a hold of Helen's hand as they became separated from the rest of their group. Guests laughed and greeted each other, comparing costumes and expressing their excitement for the Season. Meg and Helen wove between people, emerging from the crowd and skirting around the edge of the entryway near the staircase. Meg stood on her toes and scanned the room, looking for her brother's red hair. She froze for a moment as a man turned toward her.

He was dressed completely in black, his face partly covered by a black mask. The way he stood—shoulders lowered, chin raised, and back straight—seemed familiar, and when their eyes met, he smiled. Carlo?

She shook her head, irritated that she'd even had the thought.

When Meg turned her eyes back, the man was lost in the crowd, and she reprimanded herself. Carlo was not here. She needed to stop pining away and imagining him in every gentleman she saw.

A moment later, Helen tugged on her hand and indicated that Lucinda, Lord Featherstone, and Daniel were approaching. Meg cringed as she remembered her last meeting with the earl.

Daniel smiled at Meg beneath his mask. "Good evening, Queen Bess." He wore a simple waistcoat and jacket in dark gray. Furry wolf ears extended from the top of his mask. He turned toward Helen. "And a lovely Egyptian ruler as well. I will need to watch my behavior tonight in the midst of so many monarchs."

Lord Featherstone took Meg's hand, and she reluctantly turned her attention to him, mustering a semblance of a smile, even though his touch made her scalp prickle. She was glad for the mask that hid her face.

The earl wore a doublet and hose; a large sword hung from his waist. The mask did not hide the startling blue of his eyes. "And you are . . . Romeo?" Meg ventured.

The earl made a "tut-tut" sound, shaking his head. "Miss Margaret. Tonight, I am not a lover but the brash fighter, Benvolio, set to duel with Tybalt."

Meg would have actually found herself surprised if the earl *hadn't* confused his Shakespeare. She pulled her hand away, closed her eyes, and did not even attempt to point out that Benvolio was a peacemaker while it was his cousin, Mercutio, who fought Tybalt. When she opened them, she met Daniel's gaze and saw from his obvious attempts to hide his smile by pressing his lips together that he had also noticed the earl's mistake.

Daniel winked before offering his arm to Meg and following Lord Featherstone and Helen up the grand staircase. Meg lifted the front of her heavy skirt to keep from tripping.

They waited in the hallway as each person was announced upon entering the ballroom. The earl and Helen stepped through the doorway, and the herald called their names: "Anthony Devon Poulter, Seventh Earl of Featherstone, and Lady Helen Poulter."

Daniel's mouth raised in a smile. "Are you ready, Meg?" he said. She actually thought a flicker of nervousness crossed over his expression.

Her own mouth had gone dry, and she held onto Daniel's arm tightly as they walked into the ballroom.

"Mr. Daniel Burton and Miss Margaret Burton of South Carolina, America."

Meg clamped her teeth tightly to keep her mouth from falling open as they walked into the ballroom. She had obviously been too involved with her self-pity to give much notice to the enormous amount of work that had gone into preparing for the ball.

Every surface glistened. Candlelight made the crystal in the chandeliers and sconces gleam, and it reflected from the mirrors. The gold-leaf of the wainscoting and the warm-hued wood floors made the room glow. Tables were arranged along the walls with long tablecloths and vases overflowing with flowers. The music that filled the air came from a small orchestra at one end of the room.

Meg could not take her eyes from the crush of people. The elegant gowns, hair pieces, sparkling jewelry, and embroidered waistcoats made the formal gatherings in Charleston seem more like barn raisings.

She still gazed, spellbound by the beauty of the decorations and the refined guests filling the ballroom, when Lord Featherstone stepped into her line of sight. He lifted the hand that was not on her brother's arm and opened Meg's dance card.

The earl's touch made Meg's muscles tense. She was glad her brother was next to her.

Lord Featherstone's gaze lifted to Meg's and then back to the booklet he held. "I see your waltz has already been claimed." He tugged on her arm as he moved the charcoal pencil to write on her dance card. "I shall have to content myself with the minuet. If we're lucky, we will find ourselves in the same group for the cotillion." He released the book but retained his hold on Meg's hand until she pulled it from his grasp.

Her waltz had been claimed? Surely there was a mistake.

Daniel excused himself and made his way toward a group that most likely contained the latest object of his affections.

Lucinda joined them, and Meg was relieved for an excuse to move away from Lord Featherstone. She turned toward the women and opened the booklet that hung from her wrist.

"Did you see the prince?" Lucinda asked. "He was here with the duchess. I am determined that he shall dance with me."

Meg scanned the page, her gaze moving down the list of dances. Lord Featherstone had signed his name, reserving the minuet, but as she continued down the page, she saw another line had been marked. The waltz was to take place directly after midnight, once the company removed their masks. Her waltz had indeed been reserved. She studied the signature, attempting to decipher the graceful script and wondering if perhaps Serena had given her the wrong dance card.

Lucinda gasped, and when Meg looked toward her, she saw that Lucinda's gaze was focused on the card in Meg's hand.

"Meg, why did you not say anything?" Lucinda raised her eyes, a glare marring her face.

Meg looked from Lucinda's scowl to Helen's wide eyes. "I don't know what you—"

"Why did you not tell us that you are to waltz with the prince?"

Chapter 18

Meg stared at the signature upon her dance card. It could not belong to Prince Rodrigo, since she had never been introduced to the man. Serena *must* have confused the dance cards.

Lucinda's glare was pure poison as she stared at Meg from beneath her mask.

"There must be a mistake." Meg turned her gaze instead to Helen. "I don't know how the prince's name came to be on my dance card."

Lucinda took her sister's hand and pulled on it. "Come, Helen. I should not like to waste my time with a concealing wench any longer." She practically dragged Helen away from Meg and toward where her mother stood talking to Colonel Stackhouse.

Meg did not allow Lucinda's words to bother her. She glanced back at the card. She would sort this out. She searched the room and finally found Serena standing arm and arm with the duke. They were speaking to a round, balding man. The man wore a fur-lined cape and a golden crown and even carried a scepter. Meg knew he must be Prince Rodrigo. Of course he would choose a costume that reminded everyone of his royal status. She decided that she would wait until Serena moved away from her brother before approaching her with the dilemma of the erroneous dance card.

Meg turned and nearly collided with a man dressed in black. "Pardon m—" she began, but she did not finish. Even behind a mask, his dark eyes made her heart skip a beat and her chest fill with fire.

"Carlo. What are you doing here?" she whispered.

A slow smile spread beneath his black mask, exposing the familiar dimple in his cheek. "I had hoped to dance with you." He lifted her hand just as the music changed, and then he led her toward the floor. "You look beautiful, Margarita," he muttered, just loud enough that only she could hear.

Meg's pulse sped up, and she worried Carlo would feel it in her hand. She allowed herself to let go of her fear for him and enjoy this moment. Her first dance at her first ball, and it was with the man of her dreams. Once they were in position, she glanced toward him. How had he done this? Did nobody notice him slip into the ballroom? She could well see how he would not be recognized. His jacket fit as smartly as any gentleman's in the room, stretching across his broad shoulders. He held himself with poise. Confidence seemed to flow from him. And with the mask to disguise his features, he surely had fooled anyone who might have wondered. Carlo looked every bit the aristocrat.

Carlo's gaze remained upon Meg's face, and she thought the night could not possibly become more enchanting. The music began. Carlo bowed then reached for her hand. They moved through the steps of the dance, and Meg felt as though she were in a dream. Carlo guided her through each turn elegantly. Whenever their hands met, Meg's heart raced, and when they separated, she could not wait until they touched again. How did a stable hand become such an accomplished dancer?

The dance ended much sooner than she would have liked, and Meg took Carlo's hand as he escorted her from the floor. The magic of the moment passed, and Meg began to worry. She looked around the room, finding the balding prince, and tugging on Carlo's hand to change their direction. If he were to be recognized, it would be a disaster.

"Thank you," she said when they reached the outer edge of the room. Her throat became tight when she realized that she would never have the chance to dance with Carlo again. She would leave for London in the morning.

When he released her hand, it felt cold.

A group of women stood nearby, and occasionally one of them would steal a glance at Carlo. Meg saw that Lucinda was among them, and their eyes met briefly. Lucinda's gaze moved to Carlo, and her eyes narrowed.

Meg turned and spoke softly, so as not to be overheard. "Carlo, you must leave. I fear the consequences to you are not worth the risk."

"I would chance any penalty to dance with you, Margarita."

Meg's heart fluttered at his words, but it just as quickly dropped. "I could not bear it if you were punished because of it."

"I will not be punished."

She shook her head. "You do not know that. The prince is here tonight. What if he discovers you?"

The edges of Carlo's mouth curled. "He will not."

She pursed her lips; the sorrow she'd felt was dispersing as Carlo apparently did not take her concerns seriously. She was becoming irritated at his overconfidence "You cannot be sure. At midnight everyone will remove their mask, and what happens then? You must be gone."

Beneath his mask, Carlo's expression altered, becoming serious. "I must speak with you before midnight."

"You are speaking with me now."

"Alone."

Meg shook her head. She could not ruin her reputation and that of the duke and Serena by taking the chance of being discovered alone with a man—and a man beneath her station at that. She could ruin everything if she took such an action. She would not. But she didn't get the chance to voice her argument before Carlo spoke.

"Please. I must."

She shook her head again but could feel her resolve wavering as his dark eyes held hers.

"Margarita, I am pleading with you. Meet me in the Oriental drawing room at quarter of twelve."

"You know very well I cannot do such a thing." Meg could not meet his gaze. She looked over Carlo's shoulder as Mr. Newton approached.

Carlo lifted her hand and bent over it. "Tomorrow you leave. I will not have another chance. Do me this one favor, Margarita." His voice was almost a whisper. Without a backward glance, he strode away.

Meg accepted Mr. Newton's invitation to dance. Forcing a smile, she attempted to carry on a conversation as her mind spun. Why would he want to speak with her alone? She could think of no reason except to bid her farewell, and the familiar aching of her heart returned in earnest.

She hardly realized the dance had ended and another had begun. Meg's mind continued to dwell on the inevitable parting as her feet luckily remembered the training the dance master had given. Carlo likely wanted to give her a keepsake, a memento to remember their time together. Perhaps he would ask for a lock of her hair to wear next to his heart as he lived a life devoid of joy because she was not in it. Maybe she would even allow him to steal a kiss. The possibility ignited a warmth in her chest.

The hours passed quickly, Meg moved from partner to partner, hardly remembering one from another and comparing each to Carlo. Although she would have loved to be swept away into a sea of bliss with each dance, it was not the case. Only one man had the ability to heat her skin with every touch.

She smiled and thanked the gentleman who escorted her from the floor, and the music changed again. Meg lungs contracted when she heard the orchestra start the minuet.

Lord Featherstone approached, reaching a hand toward her.

Meg could not even manage to summon a pleasant expression to her face as she accompanied him to the dance floor. Every time the earl clasped her hand or moved past her, Meg's muscles clenched on their own volition. She kept her eyes firmly on his doublet, never allowing them to rise to his gaze. She answered his questions pleasantly enough, amazed that he had the audacity to speak so agreeably to her after their encounter in the woods. The man owed her an apology.

When the dance finished, Meg took his hand to leave the dance floor.

The earl walked slowly, moving his thumb over the back of Meg's hand in a caress that made her skin crawl. As they passed the duke's golden grandfather clock, she realized that if she planned to meet Carlo, she would have to hurry. She pulled her hand from the earl's and bobbing in a quick curtsey, excused herself.

Meg walked in the direction of the ladies' withdrawing room, certain that Lord Featherstone would not follow her there. She slipped through the crowd as well as she could in her oversized skirts and descended the grand staircase into the entry hall. She tried to look as if she were not heading to a clandestine rendezvous with a forbidden lover, but how could one hide such a thing? The thought of Carlo sweeping her into his arms made her stomach roll in anticipation. One night. One kiss, and then she would leave him forever.

She hurried through the corridor and into the room, but Carlo was not there. Meg untied her mask. She removed the starched collar from around her neck and the cuffs from her sleeves, rubbing her skin where the stiff fabric had chaffed.

She walked around the room, studying the Chinese tapestries and carved furniture by candlelight. She would miss Thornshire and all the memories associated with it. She looked toward the couch where Carlo had hidden her cloak the night of the tower picnic, and her eyes stung. That was the night everything had changed. The night she realized she had lost her heart to Carlo and, after his kiss, known it would ruin them both if she did not stay away.

Meg turned when she heard footsteps, her heart racing. But it was not Carlo who entered the room. Her chest felt hollow. "Lord Featherstone, what are you doing here?"

The earl held his mask in his hand. "Miss Margaret, come now. There is no need to pretend. Your face was flushed, and you could not look me in the eye. Then you rushed off to a private room, very obviously expecting me to follow. How could I not?"

Meg stared at the earl. "My lord, I assure you; I had no intention of leading you here. I simply wanted a moment to rest alone."

The earl tipped his head to the side and shook it back and forth. "Margaret, we both know that is not the truth. But if it makes you feel more comfortable, I will play along with your charade of innocence."

Meg looked toward the doorway. Where was Carlo?

"My dear." Lord Featherstone continued to walk toward her. "I have wanted to find you alone for some time. There is something I should like to ask you, and it is a matter best discussed privately."

Meg backed away until the wall prevented her from going farther. Her muscles tensed, and she looked toward the door again. What would Lord Featherstone do to Carlo if he should interrupt? What would the earl do to her if Carlo did not?

The earl was near enough that she had to raise her chin to keep eye contact. "My lord, I must insist you step back."

"Margaret, your beauty has drawn me to you since the moment we met. Your passion at the Harrisons' musicale—I have not been able to dismiss it from my mind." He let out a sigh. "Though you are not accomplished as I would like and you are often outspoken, I am determined that I shall have you for my own."

Meg put her hands behind her back so the earl wouldn't see them shaking. She attempted to keep her voice calm. "Sir, how dare you insult me in such an atrocious manner and think it an acceptable proposal of marriage?"

Lord Featherstone raised a brow. "I did not intend you to understand that my offer included marriage."

A hot stone landed in the pit of Meg's stomach. Her lungs were tight when she tried to draw a breath. "My lord, when have I ever led you to believe I would consider such an appalling arrangement?"

"My dearest, I heard what you did *not* say." His gaze lowered to her lips and downward to her throat. "I have spoken with Daniel, and I understand your family's financial situation. I can be very generous." He brushed his finger over her collarbone.

She felt the blood drain from her face and leaned back against the wall for support, hunching her shoulders. "My brother would never agree to such a thing."

Lord Featherstone pressed his hand against the wall next to her head. His body trapped her in place. "It's true that we didn't discuss the particulars, but you must know, Margaret, this is likely the best offer you can hope to receive. You have no title, no money, your manners are not refined, your speech is . . . well, American. Aside from your beauty and passion, you have nothing to recommend you."

Meg clamped her hand over her mouth. She was certain her stomach would heave. She pushed at the earl and struggled against him.

The padded front of the earl's doublet brushed against the pearl beads on her bodice. He slid a hand around the back of her neck. "You should be grateful that I am able to overlook your obvious—"

He did not finish his sentence. His eyes bulged, and he flew backward with a yelp and the sound of tearing fabric.

Carlo held the earl's torn collar. His face was red with fury. He yelled at the man in a battering of Spanish words that had Lord Featherstone cowering next to the duke's Chinese tea table.

Meg thought her legs would give way. Tears rushed to her eyes. "You must not strike him, Carlo." She did not intend for her voice to tremble.

"Carlo?" Lord Featherstone said, looking back at the man towering over him.

Carlo ignored the earl. He took her arm and led her to the couch. "Did he hurt you, Margarita?"

"Margarita?" Lord Featherstone said.

Meg could not bring herself to look at Carlo. Just the thought of the earl's words squeezed her ribs and burned her skin. And Carlo had heard everything. Her humiliation at Lord Featherstone's offensive proposal turned sour in her stomach.

They were ruined. Lord Featherstone knew Meg and Carlo had a relationship. Carlo had attacked him and would undoubtedly be punished for it.

It was suddenly too much for Meg. She pulled away and ran to the French doors, flinging them open then dashing across the balcony and down the stairs into the duke's gardens.

She didn't have a purpose in mind other than getting as far away from Thornshire Castle, Lord Featherstone, and Carlo as she could. Her dress was heavy, and she tripped over the skirts, but she managed to catch herself and continue. The greenhouse seemed a good destination, since the castle was filled with people and she didn't know how much farther she would be able to run in her dancing slippers and burdensome gown.

She followed the path through the garden, nearing the edge of the woods behind the greenhouse. Moonlight shone strangely through the trees, casting dark shadows in the night. The sounds of laughter and men's voices floated toward her from the main road, which was filled with carriages and footmen tending to horses as they awaited the end of the ball.

Crunching footsteps sounded on the gravel path behind her, and Carlo called to her. She stumbled again, and he caught her arm. He pulled her toward him.

Meg's eyes ran with tears. Although she wanted nothing more than to sink into Carlo's arms, she did not allow it. She shoved against his chest, shaking her head, since her ability to speak could not be depended on. Carlo must not be found with her. She tried to yank her arm from his grasp.

In spite of Meg's struggles, Carlo pulled her against his chest, wrapping his arms around her and cradling her head. "There is no need to run, Margarita," he said in a low voice. "Everything is all right now."

Meg continued to pull away, but Carlo's embrace was warm and strong, and she didn't have the energy to resist any longer. Her muscles relaxed, and she melted against him, allowing him to hold her while she wept. Meg buried her face into his chest, and her tears soaked into his waistcoat until it was cold against her cheeks.

"I should have never come to England," she whispered.

"If you had not, I would be lonely and miserable on this foggy island." He continued to rub his hand softly over her back.

"No, you would be happily caring for Patito and not putting yourself at risk stealing into balls and assaulting noblemen."

"It was worth the risk, as I told you before. And I assure you I was not happy. Not until my *compañera de aventura* arrived."

Meg's tears flowed again in earnest. "I should not have encouraged . . ." She choked on a sob.

Carlo lifted her face, leaning back so that she could see his eyes clearly. He cupped her chin and brushed her tears with his fingers. "Margarita, I have something to tell you, and though I have practiced countless times, I still do not know how to say it."

Meg steeled herself for the words she wanted and feared. She knew the sound of Carlo pledging his love to her before they bid a tragic farewell would remain in her mind until her dying day.

His gaze was intense as he held hers. "Margarita, I am Prince Rodrigo."

Meg blinked and then squeezed her eyes shut, allowing her face to relax before she opened them. "Carlo, stop. I don't want to pretend anymore."

He raised his brows. "It is not pretend. And I am not Carlo. I am *Principe Rodrigo de Talavera*." He gave a slight bow. "When we first met, I did not tell you the truth because you assumed otherwise, and once you became friends with Carlo, I did not want to—"

"Enough!" Meg pushed him away. "This is not a game." She clenched her hands so tightly that her fingernails pressed into her palms. "We must stop this foolishness and face reality. I have seen the prince tonight, and you are not him. You care for Patito and work in the stables. And I am simply Meg, the American with nothing to recommend me to gentlemen of the *ton*." Meg lowered her eyes. "That is the truth, and an imaginary scenario will not solve it."

"I still intend to call that man out for his indecent proposition."

"This is what I am talking about. Carlo, you cannot call him out. He is a nobleman, and you—"

Carlo covered Meg's mouth with his hand. His eyes darted toward the tree line. "I heard something," he whispered in her ear.

Meg listened for a moment and then pushed Carlo's hand away. "Stop. I don't want to play anymore." This was becoming ridiculous.

Carlo reached for her, his finger over his lips, but she moved away.

"We must end this nonsense—" Meg heard a rustle and turned to see men stepping from the forest. They appeared to be footmen, although each carried a weapon—as was to be expected from another of Carlo's games. The steel of their swords shone in the moonlight. One man lowered a musket, aiming it directly at them.

"Margarita," Carlo said in a low voice. "Do not move."

Meg shook her head. Carlo needed to realize that another adventure was not going to resolve things. She was still leaving for London in the morning, and they would never meet again. A band of thieves accosting them in the woods would have been a welcome diversion a week earlier, but Meg needed to put a stop to this, for both their sakes.

She stepped toward the man with the musket. "I am sorry you went to such trouble, sir, but I need to return to the castle."

"Margarita," Carlo hissed.

"I do appreciate the gesture, but the timing is all wrong, and I'm simply not in the mood for this."

The soldier spoke to his companions, and it took a moment for Meg to realize he was speaking French. Were these men French? She could not imagine that Carlo would devise an escapade with a group of Frenchmen. The hair on the back of her neck stood up, and she took a step closer to Carlo.

The man with the musket was apparently the leader. At his signal, the four men surrounded them. He faced Carlo. "How fortunate that we should find you here, Your Highness." The man's words were sarcastic, yet he still inclined his head respectfully. "We'd planned a much more elaborate scheme to apprehend you and your sister, but just as we were secreting ourselves in the woods to wait for the guests to leave, what should we overhear but the very man we'd come to find declaring his name aloud?" The Frenchman shrugged his shoulders. "It was as if you were asking to be captured."

"But he's not really the prince. Tell them, Carlo," Meg said.

Carlo took Meg's hand and pulled her closer and slightly behind him. "You must know, *monsieur*, that the estate is surrounded by Spanish and English soldiers. You and your small group do not stand a chance."

The man lifted the end of his musket into the air and set the weapon to rest on the ground, appearing quite unaffected by Carlo's words. "With a hundred carriages coming and going tonight, I am afraid I disagree with you, Your Highness. We were not searched as we entered, and I am confident it will be just as easy to depart." He swept his hand in front of him. "If you would be so kind as to accompany us."

Carlo tensed.

"Ah," the Frenchman said, raising his brows. "I had not considered that you might resist. In this, you are very unlike the rest of your family." He motioned to one of the men, who seized Carlo's arm.

Carlo pushed the man away, swinging his fist into his jaw, and managed to shove another to the ground before the third man clubbed Carlo over the head. He wobbled, and the three managed to restrain him with rope.

Meg stood frozen to the spot. Should she attempt to help Carlo? What could she possibly do against four armed men? She turned, intending to run for help, when one of the men grabbed her around the waist, lifting her off the ground.

Meg screamed and kicked and scratched at the man, but it did no good. He clamped a hand over her mouth and held her tightly, even as she squirmed in his grasp.

Meg's heart pounded painfully in her chest. Her eyes darted around and finally found Carlo's. He glared at the man who held her and then turned his gaze to hers. His expression softened, and he shook his head slightly. Meg stopped struggling, although she could not force her muscles to relax.

The men spoke with their leader for a moment, and Meg concentrated on their words. It seemed that the men were attempting to decide if she was Princess Serena. The leader was not sure if Serena had red hair, but the man who held her argued that she wore a crown, so she must be.

The leader stepped closer to Meg, studying her face. His gaze moved to the costume crown in her hair.

"Monsieur." Even though he sat, bound upon the forest floor, Carlo's gaze held the Frenchman's, and his voice still managed to command. "Do not hurt my sister. We will accompany you peacefully."

The man nodded, and Carlo's legs were untied. They were led through the woods to a waiting carriage. Carlo was pushed roughly inside.

Meg tried to be brave, but she pulled away as the man dragged her toward the dark coach door. Her eyes darted toward the castle. The music of the ball still drifted toward her. The ball seemed ages ago, yet it was still taking place. Their disappearance would not be discovered for hours—possibly not until the next day.

Her breath came in gasps, and she heard herself whimper as the man lifted her into the carriage. The last thing she saw before the door was shut was a pearl bead upon the ground, glowing in the moonlight.

Chapter 19

RODRIGO'S EYES ADJUSTED TO THE dim interior of the carriage. He steadied his breath as he attempted to think calmly. Meg sat in the corner of the seat across from him, her shoulders hunched and arms crossed. Her eyes were wide with fear.

"Margarita?" He began to reach toward her but realized his hands were still bound, and instead he lowered them between his knees.

"Your head." Her gaze moved to where the soldier had struck him.

"It is fine." He attempted what he hoped was a reassuring smile, even though his head pounded.

"Where are they taking us?" she whispered.

"France, I imagine."

Meg's eyes widened. "We cannot go to France. What happens when they discover that we are not who we claim to be?

That precise thought was forefront in Rodrigo's mind. They had been fortunate indeed that the leader of the French soldiers had not known English well enough to recognize that Meg did not speak with a Spanish accent. They would have certainly killed her if they had known she was not Serena. That ostentatious costume crown had very likely saved Meg's life—for now.

The Frenchmen had made it clear that they had no intention of harming a member of the royal family. Rodrigo and Serena were only of value if they were kept alive, which would work to Rodrigo's advantage. His main objective would be to help Meg escape before it was discovered that she was not the princesa.

But first, the other matter still needed to be resolved.

"Margarita, you would indeed be in danger if it's discovered that you are not Serena. I on the other hand . . . I am safe for now."

Meg opened her mouth and leaned forward as if she would argue but then closed it again. She lowered her head. "It is true then. You are the prince."

"Yes." Why did he feel the need to apologize for it?

"You signed my dance card." She darted a look at him and then dropped her gaze again, to where the booklet had hung at her wrist. She must have lost it when the soldiers seized her.

"I didn't want anyone else to claim your waltz. I'm afraid the idea made me quite jealous. Although, after watching the stiff way British men dance, my worry lessened considerably. If there had been a Spaniard threatening to waltz with you . . ." Rodrigo offered a small smile, attempting to lighten the mood. He did not even want to picture Meg dancing in the more sensuous style favored by the Spanish. Unless it was with him, of course.

"Serena knew?"

"Yes."

"Who else?" Meg said in a small voice.

"Only the duke and my sister. They honored my wishes and did not reveal it to you."

Meg's voice held no inflection. "And that is why you wished to speak to me before midnight? Before the company removed their masks."

Rodrigo wished he knew how to read her reaction. "I wanted to tell you privately."

Meg simply nodded but did not lift her gaze. After a moment she spoke again. "Do you think Daniel and Colonel Stackhouse will discover we are missing?"

The abrupt change of subject told him that she was not unhurt by his deception, but he did not wish to cause her any more embarrassment. They could revisit the topic when it wasn't so fresh.

"I do not think it will be realized for hours. Unless Lord Featherstone chooses to tell that we did not return after you left the drawing room, and I cannot imagine he would mention it."

Meg flinched when the earl's name was mentioned, and Rodrigo wished it had been Lord Featherstone's smug face on the receiving end of the very satisfying blow he had given the French soldier.

"They will not know in which direction to follow us," Meg said.

"I fear that is the truth."

Meg looked around the carriage as if searching for something. She still did not meet Rodrigo's gaze. Her gaze lit upon the window next to her, and she sat up on the bench, moving the heavy curtains the smallest bit to peek out. She turned her head from side to side in order to get a view from different angles without disturbing the curtain, and then she reached beneath it. Rodrigo heard the click of the latch being opened and a rush of cool air blew into the carriage. The sound of the French soldier's voices drifted on the wind.

Rodrigo listened for a moment, but the creaking of the carriage made it impossible to hear what the men were saying.

Meg removed her gloves and set them aside, then she twisted and pulled on the large, knuckle-sized pearl beads that covered her bodice. When she had torn off a handful, Meg reached slowly beneath the curtain and dropped the beads one by one through the window. She waited, most likely to see if there was any reaction from the soldiers outside the carriage, but there was none. The voices continued uninterrupted, and Meg turned back to the row of beads, tearing the thread and working them loose.

Rodrigo watched her, amazed by her creativity, not wanting to tell her that it would most likely do no good. They would be on a boat, sailing across the channel long before anyone happened upon the beads. But if it comforted her or distracted her mind from their situation, he would not discourage it.

Meg filled up each of her gloves, occasionally pouring a collection of beads through the window. Rodrigo thought he would never tire of watching her. Her expression was determined and her eyes intent. The crease he loved sat in its place above her nose. Small streaks of moonlight darted over her as the curtains moved. The silvery bands played over her curls and highlighted the soft skin of her cheeks.

"I know why you did it." Meg's voice startled him from his contemplations.

"You do?"

"Yes." She still did not look at him. "It must become tiring to be a prince and feel as though you were always just known for your title and not as the man behind it. I suspect it's rather lonely." Meg's gaze rested on him for a moment, and then she turned back to ridding her gown of its embellishments. "I am guilty of the same—I judged you without knowing you."

Rodrigo's throat was tight. He should have never wondered if Meg would understand. She described his feelings exactly. Before he could reply, Meg continued.

"I've not been entirely honest either." Her voice was quiet.

Rodrigo leaned forward to hear over the noise of the carriage, the voices outside, and the wind blowing through the crack in the window.

"I did not tell Carlo that I was sent to England to find a wealthy husband. I find the entire situation disgusting, so I did not want Carlo to know. I could not bear it if he were disappointed in me." Meg's voice was nearly a whisper. "Ladies are expected to act a particular way around a gentleman they wish to impress. When I was with Carlo, I did not have to worry about remembering all of those things. He liked that I was different. Even if it meant listening to poetry and acting out adventures. With Carlo, I didn't have to pretend to be any other than Meg."

Meg glanced at Rodrigo and then lowered her eyes again. "I imagine it was rather the same for the prince."

"You have described it exactly, Margarita," Rodrigo said. He moved to sit next to her on the bench. "Without a title, Carlo was free to just . . . be." He studied her, willing her to raise her eyes, but she continued to work at a piece of thread, loosening the bead it held.

"I shall miss Carlo," Meg finally said. "I do not think I could act the same with the prince."

Rodrigo touched a finger to her chin, lifting her gaze to meet his. "I think you could. In fact, I know it to be true."

She shook her head. "With the prince, I would be Margaret. Not Meg and never Margarita. I would need to be a proper young lady."

"Perhaps you should give the prince a chance," Rodrigo said. "He might surprise you, and I have heard he can be quite charming."

"How could he ever trust me when he knows the truth of my situation?" Meg turned and dropped more beads through the window. "Besides, the prince and I have not even been properly introduced. There is no way to form an acquaintance." The corner of her lips twitched the slightest bit.

"Yes, I fear that is an obstacle. But I believe there is an exception to that particular rule of etiquette. You can find the entire rule listed under *formalities to be observed by political prisoners*. If two strangers happen to be bound for an undisclosed location and there is no one available to perform the appropriate introduction, it is entirely proper to introduce oneself."

Rodrigo shifted in the seat to face her and bowed, as well as he could in the cramped quarters with his hands bound. "I am Principe Rodrigo de Talavera of the Two Siciles, native to Madrid, and lately resident of the dower house at Thornshire Castle. Pleased to make your acquaintance, miss."

"Margaret Burton of Charleston." Meg offered her hand, and Rodrigo inclined his head and kissed the air above her fingers.

"And now, Miss Margaret Burton of Charleston, since neither of us has previous experience with this type of situation, I think we should depend upon our mutual friend, Carlo, to indicate how we proceed. What would you tell him right now?"

"I would tell him I am afraid." Meg looked up at him with moist eyes. "I don't want to go to France and be a prisoner and . . . the guillotine." Her face paled as she said the word sotto voce.

Rodrigo's heart suddenly weighed a hundred pounds. He kept his voice calm, and he hoped soothing. "And what would Carlo do?"

Meg looked at him through her lashes. "He would hold my hand," she whispered.

Rodrigo found her trembling hand, holding it awkwardly as his own hands were bound.

Meg slid toward him, sitting on the seat next to him and leaning her head on his shoulder. She rubbed her other hand gently over the ropes connecting his wrists. "Does it hurt? I can untie the knots."

"I do not want to anger them by removing the bindings." Rodrigo would not give the soldiers any reason to be displeased. Not when Meg's life hung in the balance.

Meg sat up and dropped more beads through the window before nestling back against him and slipping her hand between his.

Rodrigo was amazed how much such a simple action could soothe him. He pressed her hand between his palms. "Margarita, I have not formally apologized for my actions."

She shook her head against his shoulder. "It is not necessary. I know you are sorry."

"It *is* necessary. I owe you the deepest apology for deceiving you as I did. I truly did not intend for our relationship to develop into something so . . ."

Meg shifted next to him.

"I admit, if I had to do it again, I likely would not change a thing. Except your tears. Such a thing is inexcusable. I regret more than anything causing you to weep."

Rodrigo pressed a kiss to her head, avoiding the spikes of the crown and wishing that his arms were not bound and he could wrap Meg in them.

"Thank you."

"And now what would Carlo do?" Rodrigo asked softly, rubbing his thumb over Meg's knuckles.

Meg was quiet for a moment. "He would tell me a clever story, or I wonder if he might . . . quote some poetry? I think he said once that he knows Quintana." Meg sat up, her mouth forming a small 'o' which Rodrigo found completely adorable. "You don't only know his poetry, you know Manuel José Quintana."

Rodrigo smiled. "That is correct. In that, I have a point ahead of Carlo. He doesn't know any famous poets." He laughed inside at the idea of having to compete with the other version of himself, wondering when his world had stopped making sense.

Meg raised her eyebrows. "And do you know any of Quintana's poetry, Your Highness?"

"Of course. I would wager that every Spaniard does." He tipped his head. "But I only allow my soul to speak to another if she sits a bit closer. For some reason, I find it sparks my memory."

He had the satisfaction of seeing Meg's cheeks turn pink. She dropped some pearls through the window and moved next to him, leaning against him and returning her hand to his.

"And Margarita, you must call me Rodrigo."

"It feels strange."

"I am sorry."

"I know."

Rodrigo took a breath and began:

"*¿Que era, decidme, la nacion que un dia*
Reina del mundo proclamo el destino,
La que a todas las zonas extendia
Su cetro de oro y su blason divino?"

As he spoke Meg relaxed against him, and her hand softened, melting in his grasp. Though he spoke of war and of unrest in Spain, his voice was soft and the cadence soothing to both of them. He looked down at the head of curls that leaned against his shoulder and the ridiculous crown perched among them. He inhaled the warm scent that he had come to associate with Meg, and his heart skipped.

Though he had given her every reason not to, this woman trusted him, and he wanted to be worthy of such a gift. He did not know how they would escape from the French soldiers, but the burden of Meg's safety weighed heavily on him.

Meg stirred, leaning away to pour more beads through the gap in the window. "It is beautiful. I wish I understood the words."

"Yes, there is no mention of ducklings in 'Oda a España.' I shall speak to Quintana about his oversight when next we meet."

Meg smiled. "He could compose a very moving verse about a brave but gentle horse." She glanced up at him. "But I am afraid I have made you sorrowful, Car—Rodrigo. You miss Patito." Meg laid her hand upon his cheek.

He closed his eyes, enjoying the softness of her touch.

"Rodrigo?"

He heard worry in her voice, but at the same time, it was heaven to hear her say his name. "Sí?"

"How will we escape?"

The weight grew heavier as he studied her face. He lifted his bound hands and awkwardly ran his thumb over her brow, wishing he could just as easily smooth away her fears.

"I do not know. We will need a plan. And I will need a sword."

Meg's eyebrows drew back together, and he smoothed them again. "Margarita, you are very fortunate that we were apprehended together. Your old friend Carlo did not study under the greatest swordsman in Spain. But it just happens that I did."

Chapter 20

Meg dropped the last of her pearl beads out of the window and sighed as she re-latched it to keep out the cold air. The beads were most likely a pointless endeavor, but she felt as if she had to do something besides sit helplessly in this carriage.

She turned her attention to Car—Rodrigo. *Prince* Rodrigo. How had she possibly been so foolish not to realize who he was? As she thought back through the weeks of their acquaintance, there were numerous evidences that her friend was not who he claimed to be. Why had she not seen them? Perhaps she hadn't wanted to.

She squirmed uncomfortably inside as she thought about her treatment of Carlo—at least initially. She had believed his station to be below her own. Had she treated him as such? Had she been guilty of the very thing she had come to abhor about the British aristocracy?

Once Meg had realized the depth of her feelings for Carlo, she had been saddened to realize that as a poor servant, he would not be a suitable match. The wretched feeling of knowing now that *she* was the one unsuitable was infinitely more painful. Perhaps Rodrigo did not feel the same for her after all. Why would he when he knew she was no more than an American merchant's daughter who needed a rich husband? Her stomach felt heavy. Spanish men were known for their flirtatious ways. Had it all been an act? Or a game?

Meg was jarred from her thoughts when the carriage came to a halt. Rodrigo moved to the seat across from her. Was he just attempting to seem more 'brotherly' when the French soldiers opened the door? Or was there some truth to her worries about his true feelings for her?

The leader of the Frenchmen assisted her from the carriage, and Meg looked around. They had arrived at a cottage. Though it was dark, with only the moonlight and soldiers' lanterns to clarify the scene, she could smell the sea and hear the whisper of waves crashing into the shore. The nets hanging near the door led Meg to presume that the cottage belonged to a fisherman. She estimated they had traveled for nearly two hours, which was plenty of time to reach the coast.

Rodrigo stepped from the carriage and stood behind her. Even though Meg couldn't see him, his strong presence reassured her, and she squared her shoulders.

The men led them into the quaint house. Directly inside the front door was an entryway with a small parlor off to one side and a kitchen and eating area to the other. They followed the soldiers straight ahead to a narrow hallway with only two doors. A soldier opened one door and indicated for them to enter. By lantern light, Meg saw the tidy room contained only a straw-mattress bed and a chest.

Meg wondered what had happened to the occupants of the house. It didn't look as though it had been deserted. Simple curtains hung in the windows, and linens were upon the bed. Had the French soldiers imprisoned the fisherman? Killed him? Did he have a family? Her contemplations brought back the fears she had felt earlier. They were in serious danger, and Meg didn't think her legs would support her.

Rodrigo caught her just as she started to sway and led her to sit upon the bed.

Meg heard the soldier speaking in French to Rodrigo, but she felt so overwhelmed that she didn't put forth the necessary energy to concentrate with her limited understanding of the language. Her head felt as if it were stuffed with cotton.

The soldier set the lantern on the floor. He closed the door, and a key turned in the lock.

Rodrigo knelt in front of her, moving his bound hands to her cheeks, turning her gaze to meet his. "Are you all right?"

Meg tried to nod. But she felt the blood draining from her face, and Rodrigo pushed her gently back onto the pillows.

"You need to rest."

"We need to escape." She tried to speak without slurring.

"We can spare a moment." Rodrigo brushed the curls from her forehead, which she could tell felt clammy. "When did you last eat?"

"This morning," Meg said. "But I was so nervous about the ball that I only ate a bit of toast." She didn't dare to mention that the tight corset likely played a part in her light-headedness.

"And you have been awake all night."

"Rodrigo, I think I'm cured of adventures," Meg said.

"Surely not. We are just beginning." He smiled, attempting to cheer her.

With an enormous effort, Meg pushed her arms down against the mattress and sat up, blinking as her head swam, but she did not lie back down. Her stomach felt sick, and her head ached. "I had imagined it to be much more romantic to swoon," she said.

"Next time, with a bit of warning, I will catch you in my arms and spirit you away on my stallion."

Meg appreciated his efforts to take her mind from their situation, and his words caused her cheeks to heat. "Not if your arms are bound." She attempted to speak calmly as if his words had not nearly caused her to swoon again. "Come, I will see if I can untie the ropes."

He sat next to her on the bed, the straw mattress creaking noisily, and Meg worked at the knots, finally managing to loosen the ropes enough to unwind them from Rodrigo's arms.

Rodrigo rubbed his wrists as he moved to the window, pushing aside the curtains and looking out. He tightened his lips, and Meg supposed he did not like what he saw.

She stood and joined him. In the silvery moonlight, she saw that the cottage was perched upon a high cliff. The side of the house was nearly to the edge with just a small lip between the wall and a steep drop.

Rodrigo tried the window, but it did not open. Even if it had, they could both see that this route would offer no escape. He moved to the door, trying to turn the knob, and then kneeling to peer through the keyhole.

Rodrigo stood and paced, his eyes squinting in concentration. He stopped and looked at Meg. He turned to the wooden chest and, after digging around for a moment, took out some clothing that he handed to her. "It appears that the owner of this house is larger than you, but I fear that gown will make stealth an impossibility."

Meg held up the trousers and shirt, glancing around the room. The chamber was too small for privacy.

Rodrigo cleared his throat. "I will turn around while you dress. Do you need any . . . assistance?" he indicated the back of her gown.

Meg shook her head. Her face burned. The gown was difficult to unfasten, but she didn't dare to ask Rodrigo to help. As she contorted her body and attempted to liberate herself from her costume, she stole glances at Rodrigo. True to his word, he remained facing the wall.

She was sweating by the time she finished wrestling her way out of the gown and layers of petticoats. Meg finally took a deep breath, enjoying the sensation of expanding her lungs as she loosened the corset ties, removed the contraption, and tossed it onto the pile of discarded garments.

The fisherman's clothing *was* quite large. Meg rolled up the cuffs of the trousers, mortified at how silly they looked with her dancing slippers peeking out beneath them. The shirt hung to her knees, but she gathered it and tucked it down inside the pants.

"I am dressed," she said, holding the waistband of the trousers to keep them from falling off, knowing she looked utterly ridiculous.

Rodrigo picked up the rope that had bound his hands and reached his arms around her, pulling her toward him as he knotted it around her waist. He left trails of heat behind where his hands brushed against her torso, and Meg could not meet his eyes as he performed such an intimate action.

He stepped back and looked her over, nodding as the corners of his mouth turned downward, and his eyes sparkled with mischief. "If I had known how your figure would appear in men's clothing, I'd have recommended it from the beginning."

Meg was secretly pleased, but how could he possibly think she looked anything but absurd? She acted shocked at his presumptuous manners. "Rodrigo is a bit of a scoundrel, Your Highness. I wonder how Carlo would react to such brazen sentiments."

"Carlo would agree with me completely." Rodrigo winked and turned his gaze to the pile of clothing on the floor. "Margarita, I think I have a plan." When he looked at her, all humor was gone from his expression. "But it will require risk on both our parts. I do not know how long we have, and it is of the utmost importance to me for you to escape."

"For both of us to escape," she corrected.

"You are in the greatest danger, so we will worry about your safety first."

"Rodrigo, I—"

"You must trust me. Can you do that?"

"Of course I trust you, but I'll not leave this place without you."

"These soldiers, they will not harm me. I am more valuable to them alive. But if—when we should arrive in France and it is discovered that you are not Serena . . ." He rested a hand on her shoulder and then moved it up to the side of her neck, his thumb stroking her throat. "Margarita, I do not know if I could protect you, and I must know you are safe."

Meg nodded, although she did not agree. She would not leave Rodrigo with these French soldiers while she fled to safety. But she would not argue. They did not know how much time they had. "Tell me the plan."

"First we need the key." Rodrigo picked up Meg's heavy gown and pushed the train beneath the door. He looked around the room, and finally his gaze landed on Meg's crown. "May I?" he asked as he pulled it from her hair.

Meg nodded, more interested in what Rodrigo was doing than in keeping her costume tiara.

"I will replace it," Rodrigo said. His mouth curled in a half smile as he focused his attention on the crown, bending one end of the low quality metal into a tube. He pushed the tube into the keyhole, twisting it around until they heard the thunk of the key hitting the fabric on the floor in the hallway. He pulled the gown's train back into the room with the key on top.

Rodrigo handed the key to Meg and set about gathering the garments she had discarded. Meg blushed as he lifted her petticoats and corset, but he did not give them more than a hasty glance as he bundled them with the gown and arranged them beneath the bedding. If one did not look too closely, it appeared as if two people were sleeping beneath the linens.

"Who would have thought my talent for sneaking away from my governess would end up being of such value?" He placed his finger over his lips and turned the knob, opening the door slowly.

They peeked into the hall, and then Rodrigo leaned through the doorway.

Meg gripped his arm, ready to pull him back inside at the first sound of danger. Her heart pounded.

After a moment, Rodrigo doused the lantern and took the key from Meg. He held onto her hand, and they crept into the hallway, locking the door behind them. Rodrigo opened the other door and pulled Meg inside. He hurried across the small bedchamber and attempted to open the window, but like the other, it did not open.

"We shall have to escape through the kitchen," he said.

"The soldiers will see us." Even in a whisper, Meg could hear her voice rise in panic.

"These soldiers are not well trained. I think they will not be overly watchful, but we will still need to be as silent as possible."

He took Meg's hand again and listened at the door for a moment before he opened it and started through. But he stopped suddenly and pulled Meg back into the room, closing the door behind them. Rodrigo placed his hands on her arms. "Margarita, listen to me, if we are seen, you must run. I will occupy the soldiers as long as I can, but promise me you will run as fast as you are able. I will be right behind you. Follow the road, find a town, and send word to the duke. You must not stop. Do you understand?"

Meg nodded. Her stomach was heavy, and she could not stop shaking. She would agree with him, though she had no intention of leaving him.

Rodrigo brushed a kiss over Meg's lips, and her already pounding heart accelerated. What did he mean by it?

He stopped, tipping his head to the side, and moved his hand to her face. "According to your expression, there is some question as to my intentions. Or perhaps that was less than satisfactory?" Rodrigo slipped his hand beneath her ear, pulling her toward him and kissing her soundly.

When he pulled away, Meg blinked. Her breath came quickly, her toes tingled, and it took a moment for her mind to clear and remember their situation.

Rodrigo winked at her. He grasped her hand, leading her through the door and into shadows of the dark hallway.

The French soldiers' voices came from the parlor area. They sounded tired, and Meg felt a bit lighter. If the men were not alert, she and Rodrigo might be able to slip past unnoticed. They stood in the hallway for a moment, listening, and Meg wished she had put more energy into her French studies.

She felt Rodrigo stiffen and glanced up at him. His attention was on the soldiers' conversation. What had they said? Meg gave his hand a tug. He glanced to her, and the two of them slipped into the darkened kitchen.

Rodrigo moved to the window, and Meg dared a glance around the doorframe at the parlor across the hall.

The soldiers had a single lantern for light and were sprawled upon the furniture. One man snored, and the other two spoke occasionally. The men had removed their swords and set them in the corner near the front door, apparently for quick access when it was time to depart.

Rodrigo ducked down and made his way back to her. He whispered against her ear. "The sentry with the musket is directly outside. We will need to go through the main door."

Meg shook her head. "They will hear us, and even if they do not, the cold air will notify them when the door opens."

"We have no other choice. The boat could arrive any minute."

Meg's mouth went dry, and her pulse thrashed in her ears. "I have an idea." She moved quickly, before Rodrigo had a chance to stop her, because she was certain he would.

She crept across the entryway to the group of swords, lifting one at a time into her arms, careful not to allow them to bump into each other and alert the soldiers. The weapons were much heavier than she'd anticipated.

One of the soldiers said something, and she could hear movement in the room. Meg froze in the darkened hallway. Little by little, she moved backward and pressed herself against the wall.

Meg glanced back toward Rodrigo, who stood in the shadows watching her. Even in the darkness she could see by the set of his shoulders that he was tense as a spring. His gaze shifted to the soldiers and then back to her.

The sound of movement continued, footsteps followed by a glass being refilled, and finally the regular noise of the men's conversation resumed. Meg peeked into the room and then hunched over, pressing the swords against her to keep them quiet. She did not stop at the kitchen, but continued into the hallway at the back of the house.

Rodrigo followed. She could tell he wasn't pleased that she had taken such a risk. He unlocked and opened the door to the room where they had originally been detained, but Meg shook her head, indicating the other room. Rodrigo opened the door and closed it once they were inside.

He took the heavy weapons from her. He strapped one around his waist. "Margarita, you should not have—"

"I know. We do not have time to argue. As of now, there is one armed man in this house. We have the advantage. I will hide these swords, and we need to find something to bind our prisoners. The other room has a key, so it will serve us better."

Rodrigo shook his head, muttering something in Spanish. His gaze settled on Meg. "Heaven help me, how did I get involved with such a woman?" His mouth turned in a half smile. "I should have known you would devise a plan, Margarita."

A warm glow started in Meg's middle at his praise.

In a few minutes, they had sliced a bed sheet into strips, and Meg pushed the swords underneath the bed. They crept across the hall again to their original room. Rodrigo locked the door from the inside and pushed the key beneath. If the soldiers believed they were still locked inside and the key had simply fallen, they could maintain the element of surprise until the last possible moment.

"I will say it again, although I don't expect you to actually listen." He muttered some words in Spanish. "You must follow my lead, Margarita. Stay behind me, and do not allow the soldiers near you. I would have a difficult time refusing to surrender my sword if you were seized. A man could be convinced to do anything if the safety of a woman he cares for is threatened."

"I understand." In spite of the circumstances, Meg's heart tripped at his words. Rodrigo cared for her, and even though it was not a declaration of his undying love, the simple statement wrapped around her heart and gave her the courage she needed.

He stood behind the door and motioned for Meg to move behind him. "Ready?" Rodrigo asked as he unsheathed his sword.

Chapter 21

Rodrigo hefted the unfamiliar weapon, testing the weight. It was different than the swords he had trained with. He had always insisted on the highest quality Spanish steel, and his costly weapons had balanced perfectly. This military-issue sword felt bulky and unwieldy in comparison. The leather of the grip was worn, and the hilt had no hand guard. The rapier he'd worn in Spain—a Toledo blade with elegant filigreed hilt—had been more of a fashion accessory, and even though he had trained extensively in fencing, he'd never fought without the protective gloves and padded waistcoat.

He glanced toward Meg, whose eyes shone as she looked toward him. The trust in her gaze gave him a boost of courage. She had complete confidence in his ability to save them. If she knew that he was in truth a pampered, overindulged man who, until the last year, had never worried about anything more significant than whether his boots were the latest in style, would she still look to him as her champion?

He took a breath and banged his palm on the door, calling for the soldiers.

A moment later, a man opened the door and entered looking rather irritated. In an instant, he was kneeling on the ground. Rodrigo pressed his sword to the soldier's throat, watching carefully as Meg bound his wrists and ankles with strips of bed linen then tied a strip around his mouth to keep him from crying a warning to the others.

He did not remove the blade until Meg was well away from the man.

More pounds on the door produced the other two soldiers, whose tired faces transformed to surprise followed by anger just as quickly as their comrade's.

Rodrigo pushed them to the ground and held them at sword point until Meg had bound and gagged them, and then he moved her away quickly. He did not like how they watched Meg in the clothing she wore, and he wanted her as far from their wayward eyes as possible. He was amazed the soldiers hadn't bothered to look for their weapons, attesting to the fact that they had not thought a prince and princess would oppose them. They'd likely been assured their assignment would be effortless. Rodrigo hoped they were severely disappointed.

Meg turned the key in the lock behind them, and they hurried through the house. It would be only a matter of time before the soldiers freed themselves from their bonds and broke down the bedchamber door to come after them.

Rodrigo cracked the front door open and studied the shadows in the darkness. He risked opening it farther with no consequence. For a split second, he was torn. The soldiers had spoken of Pierrefonds as his parents' prison. The men bound in the bedchamber were his only link to his mother and father. Part of him wanted to return and allow them to take him to France. It was the closest he had come to discovering his parents' whereabouts, and he was not certain if he'd have another chance. Prisoners could be relocated at any time.

Meg held onto his arm, and he felt the weight of her safety again on his shoulders. He glanced at her, and his heart constricted. Nothing was as important as Meg's protection. It would be a different story if she were safe. He pushed thoughts of Pierrefonds from his mind and nodded, taking Meg's hand and pulling her through the door. They crouched in the shadows next to the house for a brief moment until their eyes became accustomed to the darkness.

Meg shivered, rubbing her arms through her thin shirt, and he shrugged off his coat, helping her put it on. The coattails nearly touched the ground, and the sleeves fell well past her hands. Meg lifted one arm, shaking it to free her hand, and she clasped Rodrigo's again.

From the side of the house, a path led down the cliff to the water below. A boat bobbed on the waves, apparently waiting to take them to the ship when the signal came. There was still no sign of the sentry.

Rodrigo pointed toward the road they'd arrived on. It followed a straight path through the field in front of the cottage and then disappeared behind a shadowy clump of trees. They would be exposed but only briefly. "Run for the trees," he whispered in Meg's ear.

Meg nodded, but her hand trembled in his.

He glanced around once more before breaking out of the shadows and dashing across the open space. Meg followed as closely as she could, stumbling once, but he pulled her on, wishing he'd found a pair of shoes to replace her dancing slippers. The thin soles offered no protection from the rocky ground. He slowed his pace slightly to keep Meg next to him.

The crash of a gunshot echoed behind them, and Rodrigo threw Meg to the ground, lying next to her and holding her head against his. His heartbeat thrashed painfully in his ears as he tried to push aside his panic and assess the situation.

Meg shook next to him. Her hands covered her face.

"Are you hurt?" he asked, dreading her answer.

She shook her head, moving her hands to look at him with bulging eyes. "You?"

"No," Rodrigo said, and Meg breathed a sigh. "We must not allow him time to reload." He jumped to his feet, pulling out his sword and whirling around, searching for the soldier who had fired at them.

Meg screamed, and Rodrigo turned, lifting his sword instinctively as the sentry leapt from the trees and brought his own sword crashing down upon Rodrigo's. The force of the blow jarred him, and it was quickly followed by another, which Rodrigo just managed to parry. The hours of training were the only thing protecting Rodrigo. He was completely out of his element.

The man obeyed none of the rules of swordplay. His thrusts were not graceful, his footwork ugly. Each blow was accompanied by a grunt, and spittle flew from his mouth when he made contact.

Rodrigo knew that while he had better training in gentlemanly combat, this man carried a wealth of experience. He'd fought in actual battles, real contests of life or death. This soldier intended to kill him or at least wound him badly enough that he wouldn't be able to escape again. He delivered a battering of blows. Some Rodrigo managed to block; others glanced off his sword at odd angles, grazing his flesh.

Rodrigo's forearms were slashed, sweat covered his body, and he did not know how he could possibly compete with this seasoned combatant. A movement caught his eye. Meg stood wrapped in his coat, her fingers clawing her cheeks. A look of supreme terror had seized her expression. In that instant, Rodrigo remembered that he was not only fighting for his own life. If he was defeated, Meg would be left in this man's control.

She would be taken to France, revealed as an imposter, and sent to the guillotine. The knowledge steeled his insides.

He allowed the emotions he had held in check to surface. The anger, fear, and frustration for his family, his country, and the woman he loved all combined. Energy surged in his veins, and with a yell, Rodrigo brought his sword down. The soldier blocked it easily and twisted, slashing at Rodrigo's torso and slicing his waistcoat. Rodrigo lunged, but the man kicked his feet out from beneath him, and he dropped to the ground.

Meg screamed his name.

The soldier lifted his arm to deliver a killing blow, but Rodrigo lurched and thrust his sword upwards through the man's body. He was mildly surprised at how easy it was to drive a sharpened piece of metal through another human being. Rather like slicing a cake. The soldier's eyes glazed, and he fell backward, pulling Rodrigo's sword with him.

Rodrigo released the weapon and slumped to the ground. His stomach churned, and he shook as the realization of what had just taken place crashed over him.

His mind began to go numb, and ice spread from his core. To say that he was shaken was a gross understatement. He did not feel heroic and strong. Instead he was horrified and thought he'd be ill.

He looked toward Meg, afraid of seeing the fear in her eyes directed at him. Would she think him a monster? Before he had a chance of more than a glance at her expression, Meg flung herself at him. She wrapped her arms around him, pressing her face into his chest. The noises she made were a strange combination of laughter and weeping, and irrationally, the sound calmed Rodrigo.

"You are safe now," he heard himself say, as he patted her back.

Meg lifted her head. Trails of tears streaked down her cheeks, shining in the darkness as she knelt in front of him. "*I* am safe?" She pressed her palms on his cheeks, leaning her forehead against his. "You silly prince. I am not concerned one fig about my own safety, not when—" Her eyes darted toward the man on the ground. "I have never been so terrified." She moved backward and examined Rodrigo. Her eyes narrowed as she lifted his arms, studied the cuts, and then poked her fingers into his slashed waistcoat. "I do not think you're seriously injured," she said. "But we should find a surgeon to wrap your wounds."

She stood and offered her hands to help him to rise. Rodrigo shook his head, a tired smile playing over his mouth. How did this little woman lend him such strength? He stood and angled himself to block Meg's view of the dead soldier. He didn't want to pull his blade from where it protruded out of the man's body, finding it easier to take the weapon from the soldier's hand. Luckily the sword appeared to be standard issue and fit into the scabbard at Rodrigo's waist. He found that he could not look at the man's face and turned back toward Meg.

Her hand slipped into his. Rodrigo glanced down at her. Her hair was untidy. Most of the curls had come loose and hung over her shoulders. She wore a fisherman's rough clothing and Rodrigo's oversized jacket. Her eyes were swollen, and her shoulders drooped in fatigue. Rodrigo could not imagine any sight more lovely.

Rodrigo glanced back toward the cottage. The men could escape and pursue them at any moment, but he was too exhausted to do more than walk down the road. Luckily they were near the copse of trees, and soon the cottage was blocked from their view.

"I thought I had lost you," Meg said softly. "I do not want to ever feel that way again."

Rodrigo stopped and pulled on their joined hands until she stepped toward him. He wrapped an arm around her waist, pulling her close. Lifting her chin, he skimmed his fingers over her forehead, brushing the loose hair from her face. "You will never lose me, Margarita. No matter what may happen.

Meg closed her eyes, and her face relaxed.

It was the perfect scenario. What else could Rodrigo do but kiss her? He swept his lips over hers, eliciting a small feminine sigh that propelled a flash of heat through his veins. He pushed his fingers into her soft curls, cradling her head, and pulled her close until her lips were a breath away.

He jerked at the sudden sound of hoofbeats and pulled Meg into the cover of the trees. They crouched behind a bushy undergrowth and waited for the horses to approach, whether from the cottage or the other direction, he could not tell. Had the soldiers escaped already? Were French reinforcements approaching? How could he possibly defend them if they were discovered? Remaining hidden was their only hope. "Do not move," he whispered, certain that the banging of his heartbeat would reveal them.

Meg hid her face against his shoulder; her hands were clamped painfully around his arm.

The riders approached, not from the cottage, but from the main road, and once they were near enough to perceive, Rodrigo nearly laughed aloud as his tensed muscles slacked. He moved to stand, but Meg's iron grip pulled him back.

"We are saved," he said, pressing a kiss to her forehead. "Come, Margarita." He pulled her to her feet, and they stepped from the tree cover to hail the horsemen.

A large detachment of Spanish and British soldiers stopped at his call. His eyes moved over the group, and the relief that poured over him nearly caused him to slump to the ground.

Colonel Stackhouse was off his horse and at their side in an instant, and Rodrigo didn't think he had ever been so glad to see anyone in his entire life. The colonel's gaze took in the situation immediately, calling for someone to tend to Rodrigo's wounds. His eye settled on Meg, and a smile bent his lips. "I see we have the source of the pearl trail. Ingenious, Miss Burton, though I'd have expected nothing less."

Rodrigo put his arm around her shoulder and squeezed, fiercely proud of Meg's cleverness.

A soldier brought a rag and a canteen and began to clean the slashes on Rodrigo's arms. He winced and finally shook the man off.

"But how did you know to search for us?" Meg asked. "We thought it would be hours before anyone noticed we were missing."

The duke approached from the group of horses and men. He laid a hand on Rodrigo's shoulder. "Your sister was quite distressed when the two of you did not turn up for the waltz," he said. "She was certain something criminal was afoot, and I know better than to mistrust my wife's instincts." He pulled a booklet from his pocket and handed it to Meg. "Your dance card was found when we searched the grounds."

"Meg?"

They all turned toward the speaker as he approached.

"Daniel." Meg rushed into her brother's arms, and he led her away from the group. Rodrigo watched as they spoke softly, and after a moment, Daniel wrapped his arms around her, pulling her into an embrace and kissing the top of her head. A pang of jealousy shot through Rodrigo, but he stifled it. He hoped he'd have plenty of opportunities to hold and comfort Meg.

The captain of the Spanish guard approached and bowed.

Rodrigo nodded, giving the man permission to speak.

"Your Highness, I cannot begin to apologize for our error. It is completely inexcusable, and I take full responsibility—"

Rodrigo held up his hands, cutting off the man's words. "We haven't time for apologies, Capitán Fernández. I need you to listen." He told the group everything that had happened from the moment the soldiers stepped out of the woods behind the greenhouse. Colonel Stackhouse, the duke, and the capitán attended intently as he related the soldiers' conversation.

"Pierrefonds? The chateau?" Colonel Stackhouse said when Rodrigo had finished. "I had heard that the Emperor purchased it, but it's little more than a ruin."

"A well-guarded ruin if Napoleon is truly detaining prisoners there," Capitán Fernández said. "We shall formulate a rescue mission at once, Your Highness."

Rodrigo rubbed the back of his neck. "I worry that we might be too late. If they are transferred or . . ." He didn't voice his fear aloud, trusting the men to understand his concern. "If these soldiers are in reality traveling to the location where my parents are being held, perhaps—"

"You think to join them," Colonel Stackhouse said.

"No, Your Highness. It is too dangerous," the duke and Capitán Fernández both said at the same time but in different languages.

Rodrigo folded his arms across his chest, wincing at the stinging of the cuts on his forearms. "I understand the risk, but I feel as though this may be our only chance. It is the closest we have come after months of searching, and we still have the advantage. They will not expect that the prison's location has been compromised or that you follow. If I do not go with them, they could relocate my parents, and we will be as ignorant as before."

Colonel Stackhouse tapped his finger on his chin, looking toward the trees as he spoke. "The chateau is more than one hundred miles from Calais and near to Paris, which makes it a gamble. But if a company were to enter by way of Belgium . . ." He squinted his eye and turned his gaze to Rodrigo. "But I fear, Your Highness, such an operation could take the better part of a month at least. And that does not consider *after* your parents, and you, are rescued—if the operation is successful, that is. We'll need to plan for not only an escape from the chateau, but from the very center of our enemy's territory."

"But do you believe it to be worth the danger if there is even a slight possibility?" Rodrigo asked.

Colonel Stackhouse nodded his head. "Aside from the sheer folly of placing oneself willingly in the hands of the enemy and the inherent risk of traveling as a prisoner behind enemy lines, Your Highness. I can see that this is a viable plan. Risky, to be sure, but it may be the only opportunity we have. And the value of having a man on the inside, that in and of itself greatly increases the chances of success."

"I must try," Rodrigo said as his gaze slipped in Meg's direction. His chest was tight, and a sour taste arose in his mouth when he realized the consequences of his decision.

The colonel placed his hand upon Rodrigo's shoulder, which, from the colonel, was the equivalent of an effusive embrace. "I fear there is also the matter of your sister's anger to contend with. I don't want to be the one to deliver the news to her."

"Nor I," muttered the duke.

Rodrigo's heart sank further. He would be leaving behind the two people he cared for more than any other. Could Meg and Serena possibly understand?

Colonel Stackhouse continued, "You'll need to leave immediately. I do not believe you will find it difficult to be recaptured as the soldiers surely fear their commander's reprimand at having lost their prisoners. Go now, and the capitán and I will see to the arrangements for your rescue. A ship will have to drop off a party secretly on a stretch of unpatrolled Belgian shoreline. But that's what we've intelligence operatives for, is it not?"

Capitán Fernández nodded his head, though he did not look as though he agreed with the plan in the least.

Colonel Stackhouse gazed back at the trees. "It sounds like a grand operation, men. Sticking it to old Boney right beneath his Frenchy nose." He sighed, and his expression appeared almost wistful. "I'm sorry to say I'll not be able to accompany you. I am still not cleared for active duty, and there is the matter of . . ." The colonel cleared his throat uncomfortably.

"The matter of your forthcoming marriage to Lady Featherstone," the duke said, winking. "Another lady I would not want angry with me."

"Yes, well." The colonel adjusted his cravat. "You have a bit of explaining to do yourself, Your Highness." He nodded in Meg's direction. "And then you must hasten."

Rodrigo shook hands with the three men. He wished the colonel congratulations on his engagement and reassured Capitán Fernández that he was doing what was best for his parents and his country. Rodrigo's throat tightened when he bid the duke farewell and sent his love to his sister. "Do not allow Lord Featherstone near Meg," he said to the duke.

"And please care for my horse." The duke nodded his understanding, and Rodrigo departed.

His feet were heavy as he walked toward where Meg and Daniel stood. "Mr. Burton, with your permission, may I speak to your sister privately?"

Daniel bowed. "Of course, Your Highness."

Rodrigo led Meg away from the group. When they had walked far enough to avoid being overheard, he stopped and turned her toward him.

Meg grasped his hands. "Rodrigo, we did it. We can go home now!" Her eyes shone in the moonlight, and his insides sank further. Into his boots.

He lifted her hand in his, brushing his knuckle over her cheek. "Meg, I cannot go back to the castle with you."

Her joyful expression did not change except for a slight squinting of her eyes. "I do not understand. What do you mean?"

"I must go to France. My parents . . .We do not know if we will have another opportunity to find them."

The crease appeared above Meg's nose. Her carriage stiffened. "You would allow yourself to be recaptured? But you cannot do such a thing. The soldiers can find your parents."

"I am the only one who can get inside the prison. It is the best chance of rescuing them."

Meg took a step back and shook her hand from his. "No, this is a terrible idea. We just got away, and you would— It is *France*, Rodrigo."

"I must."

She looked up at him through her lashes. Pools of tears filled her eyes and spilled over, leaving trails down her cheeks. Meg brushed them away impatiently with her palms. "You said I would never lose you. We are *compañeros de aventura.*"

Hearing her voice hitch as she said the words with her drawling accent made Rodrigo's throat scratchy. The ache in his chest grew so intense he didn't know if he would be able to endure it. He framed her face with his hands. "Meg, if you ask me, I will stay."

"Then stay. Please stay." Her tears began to run over his hands.

Rodrigo touched his forehead to hers. He pressed his eyes shut but opened them when Meg placed her own palms against his cheeks.

She shook her head, the look of defiance in her eyes softened into defeat. She swallowed heavily, and her shoulders slumped. "I see that you must do this," she whispered. "I will not ask you to stay."

"I promise that I will return."

"You know you cannot make such a promise."

"But I will. I promise I will return to you, Margarita." He covered her lips with his, pouring every ounce of himself into the kiss. His heart trembled with his need for her to understand the depths of his feelings for her. Rodrigo's mind spun with memories of laughter, tears, poems, and adventures; Meg had brought back a joy for life after a cynical, proud man believed it to be gone.

She wrapped her arms around his neck, clinging to him as her breath hitched in a sob.

Rodrigo pulled away, gently loosening her arms. His throat was so tight that all he could manage was a whisper. "I promise." He stroked her cheek once more and ran toward the cottage.

He glanced back once. The sight of Meg kneeling upon the ground with her brother holding her as she sobbed caused his eyes to blur with tears of his own. He drove himself forward gasping at the force of the pain in his heart. He must return to Meg. He must.

Chapter 22

Three months later

Meg's heart flipped when the bell rang, just as it had every single time in the months since Rodrigo departed for France. She held her breath, praying that this would be the one—the letter, the messenger, even the prince himself. Looking across the drawing room of the duke's London house, Meg saw that Serena did the same.

The butler entered the room to announce their visitors, and both ladies let out a sigh. Serena caught her eye and they shared a disheartened smile, but it lasted only for an instant before Serena raised her brows, pressed her lips together, and nodded slightly. Meg recognized the gesture as one of encouragement. Over the months, the women had become quite adept in communicating with the slightest facial expressions. An essential requirement as the two of them had been virtually surrounded with the populous of London Society at nearly every waking moment.

Meg and Serena had forged a bond over the months that only heartache and anxiety can create. Serena had held her, and they'd wept when Meg returned the morning after the masque without Rodrigo. As the Season had progressed, the two women had come to depend upon each other when the crowds and questions and worry had become too demanding.

Meg had confided in Serena the secret encounters with Rodrigo, which she soon learned were not as secret as she'd believed. Serena confessed that she was delighted to finally be released from her promise to keep her brother's identity hidden. The women had laughed together, cried together, shared hopes and fears and dreams, and become as devoted to one another as sisters. Meg hoped that she gave as much comfort to her friend as she received.

They rose as their visitors entered. Meg noticed that Serena stood slowly. Her face was a bit pale. She would have to inquire about her friend's health once the callers had gone.

Lady Vernon bustled into the room followed by her dearest comrade. Meg reminded herself that she would need to remember to refer to the newlywed woman as Lady Patricia. The former Lady Featherstone's cheeks were flushed, and she radiated a glow that transformed the strict woman into a beaming bride.

Lady Lucinda and Lady Helen entered the room behind their mother.

"How lovely to see you all," Serena said, motioning for the women to be seated.

Meg returned to her position on the sofa near the window, not only because it had become habit to watch for any report of Rodrigo, but she hoped for a breeze. She had thought South Carolina to be stifling in the summer, but London was infinitely worse. It was more than simply heat; it was the smells that entered whenever a window was opened. A city of this size could not hide its odor with strategically placed hothouse flowers as most people tended to assume. The fragrance only added a tinge of sweetness to the smell of smoke, horses, and endless crowds of sweating people. What Meg wouldn't give for a fresh country wind.

"And may I offer you tea?" Serena asked.

"Yes, dear." Lady Vernon fanned herself profusely. "That would be lovely."

Serena motioned to a servant, who bustled from the room. Meg did not miss the quirk of Serena's mouth at the idea of warm tea on such a stifling day. The two of them had often wondered about the British and their mania for the hot, watery drink.

The servant returned a moment later with a steaming teapot and finger cakes.

Serena's arm trembled the smallest bit as she began to pour the tea, and Meg moved across the room to assist her in distributing the cups and offering the guests sweets.

Once they had been served, Meg returned to her seat, resolving to keep an eye on Serena.

Lady Vernon set down her fan and took a sip of tea. "Meg, dear. You looked so beautiful last night at the Chanceworth's ball. I must say that champagne gown was definitely the perfect color. And so many gentlemen sought your company."

"Thank you, my lady. It was a lovely evening to be sure. And Helen, how did you enjoy waltzing with Lord Dewhurst?"

Helen smiled shyly. "Very well. He is such a gentlemanly man."

"And likely very soon to be engaged to Miss Olivia Dewitt," Lucinda said, setting her teacup into her saucer, obviously displeased the conversation wasn't centered upon her. "Regina Foster's gown last year at the Chanceworth's ball was precisely the same color of champagne, and she turned quite a few heads. Meg, you are much braver than I to wear a color that was so decidedly the rage *last* season." She smoothed her skirts with her hand. "I was very pleased at the reception I received in my pale yellow gown. I predict it will become the height of fashion extremely soon."

"And speaking of Miss Foster," Lady Patricia said, "just this morning, our dearest Anthony proposed marriage to that fortunate young lady. Theirs will be a great match."

Meg raised her brow minutely in Serena's direction, eliciting a small twist of the lips from her friend. Lord Featherstone engaged to Regina Foster? Meg hoped the woman had a fondness for sparse facial hair and didn't mind her husband's indiscretions.

"Did you see that Mr. Newton stood up with me two times last night? And he paid a visit already this morning," Lucinda said. "He is quite partial to me. It will certainly come as a blow to many gentlemen when he offers for my hand."

Meg thought if she never sat through another conversation about ball gowns or marriage proposals, it would be too soon. She'd never had such boring discussions before coming to London, and it seemed as if such things were the only interest of ladies in Town. At least the gentlemen spoke of horse racing, the war on the peninsula, and other more exciting matters.

The thought of horses made her smile. The duke had brought Patito from Thornshire and insisted that Meg exercise him in Hyde Park every day. She'd learned quickly enough to avoid the fashionable hour, as there were so many coaches and horses and persons on foot that Patito could scarcely move in the throng. She'd seen more than a few heads turn when they saw Patito, and she could have sworn the stallion enjoyed the attention. He certainly seemed to be prancing a time or two, and Meg had thought it amusing, wishing she could laugh about Patito's antics with Rodrigo.

She wondered for a moment who would care for Patito when she returned to Charleston, but she put the thought from her mind. She would not go home anytime soon. America's declaration of war against England made it nearly impossible for her to return right now, and the idea of leaving made her feel as though she were giving up on Rodrigo, and she would not do that.

"Have you had any news from your brother?" Lady Vernon asked Serena, and Meg's head jerked toward the duchess.

"Nothing so far," Serena said, and Meg wondered if the others had heard the tremble in her voice.

"Well, perhaps he will change his mind and join us in London," Lady Vernon said, reopening her fan and waving it before her with a vengeance.

"He certainly disappeared from the masque early in the night. I believe he danced with only one lady," Lucinda said, leveling her gaze at Meg. "I wonder what could have frightened him away?"

"Perhaps the fear that he'd have to dance with another," Meg said.

Helen snickered but was shushed by a glare from her sister.

"I'm afraid Rodrigo had other business to attend to that night," Serena said quietly. Meg gritted her teeth, furious that Lucinda would hurt Serena's feelings, albeit unknowingly.

The colonel had thought it best that Rodrigo's mission be kept a secret. "News travels fast in London, and secrets travel faster," he'd said. As far as the rest of the party knew, Rodrigo had declined the offer to accompany them to London, choosing to remain at Thornshire instead. None had asked why the prince had not kept his horse, but Meg was certain the duke or Serena would think of the perfect answer to any questions, should they arise.

Meg had scoured the periodicals and the *Times* every morning, hoping there might be some mention of the Spanish royal family, but there was nothing. She supposed in such a case, no news was good news. One could not exactly post a letter from an enemy country in the middle of a secret rescue mission, but she wished they'd heard something. Anything.

"Do you not agree, Meg?" Serena's voice pulled her from her contemplations.

"I am sorry; I must be wool gathering," Meg said. "What were you saying?"

Serena smiled. "Lady Patricia was just telling us that she and the colonel are to leave for India when the Season ends."

"How thrilling," said Meg.

"Yes, the colonel has received a commission and a new assignment," Lady Patricia said. "And I confess I am rather eager to see new places."

Lady Vernon crossed her arms, continuing to fan herself awkwardly. She looked displeased with the idea of separation. Meg felt a twinge of sympathy. She knew how it felt to be left behind.

"Helen, will you go to India too?" Meg asked.

"I do not know." Helen said, twisting her fingers together in her lap. "Mother and the colonel have not decided whether I should accompany them or if it would be better for me to remain in England."

Lucinda threw up her hands, grimacing. "It would certainly not do you any good to journey to such a barbarous place. What chance will you have of finding a decent husband in India?"

"I—" Helen began.

"You would do much better to stay in England and allow me to help you secure a gentleman of means, such as my Mr. Newton."

Meg shifted her position, deliberately turning her body toward Helen and excluding Lucinda from her line of sight. "What do *you* wish to do, Helen?"

Helen held Meg's gaze, purposely avoiding her sister's. "I've never journeyed farther than Brighton, and India sounds . . . well, I should like to give it a try." She spoke in a quiet voice.

Lady Patricia nodded in her brisk manner. "Well, then it is settled, dear. And I will be very glad to have one of my children with me."

Meg wondered if no one had bothered to ask Helen's opinion on the matter before. She opened her mouth to expound on the glories of new experiences and seeking outside one's comfort level but stopped short.

Serena had stood to return her teacup to the tray but faltered, setting the dishes down with a clatter and placing her hand on her forehead. She looked as if she might collapse, and Meg hurried to her, wrapping an arm around her waist and easing her back into her chair.

"Serena, you are so pale. Shall I send for a doctor?"

"I do not know. I am tired and dizzy. And my stomach is so ill."

Lady Patricia knelt in front of Serena. "How long have you felt this way?"

"Only two or three days. It usually passes in a few hours," Serena said.

Lady Patricia and Lady Vernon exchanged a look.

"What is it? Will she be all right?" Meg felt the beginnings of panic growing in her chest. She lifted Serena's hand into her own, patting it and wishing she had an idea of how to help her. "Shall I fetch a doctor?"

"Yes, you should meet with a doctor, and I wonder if you should begin to ask around for a suitable midwife, dear," Lady Patricia said gently.

Serena's eyes widened, and her mouth formed an "o." She looked from Lady Patricia to Lady Vernon and then to Meg. "I had not considered, but . . . yes, I suppose I should send for a doctor."

Lady Patricia rose. "I will mix an herbal blend to help with the nausea. And you must get plenty of rest."

Lady Vernon clapped her hands. "A baby! I know my brother will want an heir, but a lovely niece to spoil and dress up . . ." She sighed.

"Please do not say anything to Charles," Serena said. "Not until I meet with the doctor. I want to be certain."

"Of course. You will want to tell the duke yourself. We will not betray your confidence." Mrs. Stackhouse turned to her daughters, placing a finger over her lips. "Come, girls, we must allow Her Grace to rest."

"Thank you," Serena said, squeezing Meg's hand.

Meg stood and curtsied as the ladies departed and then sat back on the sofa next to Serena.

Serena wiped tears from her cheeks. Meg put an arm around her, and Serena leaned against Meg's shoulder.

Meg bit her lip, unsure of how to comfort her friend. She had heard that sometimes when a woman was in a family way, she wept for no reason. "Are you . . . is there anything I can do for you?" she asked. "Would you like a cup of tea?" Meg teased, hoping to elicit a laugh.

Serena shook her head. "I only wish *mi mamá* was here," she whispered.

***

When Meg entered the dining room the next morning, she found the duke sitting at the table reading the *Times*.

"Good morning, Your Grace," she said, unsure of how to proceed. Was it proper for her to eat breakfast alone with a man so decidedly above her station? Or should she wait for Serena?

"Miss Meg," he said, folding the paper and standing. "I was hoping to speak with you."

"Of course." Meg's mind spun. In the time she'd known him, the duke had been pleasant, friendly even, but had never sought her out. Was he planning to terminate her stay with him? Had Daniel gotten into some mischief? Was there news of Rodrigo?

He indicated a chair. "Please, have a seat." Once they were both seated and Meg had been served breakfast, the duke spoke again. "Serena told me last night about her, ah . . . condition." A wide grin spread over his face, but it was replaced by a furrowed brow. "I fear she is unwell. Nothing too serious, the doctor assures us it will pass. But Serena wishes to return to the fresh air of Thornshire." The sides of his mouth pulled down in a frown. "And this is where I should like to beg a favor of you. The committee I represent will require my presence in Parliament for a minimum of another month." He rubbed his eyes. "Miss Meg, Serena adores you. She thinks of you as a sister and would dearly love you to accompany her home to the castle."

The thought of returning to Thornshire warmed Meg, and she could not help but smile at the thought. "I would be most happy to, Your Grace."

"Thank you, miss. I apologize for terminating your Season, but I do appreciate your willingness to attend my wife."

"As much as I have enjoyed London, I would prefer to be at Thornshire to nearly anywhere in the world."

"I completely agree," he said, a relieved smile forming on his face. "And Daniel is welcome to remain here as long as he likes. He has quite taken to London Society, has he not?"

"Yes, Your Grace, and I hope . . ." Meg rubbed her arm. "If you don't mind, will you look after my brother?" The truth was, Daniel had taken to London like fleas to a rat, and she seldom saw him. She worried Daniel was finding the gaming halls too much to his liking.

"Most certainly." The duke nodded knowingly. "I believe this situation will be advantageous to each of us, don't you?"

"I do, Your Grace."

"I have spoken to Colonel Stackhouse, and an extra detachment of guards is to be assigned to Thornshire. You will have no reason to fear. The two of you will be the safest young ladies in all of England."

"Thank you."

"If you will excuse me"—the duke rose—"I must be off." He placed the *Times* next to Meg's plate and then patted her arm. His face softened in concern, and his eyes moved to the paper then back to her. "I am afraid there is no mention of our mutual friend in the news today."

Meg nodded her understanding. She stood and curtseyed as he left the room. She was touched by his consideration for her feelings. The duke had been nothing but considerate during their entire stay, helping her navigate the social whirl of London, occasionally turning away a suitor who became too interested. But his greatest act of kindness had been a letter he'd written to her parents, promising to remain Meg's guardian as long as she should have need of him and pledging to help with their financial troubles until her father's business recovered.

Meg was to return to Thornshire. If there hadn't been a servant watching, she might have clapped her hands.

Thornshire. Where there was fresh air and no more ball gowns, gossip, or rich gentlemen.

Chapter 23

Meg took her time brushing Patito after their morning ride. She loved the feel of his silky mane when she teased out all the tangles. The stallion pawed his foot, impatient to be fed, and she finally put the brush and comb away and left him to his bucket of oats. "*Hasta mañana,* Patito."

Meg had thought it would be painful to return to Thornshire with reminders of Rodrigo everywhere she turned, but she felt closer to him in this place where the memories of their time together floated all around her. Meg could not understand why anyone would leave their country estate to visit London in the summer. With the flowers in bloom and everything a vibrant green, Thornshire was absolutely lovely.

In the three weeks since they'd arrived, Serena's sickness had eased, but she still tired quickly, and Meg found herself alone much of the time. She did not mind in the least. She spent her time reading or walking or taking care of Patito and Bonnie. She didn't miss the London society one bit.

Aside from servants and guards, she and Serena were alone at the castle, and Meg had taken to wearing trousers and boots on her morning ride. It was simply easier to control the horse when she could sit astride, and there was no one to impress.

As she turned around the corner of the stable, Meg saw a carriage in front of the castle entrance. Who would visit so early in the morning? It did not look like the vicar's carriage. Perhaps one of the ladies from Southampton had thought to pay an early-morning call. Meg hurried toward the entrance to change her clothes and make herself presentable. She was certain the duchess was not awake, so Meg would need to assume the role of hostess in Serena's place.

A servant met her when she neared the steps and handed her a roll of parchment.

"What is this?" Meg asked, but the man simply shrugged, bowed, and returned inside the castle.

Meg slid the twine from the scroll and unrolled it. The images on the parchment looked familiar, and in an instant she recognized the map as a duplicate of the one she had given Rodrigo months earlier. Her heart began to pound, and her fingers became painfully numb.

The labels were not the same as those she had written then, however. Atop the tower were the words, *Moonlight Picnic.* The depiction of the greenhouse said *Christabel.* Meg's throat swelled, and her vision blurred.

Rodrigo.

She studied the map for another moment. The dotted line led around the castle through the trees and into the forest. She didn't follow the path but ran directly to the gazebo, which on the map was marked with an X and the word *Treasure.*

Meg flew through the trees, past the pond, and up the steps into the gazebo. Upon a bench she found an envelope and, beneath it, a small box.

The script on the envelope read: *Margarita Burton.* Meg's hands shook as she lifted the flap and slid out a folded paper. She looked around the clearing but, seeing nothing, unfolded the paper. Her heart had somehow risen into her throat, and she sat upon the bench to read the words.

Margarita,

In the months we've been apart, I have thought of little besides you. I have attempted numerous times to write a letter from my heart to explain my feelings. But I realized that there was only one way my soul would speak to yours. Please excuse my pitiful attempt at poetry.

A proud man, lonely, frustrated, distrustful
His heart a battered shell.
A ginger-haired companion looked deep within;
She discovered the worn husk.
With smiles, turrón, games, she poured light inside.
Each droplet filling, until it was nigh to burst
He reclaimed the joy he feared had been lost.
For his heart was hers all along.

Meg held the letter to her breast, savoring the bliss of the perfect romantic gesture. The words wrapped around her heart. She jumped to her feet when she heard a noise behind her.

"Rodrigo." She didn't know whether to laugh or cry. He stood with his arms crossed, leaning a shoulder against one of the pillars. Worn clothing and a thick beard could not disguise his regal bearing.

Meg was suddenly aware that she wore breeches, and her hair was untamed. She didn't look any better than the last time he'd seen her.

He gestured to the paper she held. "It is a poor attempt, but Señor Quintana, he would not help in the least. He told me I had to do it all on my own, and that wretched thing is the result. It sounds much better in Spanish."

"Do not call it wretched when it speaks to my soul," Meg replied, and then realizing what he had said, she squinted her eyes. "You were at Cádiz?"

"Briefly." Rodrigo stood straight and took a step toward her. He tipped his head, considering her, and his mouth curled in a roguish grin. She could imagine the crease in his cheek beneath his whiskers. "I was correct when I told you men's clothing favored you. It appears that you have adopted it as your own personal style."

"I tend the prince's horse, you see." She shrugged her shoulders but allowed a teasing sparkle to show in her eye.

Rodrigo took another step toward her. "The prince does not exercise his own horse?"

"I am afraid he neglects his animal most terribly."

"A pity."

"Quite. And you, sir, you look like a pirate." Meg could not prevent her lips from twitching at his expression of surprise.

"This spot is rumored to be the location of a treasure, and I am searching for mine."

Meg's ribs ached from her heart beating against them. "Would you like some assistance?"

"First you must open the box." He took her arm and pulled her back to sit upon the bench next to him. Fire spread from his touch, and Meg tried to keep her hands from trembling as she lifted the lid of the box. Inside on a satin pillow sat a golden tiara. Meg sucked in a breath. She lifted it and studied the delicate designs and shape of the metal.

Rodrigo took it from her and placed it atop her head, adjusting it to fit into her curls. He tipped his head, studying the effect. Then he rested his hands on Meg's shoulders. "Ah, and now I have found it."

Meg's heart had begun to perform cartwheels, and she fought to keep her voice steady. "This crown is your treasure?"

"No, I have searched for *una princesa.* And here she is." He moved his hands up her neck, cupping Meg's cheeks as he leaned toward her and pressed his lips on hers tenderly and then more firmly as he drove his fingers into her hair.

Meg reached her arms around him, clinging tightly as if Rodrigo might disappear at any moment. Every fear, worry, and doubt she had harbored since the day she had covered his trousers in mud dissolved. Meg felt as if she were on fire and at the same time lighter than air.

Rodrigo drew back, tracing his thumbs over her jawline. His eyes were a deeper shade of brown, if that was possible, as his gaze held Meg's. She wondered if such a look had ever caused anyone's insides to melt the way she felt hers surely would.

He pulled her to him again, holding her in a tight embrace.

Meg buried her face against his neck. "I was so worried. I thought I would never see you again."

"I promised I would return."

"I knew you would try." She settled her head against his shoulder, finding that even after months, she fit perfectly in his arms. "And your parents?"

"They are here—at the castle with Serena."

"I am so glad. She has wanted her mother." Meg lifted her head to study his face. "And was it so very thrilling?"

"Ah, *mi compañera de aventura,* you did not miss any excitement. The escape was extremely uneventful as the French guards did not consider us capable of such an action. Most of the time, we were either walking or hiding. My mother was very unhappy with her disguise as *una maja*—a peasant."

"But you are safe, and that is all that matters."

"Sí, although I think it is time to plan another adventure."

Meg pulled back quickly, holding the tiara to keep it from falling. "I told you I am cured of adventures, and if you think to return to France—"

He placed a finger to her lips to stop her words. "I have a much more enjoyable adventure in mind. I do not believe I mentioned that my mother refused to leave España without a priest. She was worried one would be difficult to find in England. Padre Ventura was most kind to accompany us, and I am sure he would be willing to perform a marriage."

Meg flung herself back into his arms, wondering why she had left them in the first place. Her heart expanded until she worried it might blow to bits.

Rodrigo lifted her chin. "I do not have much to offer. I am a man without a country or a home; I may forever live in my sister's dower house. I do not know what my future holds, but I want my Margarita in it. My heart, it belongs to you." He brushed away the tear that escaped her eye, feathering kisses along her cheek.

"If I were to become una princesa, would I still remain your *compañera de aventura*?"

"*Si, mi amor*," Rodrigo murmured, tilting her head back and stopping further questions with an earth-shifting kiss that put every Gothic hero to shame.

About the Author

Jennifer Moore is a passionate reader and writer of all things romance due to the need to balance the rest of her world, which includes a perpetually traveling husband and four active sons, who create heaps of laundry that are anything but romantic. Jennifer has a B.A. in linguistics from the University of Utah and is a Guitar Hero champion. She lives in northern Utah with her family. You can learn more about her at authorjmoore.com.